Oil Dusk

A Peak Oil Story

John M. Cape & Laura Buckner

Cover illustrations created specifically for **Oil Dusk** by George Buchanan. (georgebuchanan.com)

Cover design by Eden Communications Inc. (edencomm.com).

Suggestions for interior design provided by TLC Graphics. (TLCGraphics.com)

Website design for the official **Oil Dusk** web site (oildusk.com) provided by Saachi Roye. (saachi.roye@gmail.com)

All rights reserved. No part of this book may be reproduced in any form or by any electronic or mechanical means, or the facilitation thereof, including information storage and retrieval systems, without permission from the publisher, except by a reviewer, who may quote brief passages in a review. Any members of educational institutions wishing to photocopy part or all of the work for classroom use, or publishers who would like to obtain permission to include the work in an anthology, should send their inquiries to:

Singing Bowl Publishing
20415 Perryoak Drive
Humble, Texas 77346
oildusk@aol.com

Library of Congress Control Number: 2009905290

© 2006 & 2009 John M. Cape and Laura Buckner

Printed in the United States of America, First Edition, July 2009

ISBN 978-0-9787893-0-5

Table of Contents

CHAPTER ONE
Rumblings..1

CHAPTER TWO
Taking Stock..8

CHAPTER THREE
Adjustments...15

CHAPTER FOUR
An Unexpected Gift..24

CHAPTER FIVE
Day Talkers and Night Stalkers..36

CHAPTER SIX
Everyone Coping..47

CHAPTER SEVEN
A State of Emergency..58

CHAPTER EIGHT
Planning..64

CHAPTER NINE
The Journey...70

Table of Contents

CHAPTER TEN
On the Road......77

CHAPTER ELEVEN
Home Sweet Home......89

CHAPTER TWELVE
Breaking Ground......97

CHAPTER THIRTEEN
The Grasshopper and the Ants......112

CHAPTER FOURTEEN
Company......120

CHAPTER FIFTEEN
Reality Sets In......124

CHAPTER SIXTEEN
The Celebration......133

CHAPTER SEVENTEEN
Summer Time, and the Livin' Ain't Easy......154

CHAPTER EIGHTEEN
An Invader......167

CHAPTER NINETEEN
A Harvest Hunt......178

CHAPTER TWENTY
Floyd Fixes a Failure......188

CHAPTER TWENTY-ONE
Hitting the Wall 198

CHAPTER TWENTY-TWO
The Meeting 213

CHAPTER TWENTY-THREE
A Christmas Surprise 216

CHAPTER TWENTY-FOUR
Business of the Day 234

CHAPTER TWENTY-FIVE
The Stranger 238

CHAPTER TWENTY-SIX
Spring 250

CHAPTER TWENTY-SEVEN
A Change for the Better 260

Authors' Notes 267

Acknowledgments 270

References 272

About the Authors 273

CHAPTER ONE

Rumblings

October 2015, Omaha

"Remember that there is nothing stable in human affairs; therefore avoid undue elation in prosperity, or undue depression in adversity."

— Socrates

When they stopped posting the price of gas, I figured either the going rate was changing too often or they knew I'd pay anything after sitting in line for an hour. It took me several days to realize the signs didn't have space for double-digit dollars. Still, when I finally reached the pump in my wife's Ford Mustang, I blinked my eyes and stared helplessly. Seventeen dollars for a gallon of gas! What the hell was going on?

My gut knotted as I stuck my credit card in the pump. The sun was low in the sky, and shining directly onto the pump. I squinted, trying to make out the LED pump instructions in the late-day glare.

"Lift nozzle and select grade." Relief flooded my lungs as I realized I'd been holding my breath, hoping our credit card would still work. Otherwise, I'd have waited for nothing.

The line of cars behind me wove out of the gas station, blocking the entire right lane of the four-lane street. Most of the waiting drivers sat in their cars with the engine running. Loud bass notes from the music from several cars competed with each other in different throbbing pulses.

The dollar digits on the pump face flashed by like seconds on a digital watch, as the gallon numbers slowly followed. Fifty-one dollars for three gallons! Yeah, this was really happening! I lightly released the pump lever, and the rate of gas filling the car slowed.

My instinct was to stop pumping gas all together – these prices were too grim. I looked back at the line behind me waiting impatiently to fill up and pressed on. With three drivers all using about a tank of gas a week, our bill was going to be... over $3,000 a month.

My dark thoughts were interrupted by the distinctive rising gurgle and click of the pump indicating a full tank. I shook the nozzle, making sure every drop found its way into our tank and returned the handle to the pump. $272.57 for sixteen gallons. No way we'd be able to keep filling up each week.

As I circled to the driver's side, an oversized SUV waiting behind me blasted his horn encouraging me to get out of his way a little faster. I shook my head. Yeah, I'd be blasting my horn too if I were unlucky enough to be driving a gas guzzler like that.

I climbed in, buckled up and hit the horn too. Why not? It's not like we can do anything about the lines and high prices. The SUV driver flipped me off as I headed out to the train station.

Leslie, almost seven months pregnant, was returning from a long business trip overseas. She got stuck in Cleveland on the way home when the airline she was booked on went belly-up. Normally her tickets would have been honored by another airline and she would have arrived home a couple of hours late. Not this time.

She had called me from the Cleveland airport two days ago, sounding calm but I could hear tension in her voice and loud noises in the background.

"Alex, I've tried every other airline here. No seats open for at least a week on any of them. I have to be in on Monday for the directors meeting! All rental cars are booked and I'm stuck here at the terminal."

I heard some loud noises through the phone and a yelp from Leslie. "Are you okay? What's going on there?" I yelled.

"Fine, just startled. Some guy's pitching a fit at the first-class ticket counter."

I could make out the muffled sounds of angry yelling coming through, but I could only imagine the chaos at the terminal. People got stressed or crabby when traveling under normal circumstances. "It sounds like he's pretty upset." I said. "Can you grab a cab?"

Leslie replied quickly, "I'm headed that way now. Maybe I can… Oh hell, people are fighting to get a taxi! I've never seen anything like this. It's really getting ugly. Crap, where is security when you need them?"

"Can you get out of there?" I asked her, worried that she would be jostled or even knocked down in a mob scene.

"Not by taxi or rental car. I can't even go to a hotel. I've heard other travelers complaining that all the local rooms are now booked."

I relaxed my grip on the phone and ran through options in my head. "How about bus or train schedules?"

"The train?" Leslie asked, then immediately said, "Let me check. Wait, there's a sign about some sort of red train in the terminal. I'll call you back, my battery is getting low."

"Okay, hon. Just be careful."

She had called back to tell me she'd boarded the city's rapid transit headed to downtown. She would go to the Amtrak station and come home by train.

Once I reached the Omaha station, the loudspeaker crackled into life, announcing the arrival of Leslie's train on track one. I couldn't remember the last time I had been on a train. I only hoped Leslie had been comfortable.

The train blew its whistle at the last crossing and screeched to a clanking halt at the platform. I scanned the length of the silver-sided cars, watching for Leslie to step down. No one else was waiting for a passenger, so I was surprised to see a group of men with briefcases, overcoats, and computer bags disembark and walk into the small station. I wonder if their flight had been cancelled, too.

Soon I spotted Leslie being helped down by one of the porters. Now thirty-nine, she was every bit as beautiful as when I married her. She was five foot four with glossy auburn hair worn short, yet loose, unlike the tightly permed helmet hairstyle preferred by my mother. Her brown leather coat was open, revealing a crisp business suit that allowed for her expanding abdomen. Surprisingly, she looked fresh and relaxed. I waved and smiled when she caught sight of me.

I quickly headed toward her, gave her a kiss and held her. She'd been away too long this time and I had missed her. We hugged each other for a good long time and then she pulled away to look up at me.

"We need to take a train trip with the kids!" she said. "It was a great suggestion – very relaxing!"

I took her bag and steered her toward the parking lot. "How was business?"

She frowned at the memory. "I won't be recommending a move of our operations. Almaty is a beautiful city and the people are really wonderful, but Kazakhstan is too remote."

I nodded ahead toward our car. "Can you believe I paid seventeen dollars a gallon to fill up today?"

"Alex, you didn't!" Leslie's exclamation was accompanied by a look of horror, and I could see her mind calculating the weekly expense, just as I had done an hour earlier. She grimaced as reality set in.

"What choice did I have? If I wait until tomorrow, the prices might be even higher – why else would there be a gas line at these prices?"

"But these prices will blow over soon, right?" she asked. I hesitated before answering. My father had always said to look out for signs when our oil-run economy started to skid. He had been an original oil conservationist, and my formative years in a home as minimally oil dependent as possible had been odd to say the least.

"And if they don't?" I replied cautiously.

"Alex, they have to!"

"Not to hear Mom tell it."

"She's not still on that?" I knew Leslie was referring to my mother's endless worries conveyed, on a daily basis, in support of her long-dead husband's ideas.

"Here we are." Glad for the change of subject, I loaded her bag into the trunk. Leslie moved straight for the driver's door, maneuvered her protruding stomach behind the steering wheel, and adjusted the seat. She held her hand out for the car keys. But I didn't relinquish them.

"Leslie, shouldn't you let me drive? You've got to be tired." I looked at her eager face and knew her answer before she said it.

"Not that tired, I slept on the train. Just give me the keys, sit back and let me remember what it feels like to drive this baby."

I sighed in resignation; this was a familiar issue. "Well, it is your car."

"Yes, I know." She smiled as she adjusted the seat belt to accommodate her shape.

She backed the car out, merged into city traffic at the corner, and headed quickly toward the freeway, accelerating by a slow-moving truck to beat him to the turn. "Can we stop and pick up some fruit?" she asked. "I'm dying for something exotic like a papaya or a mango."

I laughed. "Is this another craving? I thought you were past those."

She grinned, "Yeah, me too. Maybe it's just the limited selection overseas. The Whole Foods Market is on the way."

"Sure thing." I told her.

We soon reached the supermarket and went inside. I let her use the shopping cart as a walker. We headed to the fruit aisle.

"Alex, where are the bananas and the kiwis? They're usually right here." she exclaimed, pointing to the rack holding only a couple of pineapples and some whole coconuts.

"That's odd, let me ask the clerk." I turned and questioned a stock boy who was loading apples on my left.

"No, we're out again and we didn't receive any with our last shipment either," he said. "Maybe you could try back tomorrow?"

I turned back to Leslie. "Sorry babe. You want to check the Bag n Save?"

Leslie made a sour face and shook her head. "Nope, you know I like the quality here better. I can live without them for another day. This pineapple will do for now."

We proceeded to the checkout counter, and Leslie whipped out her credit card to pay while the cashier quickly whisked everything through.

The bagger glanced at our purchases, then looked at me and silently motioned toward a rack of reusable shopping bags.

I pulled a parachute cloth shopping bag out of my pocket and handed it to the bagger who quickly filled it with our items.

Leslie was recording something in a small electronic notebook when suddenly a guy in a large parka careened into our cart, knocking it sideways and spilling our bags. Leslie managed not to fall, but the man had tripped and fallen to the ground. He was scrambling to get back on his feet when the security manager that had been chasing him grabbed his coat. He pulled on the man's arm and a can of clam chowder fell to the floor.

"You can't steal here!" the security guy shouted.

"Give me a break!" pleaded the thief. The smell of wood smoke emanated from his clothing, permeating the whole checkout area. "I got a family to feed! I'm out of work."

"Well, my job is to stop shoplifters like you and I don't want to lose it! Tell your problems to the judge!" the manager replied loudly as he roughly redirected the thief toward an office accompanied by a second employee.

We headed to the car in silence, stunned by the man's desperation. As she pulled out the keys, the street lights in the parking lot unexpectedly flickered and went out. I looked back at the store. It had gone dark, too. "Another power outage," I told Leslie. We fumbled in a dimly lit area to open the car doors. Leslie eased herself down into the car, got it started, then guided it out toward the highway.

Our troubles in the dawning era of sky rocketing gasoline prices had just started.

CHAPTER TWO

Taking Stock

F*ALL 2015,* O*MAHA*

"Men occasionally stumble over the truth, but most of them pick themselves up and hurry off as if nothing ever happened."
— S*IR* W*INSTON* C*HURCHILL*

We were on high alert during the drive home in the dark. Most law-abiding citizens stopped at each intersection and yielded right of way, but some impatient drivers tried to force their way through the intersections without waiting their turn. I again wished I was behind the wheel and not Leslie, just for safety's sake. I made my mind up to have her pull over when she asked me a question.

"Alex! What's with the power?" She slowed as we came to an intersection and peered in both directions. A white pick-up rolled up and stopped, yielding as we started to cross. I kept a wary eye on the opposite side of the intersection. I answered her as we safely made it across.

"I don't know. It's been doing this a couple of times a week. Started right after you left on your trip. The power outages don't usually last long, though. Most have been just ten or fifteen minutes." As if listening, the streetlights glowed then flashed on. "See, I told you," I said relieved. We turned the corner and headed down the street to our home.

We lived in a typically middle class area and our home backed one of the holes of a public golf course. The yard was fenced and a screen of trees protected us from errant golf balls. The house itself was two stories, a gray stone façade against white siding with black trim, though you could hardly make this out in the dim street light.

Leslie swung into our driveway and honked the horn.

"Mommy! You're home!" Sean dashed out of the house to give Leslie a big hug. At nine, he was still open with his displays of affection.

Cameron sauntered slowly out the door behind his brother. Now thirteen, he was reluctant to show any emotions. The closest he got was the smile on his face. His hands remained firmly jammed into his jean pockets, but Leslie hugged him anyway.

We exchanged glances over her shoulder. He rolled his eyes and I just grinned at him. "Hey, help me with your mom's luggage okay?" I asked. He gladly broke free of her embrace and took the bag from me.

I noted Leslie's frown when my mother appeared in the doorway. Janine MacCasland was a petite but astute lady. Her silvery hair and big blue eyes belied the steel within. She and Leslie were very similar – which explained why they were frequently at loggerheads with each other.

My father, Aiden, had died unexpectedly just after I graduated from college. Mom focused on raising Ace who was fifteen years my junior. But once he had graduated high school and gone off to UCLA, Mom had gotten lonely. She had visited us several times, and those visits had gone much smoother than Leslie or I had anticipated. Surprisingly, they operated well as a tag team with the boys.

Eventually we made the decision to have her move up to Omaha to help manage the boys since Leslie was out of town so often. Leslie hadn't been thrilled, but saw the practicality since Janine could take over so many of the household chores, especially the cooking. We were now three months into the new living arrangements, and things weren't quite working out.

"Hello, Janine," Leslie said coolly. "Did you have any trouble with the boys?"

"Nothing I couldn't handle. They respond well to hands-on mothering," she replied. I cringed at the smugness in her tone and saw Leslie's jaw tighten as she walked stiffly past my mother and into the house.

"Mom!" I objected. "She just got back. Just give it a rest."

A few weeks later I was finishing breakfast with the boys when the phone rang. Mom got up and hit the speaker button.

"Alex?" Leslie's alarmed voice reverberated through the phone. "The schools have closed. Quick, turn on a TV!"

I motioned to Sean, who was closest to the kitchen TV, to switch it on. "Find local news," I told him. He flipped through several news channels until I spotted what I was looking for. "That's it," I said, spotting a breaking report running across the bottom of the screen.

A reporter stood in front of a school building announcing that school districts city-wide were closing due to budget reasons. The higher costs of fuel and food had eaten through the full year's budget in just four months. The station flashed several pictures of school buses parked at gas pumps and teachers with school staff members huddled in heavy coats inside classrooms and offices.

"Darn!" Mom said. "You guys won't be going to school for a while."

Cameron and Sean looked at Mom as if she were Santa Claus. They whooped with delight and Sean danced around the kitchen, chanting that school was out. "I got first dibs on the Wii!" he yelled, heading out the kitchen door, followed closely by Cameron.

"Oh no, you don't, boys!" I yelled. "Get back here and finish your breakfast."

A few weeks later, Mom popped her head into my office shortly after lunch. "Alex, we need to get some more food."

The deeply worried tone in her voice triggered memories of my father.

Dad had been a geologist who knew that the world would start running out of oil at some point, and suspected that this point was a lot sooner than many realized. The world's oil deposits had taken millions of years to create, he had told me, and once they were gone, they were gone for good. From Dad's vantage point, once the world had reached maximum oil production, or the *peak oil* point, the subsequent decline in production would precipitate all types of chaos as everyone fought over dwindling supplies. Once oil prices collapsed in the mid eighties after more than a decade of energy-related shocks, though, few people paid any attention to him as most wallowed in cheap oil and forgot about the long term energy realities.

Dad had diagrammed the way an economic collapse would propagate outward and ripple across multiple sectors of the economy. Schools, stores, the government and businesses, all would progressively experience difficulties that would in turn impose difficulties on the other sectors. It was essentially an economic chain reaction and its pattern was somewhat predictable.

If these events were in motion... My thoughts raced as I followed Mom back into the living room. She turned and handed me a fat envelope.

"What's this?"

"I want you to take that and go to Sam's Club or Costco and get everything on the list."

Astonished, I pulled out a wad of $100 bills and a detailed shopping list. There were several categories and everything on it had bulk amounts or large sizes listed.

"Mom, what is this for? We have food in the pantry."

"It's the only survival-related thing your Dad ever asked me to do for him. He wanted a list of food needed for ten to twelve people for six months of menus. And all of it had to be canned, boxed, dry, or preserved. He didn't cook much, so he needed my help. I always thought it was a strange request, but you know how he was."

"There's $10,000 dollars here! What the…?"

"Alex, I'm just an old woman with an active imagination. But if you could simply grant a dead man one of his last wishes, I'm sure I'd sleep better at night. Can you just do this for my peace of mind?"

I stared at her as I processed all the strange incidents that had been happening lately. Who was to say a shortage in bananas would not be followed by a shortage of true essentials?

"I'll go hook up the trailer."

Mom nodded and gave me a hug.

We drove far away from our normal supermarket. Mom suggested that we not see anyone we know when we bought all this stuff. I hated to waste the gas, but if we were going to stockpile, we needed to do it discretely.

The warehouse food store was crowded as always, but no one seemed to be grabbing stuff off the shelves. We spoke to a floor manager and told him we were making a large cash purchase and needed a place to put our carts as they filled up. He showed us a doorway to a storage area and gave us a handful of cards.

"Just slap a code card on each cart as you put it here. We'll know it's a large buy. Come get a manager when you are ready to check out."

The list had been stark in its simplicity and detail. Each major food group was identified. There had even been a section on infant and toddler foods. Everything was itemized by variety and amount to purchase. We had added our own essentials like matches, soap, zip lock bags, and diapers, assuming the worst. It felt like we were going on a very long camping trip.

Four hours and twelve carts later, we paid for everything and a team of stock boys helped us load the trailer and the car. So much food filled the car, we couldn't see out the back window. We made a point of returning after dark so no one would see us offloading this food into the garage.

We arrived and backed the trailer into the garage. The car jutted out into the driveway and was only partly visible from the street. We immediately set the boys to helping us unload it into Mom's room and on shelves in the garage.

Suddenly, a voice rang out from the darkness in front of the garage. "Hello? Anyone there?"

Mom stiffened.

"Wow, look at all the food!" the voice said. We still couldn't make out a face or connect a name to the voice.

I rushed toward the voice, trying to block the interior view of our garage and back the visitor farther out into the driveway. I was still trying to see through the darkness to identify the person.

"Hello? I asked cautiously. "Who are you?"

"Oh, I'm sorry," said the man, stepping into the pool of light cast by our exterior garage light. "I'm Martin Anderson. I was just walking by and noticed all the activity. I live a couple of streets over. I think I've seen this peppy little lady" – he nodded toward Mom, standing at the side of the wagon – "walking down my street a few times. Thought I'd look her up if I got the chance. Just happened to be out for an evening walk and saw all the lights on." He smiled and gave Mom the eye. Probably a widower looking for a neighborhood hook-up, I thought.

"Well, we're kind of busy right now," I said, annoyed. All our efforts to keep this stash a secret were now shot.

"Yeah, I can see that. Just thought you might be carrying something heavy and maybe I could help." He paused, then asked, "Why are you buying all that food?"

Mom stepped forward. "Martin, you don't know me from Adam, but let me tell you why we've bought all these food supplies." She took Martin's arm and deliberately walked him back toward the street.

As she maneuvered this nosy neighbor down the drive, I quickly unhooked the trailer, then got in the van and moved it into the garage next to the trailer. I hopped out and motioned to Cameron to lower the garage door while I went out to check on Mom, he nodded in understanding and quickly moved to the side door to hit the garage opener button on the wall. I heard the grinding gears as the garage door started to close behind me. By the time I reached the end of our driveway, Mom was returning from the street. She had what looked like a business card in her hand.

"Are you okay?" I asked, tense with concern, both for her and for our secret.

"Yes, I tried to explain to him about your dad's energy theories and strongly advised him to go and get a food stash of his own. From the look he gave me, I'm sure that he thought I was crazy. Even so, I made him swear that he would never tell anyone what we had."

"Do you know this guy?"

"No, I've only seen him while walking around the neighborhood. He seems nice enough, but I really wish he hadn't seen our food reserves." Her relieved expression when she had first seen our purchases had now been replaced with worry.

I wasn't sure if we were ever going to need all these supplies, but if we did, Martin might cause a lot of trouble. "Do you think there's any chance he'll actually get his own provisions as you suggested?"

"God, I hope so." she said in resignation.

"Yeah, me too." I said helplessly as we headed back into the house.

CHAPTER THREE

Adjustments

EARLY DECEMBER 2015, OMAHA

"I'm living so far beyond my income that we may almost be said to be living apart."

— E E CUMMINGS

"So with gasoline," I said, moving across the whiteboard to the chart I had diagramed to emphasize my point, "because there's nothing that can easily replace it, the high price we're seeing is just a form of rationing."

"And what happens if our gas prices seem relatively higher here than in China because of our weak dollar?" a beautiful petite brunette named Maria asked.

"Then China gets more affordable gasoline than we do. Ironically, if the currency differences are big enough, they might not even realize that we're experiencing an oil shortage. It will simply seem like business as usual for them."

The familiar vibration at my hip broke my train of thought, stopping my lecture abruptly. The screen's vaguely green glow showed a number that wasn't familiar, but the Toyco Corp ID let me know it was someone at Leslie's job. "Excuse me a moment," I told my class while flipping the phone open. "Alex MacCasland," I said then listened intently.

"Damn, she's three weeks early. Which hospital?" The students who weren't talking to each other stared at me with growing interest. I remembered how curious I had been when my eighth-grade science teacher had gone into labor during a lab experiment.

Adjustments

Some things never change. "Thanks for the call. I'll get there as soon as possible."

I hung up the phone and announced to the class, "Sorry, I've got to cut the review short. My wife just went into labor. Please send me an email if you have any questions. I should be able to check them tomorrow. Good luck on Friday's exam."

Several students wished me luck as I raced for the door.

I had ridden my bike to work in an effort to conserve fuel. Home was only five miles from the University of Nebraska at Omaha campus, meaning a good thirty minute delay if I went home to get the car. The hospital was closer, about three miles straight west, so I gave Mom a call as I packed my lecture notes and books into the bike's sidesaddle.

"Mom, Leslie's in labor. I got a call from her secretary. Her water broke and they took her directly to the hospital. Can you grab her bag?" When she asked where it was, I responded. "Should be on the shelf in the closet – throw in her toothbrush and night cream, will ya. Yeah – less than thirty minutes." I hopped on and started peddling like mad for the hospital. It was cold, but at least it hadn't been snowing.

Mom met me at the emergency room with Sean and Cameron by her side.

"Alex, here's her bag and some things I thought you might need. We'll put your bicycle in the car."

"Thanks, Mom. I turned to the boys and smiled. "Don't worry. Your mom is going to be fine."

"Don't worry about us. Give Mom a hug."

"Okay guys. I'll call you as soon as there's news. Sorry you can't be in the room with us."

"Eeww!" Sean said. "Why would we want to watch that, Dad?"

I smiled at Mom and dashed up to Labor and Delivery. I found Leslie already settled in the birthing room. It was a well-lit room with no windows and lots of specialized baby-delivery equipment planted around the walls. This setup allowed her to labor and give birth in the same room, which was apparently easier on the mother and cheaper for the hospital. Unlike Cameron and Sean's births, which had both come in the middle of the night, this one would occur in broad daylight. Leslie looked wide awake but worried.

"Hi babe. How are you doing?" I asked.

"I'm okay, except for about every three minutes or so." This last word tapered off as a contraction grabbed her.

I took her hand and slowly kneaded her fingers as I glanced at the clock. "How far along are you?"

"Only three centimeters," came the response from the nurse.

Having been through this drill twice before, I knew that when her cervix dilated to ten centimeters, she'd be ready to push. We had a ways to go yet.

"How'd you know I was here?" Leslie asked when her face relaxed again.

"Your secretary called me. Said you were in labor," I replied, watching her abdomen squeeze into basketball firmness. I noted the time. She was still at three minutes between contractions.

"Yeah, we were in executive session for closing or moving operations overseas. Having my water break wasn't the most professional thing I've ever done. You should have seen the floor." She managed a wan grin.

"So was any decision made?" I asked, knowing that the discussion could distract her from the growing pain for a little while.

"Yeah, they're moving overseas." She nodded as I looked over in alarm. "It was just awful. Steve, the CEO says, 'Let's face facts. We have two choices at this point. We can either shut down the company or move all of our operations outside the United States.' Several of us objected. Jerry, the Resources VP, said that sounded a little premature. Steve just growled. 'Premature? Have you seen our quarterly results?' You could have heard a pin drop in the room."

She paused as her face contorted. She held her stomach and then spoke up as it passed. "Our production is way down because employees can't get in to work, and we're having serious logistic issues. Most of our imported components stopped arriving in September, and shipping costs for the domestics between plants has quadrupled. Long story short, they're moving operations to Kazakhstan... It's a strong oil production region with close proximity to markets in Asia. Our US workers are outta luck, though. It makes me so mad... aaaaugh!"

"Breathe, babe," I told her. A nurse examined her and reported that her cervix had dilated to five centimeters. "She'll transition into heavy labor soon. You should get her to rest while she can." I nodded and she dimmed the room's lights.

Two hours later she was at nine centimeters and almost fully effaced. She was deeply focused and the contractions were coming every thirty seconds. "You're really close, hon! This is going to be a piece of cake."

"God," She said as she blew out little panting puffs to get through it. "Can they give me some more medication?"

"There's no time for it," the nurse said. "The baby will be out before it takes effect. You're almost ready to push."

"Give it to me anyway!" Leslie begged.

"Babe, relax. The nurse is right. It's almost over," I said as confidently as I could.

"What do you know about giving birth? Have you ever had your legs spread to the world and felt like shitting a softball? Ahhhh! Give me an epidural!"

"Leslie, it's okay, you're doing fine. Just breathe..." I looked at her with a feeling of wonder for what she was going through. Twice before she had been through this, and while labor was never routine, I wasn't as particularly worried for her health. She just took terrific care of herself. She had people that clipped her nails, cut her hair, expertly adjusted her back, and every time she suspected the slightest medical issue, she made time to see a doctor. She also had been active with exercise throughout this entire pregnancy. Leslie returned to her strong rhythmic breathing as I held her hand and wiped her face with a moist wash cloth.

Suddenly the power failed and we were thrust into darkness.

"What the hell?" Leslie cried. I looked up anxiously at the blank baby monitor.

"Just a power shortage, ma'am, they happen all the time," the nurse said. Our generators will kick on in a second." She pulled out a flashlight and its beam illuminated Leslie's face.

"Ten centimeters, now. You're almost there," announced a second nurse. The lights had still not come on. "But don't push yet."

"What happened to the power?" Leslie moaned again as her muscles tightened again. "I want to push!" She clutched my hand until her nails were biting into my skin. I gritted my teeth from the pain.

"Leslie, I love ya, but you've got to stop putting your nails through my hand." I pried her fingers open to adjust her painful grip on my hand and turned to the nurse. "Where's the doctor?"

"He's on an emergency C-section. I'm seeing if we can locate another one that's available. In the meantime, I've been through a lot of births. She's in good hands."

"No freaking doctor! Where's my doctor? Ahh!" She let loose a wail in the darkness that was heard down the hall.

"Leslie you've got to calm down." The nurse firmly said. "Let's take good deep breaths and you can start pushing in a couple of minutes."

The fetal monitor remained mute without lights flashing or the comforting beeps I was used to. This was going to be a real traditional birth.

Adjustments

The nurse focused the flashlight on the area between her legs and illuminated the birthing in an eerie glow. The crown of the head could be seen emerging.

Someone came rushing in the room. "Hello, I'm Dr. Phandra, how are you?" He immediately took up a position just in front of Leslie. "Nurse, please proceed."

A minute later, the baby whooshed into the waiting hands of the nurse. "It's a girl!" she announced happily. They continued to work with Leslie to help her expel the placenta. The activity in the room was slow and deliberate in the near darkness, and the flashlight was taken to a table to study the baby in detail. Leslie leaned back in the dark while I stood next to her, massaging her shoulders.

Once satisfied that the baby didn't require an incubator, they handed Leslie the tiny baby. I held both of them and tried to reassure Leslie that everything was going to be okay. Someone opened a door to the hallway to let light in.

"Have you made up your mind what you would like to call our daughter?" I asked.

Leslie was awfully pale, but she managed a smile. "I've got a short list of ideas. What are you thinking?"

"I just hope..." I started to say when the electricity came back on. The hospital generators were now offering minimal lighting. The nurse stepped in to apologize for the inconvenience.

"Hope. I like it," Leslie said as the baby blinked in the dim lights. "Hope, welcome to Omaha!"

We had not received the mail for several days, and when the postman came, he brought a large sack of our mail up to the front door. I threw out the usual junk mail and segregated everything that looked like a bill to the side and started to work through the pile. The first envelope contained our electrical bill. Not only was the new electricity rate three times the previous one, but they were asking for a five thousand dollar deposit to keep our service on.

I opened another envelope. It contained the hospital bill. Given the fact that the nurse delivered the baby in front of a podiatrist in the dark, I had hoped for a significant discount, but none had been given. At least we had health insurance to help cover it.

The next bill was our heating bill. This one was truly staggering. It was more than three times as high as our bill had been the previous year for November, and they too were demanding a five thousand dollar deposit.

These deposit demands made no sense to me. We had always paid our bills on time, and Leslie and I were employed, weren't we?

The last bills were even more ominous. They were from three of our four credit card companies, each demanding that we pay our outstanding balances immediately and informing us that our credit cards were being cancelled. What did they know that we didn't?

Leslie came into the living room and I pushed a small stack of mail addressed to her in her direction. She sorted through it and pulled out an envelope from Toyco. Her hand was shaking as she used a letter opener to rip the top of the envelope open. She read carefully and her face fell as she read it.

"It looks like I didn't make the cut," she said as she handed me the envelope.

I read through it quickly. They had terminated Leslie and thanked her for her time. A mediocre severance check was included.

"Well, I guess this means that we're not going to Kazakhstan," I said dryly.

"No, we aren't." She sat down heavily in a chair. I noticed she didn't seem shocked.

"You knew about this?"

She turned back to face me. "Yes, I got a call from the office just after I gave birth."

"And you didn't tell me?" I stared at her in disbelief at what I thought was an unnecessary surprise.

"I had hoped my report would help them change their minds," she said unemotionally, blankly.

"Well, obviously it didn't." A well of anger bubbled up from nowhere, and I inadvertently struck a lamp which fell over in a crash.

Mom came rushing in and looked curiously at Leslie, then me. I handed over the letter.

Mom read it and her face fell. She sank dejectedly into the chair next to Leslie. "Oh dear, I'm sorry, I didn't realize this was one of their options."

I handed her the bills from the gas and electric companies.

Mom read them and gasped. "Look," she said, "I can help with these if you like."

Leslie just looked sick. She had never expected to lose her job and certainly never expected to be floated by her mother-in-law. She put her head in her hands.

I filled the ominous silence. "Mom, if you don't mind covering the deposits, we'd be truly in your debt."

"Lord, son, that's ten grand. Let me think." She did some quick mental math and replied, "Yeah, I can manage it, but I'll be pretty much tapped out after that."

"Look, I think Alex and I can swing the electricity deposit," Leslie said, "if you could get the heating bill. Hopefully we'll be back to normal shortly. With a little luck, I'll have another job and can help out."

My mother nodded at this offer. She was always practical. "Okay, it's settled. We'll just have to really reduce our energy usage to keep our bills small," she said. "What about your car, Leslie? How are we going to make the payments on your Ford lease?"

Leslie pulled back, shaken. She then said sadly, "I guess we'll need to give it back to the dealership. I'll call them and tell them to pick it up from my office – that will save us a trip."

"What about the house and van payments?" Mom asked, looking at me.

"I've still got some income coming in from my salary. If we keep our expenses down we should be able to keep making them."

Leslie stood up and started pacing. "What about the cell phones, cable TV, or our athletic club membership?"

The athletic club membership? Now it was my turn to be startled. I liked to work out and it was a great way for me to handle stress, but it was something that we absolutely didn't have to have. Yet for some reason this revelation struck me the way that Leslie's losing her car deflated her. I found myself hoping that all this energy business would blow over by the spring so that we could rejoin.

"Other than a single cell phone and our home phone, I think we need to cancel the rest of those services – I'd like to keep Internet access too." I picked up an empty envelope and started making notes. "Hon, can you start calling these changes in? We'll need to drop our second home phone line last. Mom, make sure Ace has the number we keep. Are you going to keep your cell?" I asked her.

"I think I will for now – just until the contract runs out. That's only four months. After that, I don't know. We'll see. Give me the heating bill and I'll make the appropriate cash transfers."

I handed her the bill and gave her a hug. She smiled and gave me a motherly peck on the cheek, then whispered, "You need to keep an eye on Leslie. Her world is coming apart at the seams." I nodded, glancing over to my wife who was staring blankly out the living-room window. No, she wasn't taking this very well.

CHAPTER FOUR

An Unexpected Gift

DECEMBER 2015, OMAHA

"He who despairs over an event is a coward, but he who holds hope for the human condition is a fool."

— ALBERT CAMUS

I used the cell phone to transfer some of Leslie's retirement savings into her checking account. Sure, we'd have to pay a penalty for early withdrawal, but we needed to have some money to buy things for Christmas. We parked in the parking lot at the mall and for the first Christmas season in memory, only a small number of cars were scattered at the vast mall parking lot.

"That's strange." Leslie said as we entered the domed entrance. "Normally it's hard to find a place to park this time of year."

We immediately saw that many things were different. The inside corridors were unheated and dimly lit. The normal Christmas season decorations were nowhere to be seen, and I was secretly grateful that the mall speakers from whom ubiquitous holiday music was usually playing from dawn to midnight were silent. Mall management was on a minimal energy budget, too, it seemed. Security guards were posted prominently near every exit, and some were walking through the halls like cops on a beat. Here and there a few silent shoppers peered into darkened stores or scanned the nude mannequins in the windows.

Leslie made a beeline for Macy's and stopped dead in her tracks. I walked up behind her and heard her gasp. "There's almost nothing here!" Peering over her head into the gloom of the dimly lit store, I could see she was right. Racks hung empty. Shelves were bare. The shoe department had row upon row of vacant display stands and empty nooks. The makeup counter directly in front of us had posters and layered racks, but they stood barren and desolate. The store was a wasteland.

"Where is everything?" she asked the solitary clerk, who was bundled up in a heavy coat, gloves and a knit cap.

"All gone," she said simply.

"Where did it go?"

"We had a sale right after Thanksgiving. Nothing much has come in since."

That mystified Leslie. "Who would buy clothes when everyone is going crazy to get food?"

"That's what our management said. They elected to reduce our inventory, and we practically gave most of it away at that last sale." She gave us a wry look. "You'd be surprised what people will buy when they think they're getting a bargain – even if they're hungry."

"So, why are you still open?"

"Well, someone's got to keep an eye on the equipment, I guess." She gestured toward the cash register. "Since we don't have any inventory, this store is closing the last day of December. We're on minimal staffing – just a few of us here to get rid of anything else that's left in the store."

We left the store shaking our heads and headed back out into the center section of the mall. The next three storefronts were closed with the grates pulled down and locked. I could see empty shelves behind the grates, and most of the stores' signs had been removed. I looked down one direction of the long hallway and realized most of the stores were closed or nearly empty. Leslie had scanned in the other direction with the same results.

We soon left the mall and drove back toward home, hoping to find a strip mall with something worth buying for Christmas. I could tell by the sparse parking in each location that most of these stores were not really open for business either. Dry cleaners were closed, fast food joints were boarded up, and a number of automobile parts stores were shuttered. Only banks seemed to have

An Unexpected Gift

customers – probably people seeking loans or draining their already meager savings accounts.

Finally, we noticed a parking lot full of cars. We pulled in, curious to see what kind of store was actually doing business. We were surprised to discover it was a thrift shop, run for the benefit of a local animal shelter. We parked and went in.

The customers were intently sizing up the various items in the store. "The quality of merchandise seems better than I remember," Leslie said, "But the prices seem really high."

"When were you ever in here?" I asked. I couldn't imagine this type of store even being on Leslie's radar.

"In September. The boys were looking for suitable props for their Halloween costumes." She started to finger a boy's size shirt. "You never know what you'll find in these places."

The clothes and shoes were organized by size. Leslie told me to shop for the boys while she would pick things out for Hope and Mom. "Don't forget to get me something!" she called as we drifted in different directions. Nuts! What could she want or more importantly – what did she need? I started looking. I carefully picked out a sweater for each of the boys then found a small book about gardening I thought Mom would like. As I wandered toward the back of the store, a jumble of baby gear caught my eye. I quickly rooted through and found the perfect gift for Leslie. I hustled to the checkout with my treasures, hoping I could hide them in the trunk before Leslie saw them.

"Will this be cash or do you have something to exchange?" I was asked.

"Exchange? You mean I can trade in old items for new ones?"

"Yup! How do you think we're still in business? Our inventory keeps walking in the door," the clerk stated proudly.

"Interesting. How does it work?" I asked, intrigued by their success in such a down market.

"We price each item with a color tag based on its value. It's easier to adjust the color price chart over there given the recent inflation than it is to re-price everything in the store. If you have something to trade, we give it a color." She pointed to several items on the counter. "You can trade two of your items of that color for one of ours."

"So, I can trade some of my children's outgrown clothes for things that will fit."

"That's the general idea – as long as the items you're trading still have value," she said. "Some people still use cash and that helps us pay our bills, but most people trade."

"Would you accept food for payment?" I asked curiously.

"Of course, we'll trade food at par for anything in the store. You have food to trade?" His voice rose in volume at this last question and I was now drawing the attention of other shoppers.

"No, of course not, but we are hoping to plant a garden in the spring." I said quickly, avoiding suspicion that we might have a home stash.

She didn't think much of that idea. "Good luck. Did you have cash or something to trade?"

"I have cash for the clothing and book. What would this cost in trade?" I asked, hauling Leslie's gift onto the counter.

"It has a blue tag. That could be a pair of boots or a jacket?" The clerk eyed my leather bomber jacket, but I knew I wouldn't barter it.

"I have some other jackets at home. Can you set this aside for me?"

"Yes, we'll hold it for you for two hours." She leaned over the counter and lowered her voice as she took the item to mark it with my name.

I nodded my understanding and replied quietly that I'd be back before five pm. It looked like Christmas was looking up. Wondering if Leslie knew how the system worked, I took my other purchases to the car and came back in to see if Leslie needed help with any of her selections. I found her carrying a hat for Mom, a variety of assorted baby clothes under which she was holding something. She also had an old flannel shirt that could have been for herself, Mom or me. It looked warm and soft, and I hoped it was mine. Sure enough, she caught sight of me and tried to hide the shirt. "Did you find anything?" she asked.

"Yes, the clerk is holding it for me. Do you need any help?"

"No. You can just go wait in the car for me. I should be along in just a bit."

"Do you know that they will take cash or exchange things we have but don't want?"

Leslie perked up at that news. "Really? I have a couple of boxes of clothing the boys have outgrown. Maybe we should go home and get them."

"Just tell that clerk in the red blouse that you're with me and we are coming back with a box of stuff to exchange. She'll give us a couple of hours."

"Wow! We could really have a decent Christmas!" Leslie exclaimed as she headed to the checkout line.

We were about to enjoy what was essentially a Salvation Army Christmas and Leslie seemed to be excited about the prospect. It struck me how quickly we had been able to accept and adapt to our changed circumstances.

Christmas was subdued in general, a far cry from the material and decorative excesses of past years. We didn't even have a tree, as the tree lots that normally popped up after Thanksgiving hadn't appeared, and I wasn't willing to chop one down from the golf course. We held a small service at home having little interest in making the long, cold walk to church. We lit a couple of candles, read the nativity story and sang some carols. Leslie prayed for our future.

Leslie and I had gotten the boys bicycles during a sale in the early fall before everything had gone to hell. We had hidden them in our storage space under the stairs to wait until Christmas morning. Late last night Mom and Leslie tied a bow and a long piece of yarn to each, leading out of the closet and into the living room. The boys would find a lock in their stocking with the yarn attached. The rest of their presents were more mundane, consisting of warm clothing and shoes we'd found at the thrift shop. When possible, we'd picked out items that were a couple of sizes too big. The boys were growing and who knew when we might find affordable clothes again.

Oil Dusk

The boys were excited about their bikes, especially since their old bikes had inexplicably disappeared recently – when Leslie and I had traded them to the thrift shop for other items.

"Guys, just leave that ribbon on your bike so whoever steals it will know that it was a gift," Leslie said.

"Mom!" Cameron groaned. "We'll lock up when we park them, okay?"

Sean didn't even look up from checking out the derailleur and gears.

"Sean!" My tone was stern, but he needed to understand. He jerked his head up, looking startled. "Huh?" he inquired with a tilt of his head.

"You must lock your bike every time you get off! Do you understand?" I said. "Do you know why that's important?"

"Because someone might steal it and I wouldn't get another one?" he asked after thinking a moment.

"That's right. Now don't forget it," I warned. "Cameron, can you take Sean out and show him how to shift gears?"

"Sure, Dad! Come on, Sean, let's go show Bob and Danny our new bikes!"

The boys put on heavy coats and wheeled the bikes out the front door and down the walk. I thought briefly about their safety, riding around unaccompanied, but we could only protect them so much. Hopefully they had paid attention to my guidance about the types of people they needed to avoid.

Our gifts to each other were functional and simple. I had purchased Leslie a child carrier backpack with a built-in stand. It was adjustable so even Sean could carry Hope if he needed to. Mom got a walking stick I had found at the thrift shop. She had knitted me a winter cap that must have taken her a considerable amount of time. Leslie gave me some used woodworking tools.

Just then the phone rang and I picked up the receiver on my desk. "Hello?"

"Merry Christmas", came the bright voice of my little brother.

"Let me put you on speaker." I moved into the living room with Leslie and yelled to Mom that Ace was on the phone. I clicked on the speaker phone. "Did Santa bring you anything?"

"You bet. My stocking was full and the cookies I left out are gone – are the boys there?" he said in a light tone.

"Nope, just us adults. How are things really going in California?"

"Pretty weird if you ask me." He said in a much more solemn voice.

"How's that?" Mom asked as she returned from the kitchen with a large mug of tea she handed to Leslie. Leslie nodded her thanks.

"Everyone is buying gas out here like there's no tomorrow. Two of the stations near me actually ran out of gas this week."

"But, aren't your gas prices as crazy as ours are?" Mom asked

"Maybe worse, but that's not stopping them. I've never seen gas lines like this before and everybody seems to have lots of gas cans to fill."

"Are you okay?" I asked.

"Yeah, I'm fine. I've filled up my bike and some extra gas cans. I can probably go a few weeks before I have to worry about my next fill-up."

"You need any money?" Mom asked. I rolled my eyes. Yeah, when does a young man not want money? She spoiled Ace terribly.

"Uh, well... could you send me a little extra – just in case?"

"Sure, honey. I'll transfer some funds directly into your checking account."

"Thanks, Mom. Are you okay? I'm betting you're getting pretty spooked by all this."

"A little. I'm afraid your Dad's concerns may be coming true." She replied suddenly aware that the boys were listening from upstairs and Leslie was now glaring. I motioned to Leslie that we'd take the call into my office. She nodded and smiled gratefully at me.

"Hey Ace, we're having a hard time hearing you clearly on this extension. We're going to pick up in the office. Hang on a minute" I told him.

"Mom, let's try the phone in the study." I said, heading to my office.

Mom followed me and we shut the door as I hit the speaker button on my desk phone. Leslie stayed in the living room.

"Ace, I'm going to send you three thousand dollars." she said with finality. "I want you to use two thousand dollars to buy food. If you don't need it, you can always donate it to the needy later."

"Okay, Mom, it's your money." He said.

"Yes, it is." Mom said. Our conversation continued a few minutes longer, then Ace said goodbye.

As we hung up, Mom looked at me with a worried expression. "Do you think he's going to be okay?" She picked some lint off of my shirt as we returned to the living room.

"He's a smart guy. I'm sure he'll be fine." I replied.

"I just wish he weren't so far away." She said as she sat down on the sofa.

"Me too." I said. I looked over at my mother. She was hunched forward with her elbows on her knees and her hands clasped tightly together. When she looked up, our eyes met and I could see her sadness, but also a fierce defiance. She spoke quietly, so Leslie would not hear her from the other room.

"Your dad wanted you to have a full life, even if it will be very different from what we've all known in the past. I've waited years for Aiden's theories to be proven wrong; I've even prayed they'd be proven wrong, but damned if the old fool wasn't right in seeing this coming. I overlooked many of his crazy ideas. But now..." She paused and I saw tears in her eyes. "Well, at least he was crazy enough to prepare. Leslie won't agree, naturally, but I think it's almost time to head to the Ark." She stood and walked to the window, staring out at the bleak gray of the Nebraska winter. She was silent for a moment, then turned back to me.

"You are the man of the family, Alex. Your sister and her family are fine in Europe. There's nothing I can or need do for them. Ace only has to worry about himself, but I told him about Dad's Ark and gave him the address. He'll try to make his way there on his own if he can find enough gas for his motorcycle once the weather improves. He might make it out to us by summer."

"But we have food here, the house, and job options. Why leave?" I asked. I had seen the Ark, had even been there when Dad had first looked it over. I couldn't imagine us actually living there. "Have you ever been there Mom?"

"No, but Dad showed me photos and I was aware of work he had done there. It's not much, hon, but it's ours and I believe your Dad knew what he was doing. He had no confidence the country would get our energy act together and took actions to protect us. Our family's long term survival was your Dad's primary concern." She waved her head indicating our surroundings. "We can't be sure of our security here. There's no telling what people will do. How long do you think stores will have food?" She reached into the neckline of her sweater and pulled out a set of keys on a thin gold chain. "I've been wearing these for good luck, and now I want you to have them." She unhooked the chain, removed two keys and handed them to me. "Merry Christmas, son."

"What are these to?" I asked, dubious.

"One opens the front gate of the Ark and the second is to the cabin." She smiled and touched my shoulder as she went into the kitchen to see what we had by way of food for a Christmas meal.

I was left alone, filled with a strange sense of dread. My thoughts took me back to when my father and I had first seen the Ark.

Shortly before I started college, Dad hauled me up to Arkansas to look at his most recent discovery of rural property. This site was just outside Jasper, a tiny, picturesque town on a river in the northwest part of the state. The Boston Mountains bordered the region. I gathered from his attitude that this was "the" property and purchase was a fait accompli.

The property was a couple of miles north out of town off Cedar Lane, a well- maintained county road, with a gravel access drive that led back to a cabin near a rocky, fast-flowing creek. The forty partially wooded acres were situated in a small valley that sloped up gently toward foothills on either side. The cabin was on a relatively flat area of six acres or so. The Ozark hills engendered persistent wind swirls that would keep the temperature down in the summer and, according to Dad, could provide a steady source of electricity if we put up a small wind turbine. There was a well with reportedly decent water, but the pump no longer worked, so we couldn't be sure.

The cabin wasn't much, a large main area with a small room added on the northwest side visible through a doorway near the end of the kitchen counter. It had just an opening without a door to close off the room. The little room had a small window facing west, but no closet or anything else. A stone fireplace was built into the east wall of the main room. A halved log served as a mantel. A flue handle stuck out of some bricks. Dad shoved it up and a pile of dirt, leaves, and an old bird nest fell out of the chimney.

"Well, at least the chimney isn't blocked up," I snickered. What was Dad thinking? I wondered. Crap! It wasn't even worthy of vacation spot status. Mom was not going to call this home!

The cabin door opened south, and a couple of windows on either side looked out over a wooden porch that ran the length of the cabin front. The overhanging roofline provided shade and could be a nice spot to sit in the evenings… if you were ninety!

A kitchen area was in the northwest corner, with space for a table. "Kitchen" was far too generous a description for the drab area. A counter with some open shelves and a rack of drawers backed under a small western window. What passed for a sink was a recessed spot in the counter top with an old rusting bucket sitting in it. An ancient, brittle hose snaked down from a small hole near the ceiling. A check outdoors revealed a beat-up fifty-five gallon drum in a rickety frame secured to the roof and serving as a rainwater cistern. Gravity fed the flow of water down to the bucket indoors.

Back inside, I tried to figure out the little window I had seen in the upper wall from outside. The inner ceiling was made of wood planks. In the northeast corner I could see cuts in the planking. Closer inspection showed a couple of hinges and a pull ring. I couldn't reach it but guessed it would provide a pull-down stair to an attic. I wasn't interested in investigating further. The ceiling also had a few hooks for hanging stuff – probably dead rabbits or cooking pots, I thought before kerosene lanterns came to mind. There was no sign of any electricity or a bathroom!

"Hey, Dad! I gotta take a leak. Where's the john?" I asked, sticking my head around the corner.

"You have a choice – the woods or the outhouse back there." He pointed at a dilapidated shed with a swinging door hanging by one hinge. I headed for the woods.

"Yup, I think that's the spot," he said later as we headed back toward town. "Should work out just right."

"What on earth is there to like about that place!" I exclaimed as I stared at him in astonishment. "We could get that place by the lake or the one near the hot springs. Mom would love the mountain stone house in New Hampshire or the beach cove in South Carolina. Why this dump?" I could hardly hold in my outrage. "You aren't really going to retire to that hovel, are you?" My voice rose almost an octave in disbelief.

He just smiled and nodded his head. "I've got plans, Alex, big plans! You won't recognize the place when I'm done with it. Might take me a decade or so, but someday we'll be sitting pretty while others will wonder what happened." Then Dad chose to remind me once again about his favorite lesson in the Bible. It was the story of Joseph where he had correctly interpreted the Pharaoh's dream. There were going to be seven years of feast followed by seven years of famine. Under Joseph's direction, Egypt insured that some of the bounty from the feast years was set aside for the following famine years. Dad finished up his narrative and summed it up with his profound concern that some oil shock would send all of us to the Stone Age since neither the free market system nor our government was capable of building the alternate energy infrastructure that was necessary to prevent a future economic collapse. "Nope, during our feast years, when oil prices are low, nothing gets done and during the coming famine years, when oil prices will soar, it will be too late." Dad concluded. "You can't wait till it's gone!"

I don't know what was worse, having to watch him pontificate about why this dismal outpost might someday be important to our family or having to deal with the deep fear that maybe, just maybe, he knew what he was talking about.

Mom had called later and told me Dad bought the parcel "in spite of my strenuous objections." He had some basic repair work done and then had the entire boundary fenced and gated. No-trespassing signs were posted, and the taxes were paid for by an escrow fund he set up to pay out automatically each year through a bank in Houston. He also set up meetings with various engineers and energy specialists, but I never asked Mom to give me the details of his plans. As far as I was concerned back then, he could have nuked the place and I'd never have missed it. Dad had his Ark, but I was sure I'd never be there for more than a visit and Mom would be in her grave before she actually took up residence.

Might we now need to move to the Ark? I glanced out the window and noticed that Cameron and Sean were setting up a ramp to jump their new bikes. It was little more than a wooden plank and a brick, but this was no way to treat a new bike. No, they just didn't understand that it wouldn't be easy to get another one. I rushed outside to stop them.

CHAPTER FIVE

Day Talkers and Night Stalkers

JANUARY 2016, OMAHA

"The history of the failure of war can almost be summed up in two words: too late.
* Too late in comprehending the deadly purpose of a potential enemy.
* Too late in realizing the mortal danger.
* Too late in preparedness.
* Too late in uniting all possible forces for resistance.
* Too late in standing with one's friends."

— GENERAL DOUGLAS MACARTHUR

In the six weeks between fall and spring terms at the university, short courses were offered. A special program had been set up at the request of the Chamber of Commerce to present topics of interest to businesses, local government officials, and locals. The topics varied each year, and though I had been terminated the first week of January, I was still on tap to participate in a couple of half-day sessions on current events from an economic perspective. When the university set up the program, the expected enrollment was twenty-five. When my class roster arrived via email, the class was assigned one of the largest lecture halls on campus, able to seat five hundred students. People wanted to know how and why their lives had changed, and I spent a lot of time preparing for this session.

Heavily bundled up, I rode my bike to the campus and went to the assigned lecture hall. It had some impressive video and computer capabilities designed to make the entire course accessible online or over cable TV. I had used this sort of setup before, but back then most students had no problems making it to class. Now, with astronomical gasoline prices, instruction would be transmitted by Internet and would not require their physical presence. Students could also rerun the lectures at their leisure in the event that they were short of electricity or their batteries were dead at the time the class was conducted.

A wide variety of people were filling the seats when I arrived. A new list was on the podium, and I could see that some thirty additional registrations had been added. I asked the audience to raise their hand if they lived or worked nearby. Nearly every hand went up. It seemed that everyone in the local area had been assigned to the classroom, while those farther away would get the online option. I kicked off the instruction as a couple more people rushed in to find seats.

Feeling like the host of a television talk show, I switched on the record button and started speaking. I quickly reviewed the basics of supply and demand to gauge the economic comprehension of the group. They were aware of more than I thought and by mid morning I found myself immersed in a discussion about some macroeconomic points of interest.

"How many of you blame OPEC for our current oil shortages?" I asked. Almost every hand went up. This is good, I thought. "Okay. Why?"

"Bill Parlett," he introduced himself. "They've cut back on the amount of oil they are exporting."

"True, but here's a harder question – *just why* have they cut back?" I scanned the faces and recognized one of the students that wanted to speak. "Mary?"

"Well, because it makes oil scarcer and drives oil and gasoline prices higher." Mary said.

"Not bad." I told her. "But you've missed some key facts. When oil prices started going up so quickly several months ago, was OPEC still producing at full capacity?" Several students turned to see if Mary had an answer, but she just looked puzzled and shrugged her shoulders.

An older man seated near the front spoke up instead. "Wilson Myers," he said. "Yes, they were – *if* you can believe their production numbers."

"A valid concern, but for now let's just assume those production numbers were accurate," I said. "So what brought about the higher oil prices? Anyone?"

A striking blond in a tight red sweater raised her hand at the back of the room raised her hand, and I motioned to her to speak.

"It's supply and demand, right?" she said.

"All right," I said, smiling at her. "Can you elaborate?"

She nodded her head and tossed her ebony hair back away from her face with one hand, composing her thoughts. "Well, supply was staying constant until a lot of demand increases started coming from places like India and China. As these countries developed, their citizens moved from bicycles to mopeds and mopeds to cars. It's definitely progress from their vantage point, but these countries have so many people that they are really pushing up the demand for oil."

"And who can blame them for wanting to be like us? We've certainly exposed them to a lot of movies and television where everyone has a car. Also, when you buy a more fuel-efficient car – what happens to your previous gas guzzler?" I asked pointing toward the parking lot.

"I don't know, but they gave me money for the trade-in." Mary said.

"My bet is that someone else is now driving your old car. The number of cars on the planet has doubled in the past twenty years. There are now more than a billion cars in the world in operation."

"Only a billion cars? There are more than seven billion people – though admittedly at least half of those are children," Bill pointed out.

"That's right, and that ratio gives you a sense of how many people would like to drive cars, but can't. By the way, I disagree with Mary's suggestion that oil production was staying constant. In the old days, they used to find huge oil and gas reservoirs on a regular basis – but not lately. The active oil fields in the world are being depleted by roughly five percent a year. Said another way, if the oil industry didn't add any new production to the system the world's oil output would drop by five percent within a year." I pressed a button on my video remote, and a chart appeared on the screen in front of the room.

"As this chart shows, try as they might, industry can't add enough new production to keep supply level. There have been several small new finds and a variety of new production methods developed to increase the flow, if you will, but we've peaked. In short, the world's oil production is now decreasing every year." I pushed the button again and a revised chart popped up. This chart showed that worldwide oil production would continue to fall for the foreseeable future.

Bill exclaimed. "Our oil shortages are going to get worse!"

"Yes, you've hit it dead on. In addition, this next chart shows what is happening to oil prices as the oil supply is dropping. These charts suggest that oil prices should soar."

"Well, that would explain the high prices we're seeing," Mary said.

"But I haven't quite painted the full dismal picture yet." I said. "Here's a factor people commonly overlook. Most of the oil exporting countries are also using more of their oil for their own growing populations. So, *even if* the amount of oil being produced remained constant, these countries have less oil available for export to other countries."

"So, that's why oil is getting so scarce?" a middle-aged woman in a stylish suit asked.

"Well, that's a big part of it, but not quite all," I said. "Some countries, like China, have been able to purchase oil reserves in other countries for their long-term needs. These resources aren't being produced at full capacity because they are sort of on 'lay-away' for China's future extraction and use."

"Ouch!" exclaimed one student. I heard several murmured conversations begin between other students. I let them absorb the information and then put up a new slide.

"Just one last point, honest," I joked. "Here I've added a chart showing that a lot of the oil left in the ground is heavier than the much lighter oil that has been produced in the past. Getting at this oil will require us to use up a lot of energy. In other words, if you have to expend a half a barrel of oil to be able to extract a full barrel, then you've essentially only added an additional half a barrel to the world's supply – even though the production numbers suggested that a full barrel was produced."

The class was quiet as all these facts sank in. "Okay, but you still haven't explained why OPEC cut back on their production," the older man at the front stated.

"Ah, that requires a story." I said, "But let's take a break first." I suggested. "Be back in ten, okay?"

The class mobilized and the noise level increased as students started talking among themselves.

I wanted them to think about the sequence of events we had all just gone through, but I wasn't sure if any had made the connection to the dollar's drop in value around the world and higher prices for things here at home. If they grasped the significance of that last puzzle piece, I thought the whole picture would be clear.

Soon students began wandering back into the room and taking their seats. I opened the discussion with a probing question.

"Why have we seen the price of gasoline, and a number of other commodities like food, climb so high and so quickly?"

Mary knew the answer. "Well, no one wants the dollar anymore – so everything we buy costs more."

"Can you tell me why no one would want the dollar?"

"Our trade deficit is," she hesitated, then hissed out the next word, "obscene."

"Well said. Why is that?" I asked, continuing to probe.

"It means that we Americans don't sell enough to the rest of the world to pay for all the oil that we want to import."

"Yup! We've had a gigantic trade deficit for a long time, which means that we've been allowed to buy a whole lot more than we've been able to sell to the rest of the world. That worked as long as everyone believed the dollar was sound. Now that the dollar's value is falling, a whole bunch of investors stuck with dollars are trying to jettison them before the dollar loses more value. The net result is that the world is now flooded with cheap dollars."

"Won't everyone want to buy them back when the dollar starts to rebound?" Wilson asked.

"Maybe, but our economy is now in a serious depression and it doesn't look like we're going to rebound anytime soon. Throw in the fact that the feds will likely print a lot of money to cover our national requirements and you've got a strong argument that it will be a long time before we hit bottom."

"So Professor MacCasland," a man's voice piped up, "how do we get the dollar's value back up?"

"I don't know. That will take some doing. A lot of money was lost when the dollar collapsed, and my bet is that foreign entities won't be interested in holding dollars again for a long time."

"But we'll be able to buy oil again eventually, right?"

"Well, unfortunately the rest of the world's demand is still growing. OPEC will slowly turn their production back on over the next few years, and the rest of the world will eventually be able to use all the oil that we once imported."

"Was this all inevitable?" a man in a business suit asked.

"I don't know," I answered, "but our lack of a proactive energy plan exposed us in the long run and has made us especially vulnerable. We're only five percent of the world's population, but we produced ten percent of the world's oil and consumed twenty

41

five percent of it. We are oil junkies. Now we can't pay and we're going through withdrawal."

Another man in an old fatigue jacket spoke up. "What about using force to get the OPEC countries to sell us more oil?" Several heads in the room nodded and I overheard comments about how things would be different if the Air Force's Strategic Air Command still operated out of nearby Offutt Air Force Base.

I quickly replied, "You know, with our manufacturing sector in the dumps, I think it would be military suicide to take on the other major powers, who have warned us not to mess with OPEC. Wars tend to waste tremendous amounts of oil, and we don't have enough anymore to even be a threat with our conventional weapons."

"So, you think it's going to take a while to get past the problems we're having?" he asked.

"Let's just say that we have our work cut out for us. It would have been a lot easier to implement alternate energy solutions when we had access to cheap oil and a strong dollar." I glanced up at the clock, noting we were almost out of time. I closed the class with a final comment. "If any of you were Scouts, your skills may come in handy soon."

Theory became practice the next day. A blizzard dropped a foot of snow, but there wasn't any fuel to run the plows. The city had been operating on only one leg; the storm essentially took it out. People were isolated in their homes and in trouble.

Heat was our biggest concern. We dug out all the blankets in the house and passed them around. I moved Hope's bassinet down to the warmest room, the living room, where we had a fire going each morning. We wore layers of clothing and waited for the sun to free us from the snow.

I had hopes that the bad weather would diminish the escalating crime of the past month, but they were dashed as soon as the storm let up. I looked out the master bedroom window over the snow in our backyard and noticed something strange. The backyard wasn't a pristine white surface. Footprints crisscrossed the yard leading from a huge gaping hole in our fence up to the back deck. I dashed downstairs and opened the kitchen blinds. The hole in the fence was real. A good ten feet of boards had been pried off and stolen. Even worse was the realization that whoever had stolen the fence had also casually inspected the back of the house. My sense of vulnerability was at an all-time high. When we went to sleep that night I brought the shotgun upstairs with me.

I woke in a panic; my heart pounding and body tensed to react. Was it a nightmare or a real sound alerting me to danger? I tried to focus, but fear and fatigue overlapped in my mind, giving me a hung-over feeling. I lay still and listened – nothing. Glancing over at Leslie, I could just see the wispy curls on top of Hope's head in the curve of Leslie's arm. She was sleeping soundly, keeping warm the way people had kept warm for tens of thousands of years – snuggling close to her mother's body to take the edge off the cold. A worn synthetic blanket of woven green fleece covered them, offering just enough heat retention to allow deep sleep. The old blanket, previously squirreled away in some closet, had now become a precious family resource.

There was little source of heat, other than our bodies, in the house anymore. Nor was there much of anything else. The perishable and short shelf life food we had managed to buy before Christmas was almost gone. Our closest food store manager had done his best but shipments were so sporadic that he had finally called it quits. He arranged one last restock of whatever he could get as a Christmas thank you to his customers. He put notices around the neighborhood and had a final closing day. We spent everything we could afford to part with to stock up again. I prayed no other neighbors besides that Martin guy had seen us unloading the ten grand in non-perishables into the garage last fall; we had done it at night, but others could have been looking and who knew who Martin might have told. We'd briefed the kids not to tell their friends about our stash.

Electricity was sporadic at best and very expensive for our limited resources. While natural gas was still pretty cheap and inexpensive nationwide, our local electrical production system relied too much on coal which had been transported by diesel run engines.

My fears for our survival were growing, compounded now by the thought of someone breaking into the house. Listening for a repeat of the noise that must have woken me, I scanned the room for any means of hiding the girls if things got dangerous. Maybe I had been dreaming. Everything seemed to be quiet now.

A muffled scratching sound brought me back to full alert. Something was definitely moving in or very near the house somewhere. My thoughts again turned quickly to safety. The noise that woke me sounded again, a weird whistling, followed by an audible "thunk" on wood and some soft clicks. It could be a signal, but I couldn't tell exactly where it was coming from.

Getting up carefully, so as not to wake Hope and Leslie, I grabbed the shotgun and quietly left the bedroom. I looked in on Cameron and Sean in the room across the hall. They were both sound asleep, sprawled across the mattress with the abandon of growing boys. They didn't seem to mind the cold, as their blanket was partially kicked off.

The next room was my mother's. Nothing seemed to be moving in there.

I cautiously moved downstairs, listening for a repeat of the strange noises. The living room and entryway were silent and bare. The moon and clouds cast shifting lights across the floors, but no sound accompanied the eerie movements. Turning towards the dining room, I thought I could hear rattling noises coming from the kitchen area. It was very dark down that hall and my heart was pounding. There it was again – a scrabbling, rattling near the back door like tree limbs clawing a window, or someone trying to jimmy the door lock. I slid into the kitchen.

Silence filled the void and I squinted hard, expecting to see something moving through the darkness, but there was no sound now. I crouched by the counter and peered round the corner. Still nothing moved. I slowly opened the door and stepped quietly outside.

The moon drifted in and out of the clouds, casting shadows over the snow that masked possible movement. I scanned the backyard, letting my eyes adjust to the constantly changing illumination. Suddenly the clouds blew past and in the reflected light I could see a dark shape moving near the side door of our detached garage.

"Freeze!" I yelled. The shape at the door dashed toward the golf course.

I fired the shotgun over his head to warn him that I meant business, and he dove under the trees and escaped beneath them into the open area beyond.

Still holding the weapon at ready, I moved carefully toward the tree where I had last seen him. Lights in our house and the surrounding houses all began to flash on. I felt eyes watching me out numerous windows.

On the ground lay a hat like Martin had been wearing the day that he had discovered our food stash.

Mom came running out the backdoor with a handgun and Sean was right behind her with a baseball bat.

"What happened?" Mom asked with a wary look. Her eyes widened when she noticed the hat in my hand. She recognized where she had recently seen a similar hat.

"Just some raccoons." I said, mostly for Sean's benefit, who stood there with a groggy look that indicated that he wasn't fully awake. "Guess they were hungry. It's time to go back to sleep."

I went back inside to reassure everyone that everything was okay. Then Mom and I spent the next several hours quietly moving all of the remaining food out of the garage and into the house. By daybreak, the garage was bare.

CHAPTER SIX

Everyone Coping

JANUARY 2016, OMAHA

"In individuals, insanity is rare. But in groups, parties, nations, and epochs, it is the rule"

— NIETZSCHE

I heard a sharp rap on our door. As if someone had taken a wooden cane and popped the door with it.

Leslie was still sleeping with Hope, and Mom was in the kitchen. Going to the door to answer it, I peeked out the view hole to see an unpleasant neighbor standing there. I thought about getting the shotgun, but thought better of it. I opened the door.

"Martin Anderson" he said to reintroduce himself. "We met a month ago or so in your driveway. May I come in?"

I was absolutely not happy to see him again and didn't like the idea of letting him into our house. I closed the door behind me and stepped outside.

"Did you lose your hat?" I said coldly.

"Actually I did. I lost it in a wind gust a few weeks ago. Have you found it?

"I believe we have."

"What good luck," he said smiling slyly. "It will be nice to have it back. Sorry to bother you my friend, but I'm starting to better appreciate all the food that you and your family purchased." He said.

"I see," I said tersely. "And, how can I help you?"

"Well, you just had so much darn food and the stores have been so empty that I thought it might make sense to see if you might be willing to… share." He hesitated before choosing the right word that he was looking for.

"Well, actually, we have an entire family here and it's not as much food as you think," I responded. "Didn't Janine tell you to get some food after you left here?"

"Well, you know, I thought about it, seriously. But I'm on a fixed income and the food prices seemed to be going up so fast that I just didn't get it done."

"I'm sorry to hear that. I wish that we had something that we could share," I said.

"That's exactly why I'm here," he exclaimed. "You certainly wouldn't want everyone around here to find out that you have a cache set aside for your requirements. Especially when so many have nothing at all."

There was no mistaking his remarks. We were being blackmailed. I looked at him coldly and said. "Would you like a few items to help tide you over?" Perhaps if we could get Martin to realize that it behooved him to keep our stash a secret, he would do so.

"Son, that would be mighty neighborly of you," He said in a folksy tone. "Did I notice that you had some stew in your supply?"

"Yes, I think we could afford to share a can of that. How about some vegetables to keep it company?" I said in a tone that was clearly not hospitable, but at least it looked like we had an understanding.

"That would really be kind of you," he said with a slight tone of sarcasm. "Would you mind if I waited inside?"

"Actually, that would be a problem," I said. "Let me just get you a bag to go. I'll be right back." I quickly backed inside and locked the door before he could object.

I returned and tried to hand him a full plastic bag of food and his hat by opening the front door just a crack. He took the bag, looking pleased, but stuck his foot in the gap, preventing me from shutting the door. This time there was no stopping him. He turned his shoulder into the gap and wedged the door open, allowing him to slip into the house. Just inside the door, he stopped and took a moment to look around. I stood directly in front of him, wishing I had kept the shotgun near the door, or at least had a bat in my hands. He smiled briefly then transferred the five cans I had given him into a back pack he was carrying. He slipped the backpack on and handed the plastic bag back to me. "This will do… for now," he said ominously, then opened the door with a hand behind his back and quickly slid out the door without turning his back to me. As he pulled the door shut, I heard him call, "See you soon!"

I locked the door and peered out the front window, watching as he headed to the sidewalk and back down the street. Martin Anderson was a problem I didn't know how to solve.

Sean bounced into the room. "Mommy, Dad! Can we go to Danny's church for dinner? He says they have to bring a can of something and sit in church first but then they get to eat and there's lots of different stuff. Can we go? Pleeeassse?"

We headed to the little church on Saturday evening. Each of us had a can of food for the soup kitchen that would supply the meal after the service. It was a viable means of blending in among the more desperate in our area. I just hoped it would disguise the real reason that Martin Anderson was stopping by.

Mom insisted on staying home and guarding the stash, and she also kept Hope so that she wouldn't be out in the cold. Leslie and I dressed the boys up warmly and headed down the street. I felt uneasy about leaving Mom and Hope behind, though.

As we walked, I thought about the basic home security issues facing us. Defending our residence was not an easy proposition. I scanned the houses around us. They were essentially soft targets. Any battle or shootout between folks inside and outside would make them uninhabitable. We had windows all around the house that could easily be broken. Once broken, where would we get the glass to repair them? They could be attacked from almost any direction and there were blind spots outside the house that could screen an attacker from view from anyone inside the house. Mom was holed up in an upstairs bedroom scanning the street for potential intruders. She had a gun close at hand and the window unlocked so that she could easily throw it open and get a shot off if need be. I hoped that she would be okay without us.

I was surprised to see so many tree stumps where only weeks before trees had stood. Several wood fences also were reduced to nothing more than a few upright posts; all their wood planks gone. Many of the houses seemed deserted, though I sensed eyes staring out from behind curtains or through dark windows. Twice I saw the unmistakable blue steel gleam of a gun muzzle just inside a window as we walked by.

We arrived at the church fifteen minutes later and were met by a pastor dressed in his ecclesiastical garments. We introduced ourselves and immediately noticed the aroma of food that drifted into the church from an adjoining meeting hall. We had come to the right place!

True to the theme that there is no such thing as a free lunch, we were invited to sit down in some pews to the back of the church and were informed that the service would start shortly. The few cans of food that we had brought were deposited in a basket with other donations.

We waited patiently, noting that many of the other attendees appeared to be homeless, dressed in worn denim and soiled jackets. They were of all ages with some kids the ages of Cameron and Sean. I could hear the whimpering of a baby in a pew somewhere closer to the front. Where were these people living?

The service featured readings and hymns. The preacher spoke on the story of the Sermon on the Mount. He placed special emphasis on the idea that Jesus had fed everyone there with just a few fish and loaves of bread, though this version had some nuances I had never heard before. In this version, the fish and bread had not multiplied magically; instead all those gathered to hear Jesus had found it in their hearts to break out the fish and bread that they had brought themselves and the collective bounty fed everyone with much left over.

"So, my friends," the pastor summarized, "if you would just find it in your heart to share with everyone else in need, we will all be amazed at the bounty of the Lord. It is not the lack of food that we should fear, but the hoarding behaviors of our neighbors, our friends, maybe even our own relatives. No one should go hungry when we have the means to help. Amen."

Sean looked up at me as if he were expecting me to run to the front of the church and offer our stash to the whole lot. I gave him a dismissive look and helped him find the next hymn.

After the service, we all drifted into the Fellowship Hall and found a pot luck supper that was meager, but better than anything we'd seen for a while.

The boys were speechless with delight and rushed to the front of the line with the other kids. The pastor said a few words and we all got a full plate of food and settled down to eat it.

Sean looked up from his plate just long enough to comment, "Hey, Dad, have you ever noticed how good something tastes when you're hungry?" I nodded my head and he dove back into his food. We had food at home, but we paced ourselves and ate sparingly from it. This was a rare treat for us, and the boys in particular enjoyed both the variety and the quantity.

While we ate, I noticed that a lot of handguns being carried by the people at the table where we sat. Several men had holsters strapped to their belts and a few had knives visible as well. A few soldiers and policemen sat in rumpled and worn uniforms but I didn't ask them if they were still employed.

We ate quickly and kept to ourselves, but people at other tables chatted and seemed to be friendly. Leslie leaned over and whispered, "Looks like there are the regulars and newbies like us, huh?"

I grinned and nodded. "Let's not get to be regulars!"

"The boys might have a different idea."

We thanked the pastor on the way out, and he offered us a blessing and an open invitation to return and share what we could.

We walked down the sidewalk to the corner and crossed the street. When we were out of earshot of everyone else, Sean asked. "Dad, couldn't we share our stash with all those people? I mean, if we all just shared, no one would go hungry!"

"Sean, that's a beautiful thought," I said, measuring my words. "But unfortunately, I have to take care of our family first. Our food has to last us a long time, and if we shared, we will run out before we can grow our own food. Besides, as much as you'd like to think the best of other people, I'm not sure that anyone else would share when we needed them to. It's a hard truth, but you need to believe me when I say we need to take care of ourselves first."

It was a harsh message for the boys to accept, especially in contrast to the generosity we had just received. I was about to reinforce the message of keeping our secrets and taking care of ourselves when a voice rose behind us.

"Stop or I'll shoot. Get your hands above your head."

Leslie grabbed my arm and instantly pulled Sean close to her. We were several blocks from the church and I knew we were in trouble. No one was around to help us. I turned and faced our assailant. The first thing I saw was the pistol shaking in his hand. He was in his late twenties, a little taller than me with a dark bandana tied around his forehead. Stringy blond hair fell to his shoulders and his eyes darted over me, Leslie and the boys with a glazed look, like someone on drugs. I recognized him as someone I'd seen inside the church.

"There's no need to do anything stupid at this point." I said with my hands extended upward.

"Step over to that clearing," he ordered.

"Do as he says, boys." Leslie whispered through gritted teeth.

We trouped over to the area we had been directed to.

"Give me your wallets, your jewelry and your purse," he said. Leslie held her purse high in her extended hand.

He walked over to us, confident that we were cowed. He didn't know Leslie. As soon as he got close enough, she moved her upper body in a way that attracted his interest. Still nursing, her breasts were delightfully full and large. He stared at her out-thrust chest and appeared to be distracted. When I started to lower my arms, though, he turned abruptly to me.

It was the opening Leslie had been looking for. Her taser found his neck and he fell to the ground in a writhing fit. Unbeknownst to me, she had been carrying it in her coat sleeve as we walked. She continued to taser him as he lay on the ground screaming in pain. Finally, I grabbed his gun and gave him a solid whack on the head with it, and he lay still.

Leslie wrapped her arms around me and the boys hugged Leslie. Then we just stood there looking down at the guy on the ground. It's one thing to dispatch a bad guy in a movie and another thing to do it in real life.

"What do you want to do about him?" Leslie asked.

"I don't know, I'm not sure where we'd find any police to take care of him."

"Do you have your phone?"

"Yes, but I'd just as soon get out of here without anyone knowing where we live."

She understood the sense of that. "Okay, let's just take his gun and leave him," she said. "I get the feeling that he's not terribly good at being a thief."

"Nah, a real thief wouldn't have been so careless. Do you think he's okay?" I stooped over to examine him and noticed that he was bleeding from the spot where I had cracked his head with the pistol.

"Tell you what, we'll call the police and let them know he's here. It's pretty cold out. Surely the cops will pick him up," Leslie said.

"Okay, but let's do it on the way," I said starting to leave. "I don't want him waking up while we're still around." We quickly headed down a different street, then called 911 to report where he was without saying who we were. Leslie thought we should also call the church to let them know. There was a good chance that someone would find him before he froze to death. We all agreed that we would find a different place to share our next communal meal.

Just as I thought our money problems were stabilizing, Mom received her own financial blow. A late night news story reported that the inflation adjustment on Social Security checks had been suspended by a cash-strapped Congress. Mom's check was deposited directly into her account each month and shortly after New Year's she checked the amount of her deposit. It was about $50 dollars short of the previous month's, confirming that the inflation adjustment had been cut off.

She was sitting in her chair dejectedly when I came into the room.

"Mom, what's wrong?"

"They've killed the COLA." she replied.

"What?" I asked thinking that I hadn't heard her correctly.

"You know – the cost of living adjustment on my Social Security."

"Oh, that. Was it a significant amount?"

"Only if the cost of living starts rising fast – like now. Pretty soon the check won't come close to covering basic living costs." She slumped back dejected. "I was counting on having an income source that would be stable for us. But now it's about to completely erode away."

"Damn, if prices keep doubling each month, your check won't be worth much by summer."

"Combine that with using up most of our savings and, Alex, I think we're in serious trouble here."

"Your savings are shot? Didn't Dad have a patent or something?" I said.

She knew what I was referring to. "Yes, he had created some downhole drilling tools for oil and gas wells that paid some royalties for a few years, but better tools came along and those revenues ended." I nodded, realizing this would be inevitable. "I do have a key to a bank deposit box that I found in Dad's drawer before he died so suddenly, but it's unmarked and I've never been able to locate the bank it came from. We've looked all over Washington D.C. and Houston, but to no avail. It's a shame too, since I know there were some assets that Dad acquired that I've never been able to locate the title documents for."

I sat down in the chair next to her. "I've been trying to evaluate our options. I talked to a real estate agent today about what we could get if we put the house on the market. Once she learned that we lived in the suburbs she offered me her condolences."

She gave me a look that said I told you so. "Well, your dad said this could happen. With the dollar in free fall and inflation destroying the value of everyone's savings – especially mine – what little I had in stock is now almost worthless, except for a few international stocks. I know how important your teaching is, but I don't see a future here for us, Alex." She paused and then added. "We need to head to the Ark soon."

"The university has offered me a few more seminars over the rest of the semester, it's not much income, but it's something." I said.

She shook her head. "Yes, you're still getting paid on occasion, but the cost of everything is climbing. If you aren't willing to leave when you don't have to, we may not be able to get out of here when we really need to. Please, at least think about leaving."

I knew she was worried and wondered if Dad would have advised us to leave now, next month or maybe even last week. But

I knew once we left Omaha we'd leave behind more than our home – we'd leave behind a complete lifestyle. I needed to talk to Leslie. The sooner she accepted the inevitable the better. "I will, Mom. I will."

"The Ark?" Leslie asked when I brought up the subject with her later that night. "Are you out of your freaking mind?"

"Leslie, I know it's not exactly how you saw the future, but it's a place where we should be able to at least grow our own food until life gets back to normal."

Leslie was appalled by the idea. "Honey, I appreciate the fact that your mother called it right on the food stash, but this whole idea of moving to Arkansas to grow food..." She couldn't even finish the sentence as she tried to convey her extraordinary disbelief that all this was happening.

"Leslie," I warned, "there are just too many people here and frankly, too many of them are desperate like that idiot you tasered. I think we'd be better off in Arkansas."

"Arkansas?" she said weakly.

I pushed a wisp of hair back from her face. "Look, I don't have any better ideas, and this is what my Dad thought it would come down to. I think he was right."

Leslie hugged me and I squeezed her. She smelled sweet and flowery and her warmth seemed almost surreal given recent events.

The hug turned into something more and she started to unbutton my shirt.

"Just a sec," I said as I turned to lock our door.

We made love for the first time since Hope was born. I was extraordinarily grateful for her love, especially in these circumstances. There was something so primitive about all that had happened to us. Undistracted by career worries or long to-do lists, we were "in the moment" in a way I remembered from when we first met.

Afterward, I drifted off for a few minutes. I was awakened by a gentle shaking as she woke me. "Okay." She said.

"Okay?" I asked.

"Okay if we head to Arkansas."

"That's all it took?" I asked, surprised.

"No. Not really. But I've been thinking. What food could we grow here? How would we protect ourselves from any gang intent on robbing us? I don't have anything here anymore and frankly, this whole neighborhood is starting to scare the hell out of me."

"I don't relish the idea of moving to Arkansas either, but you're right – we're in more danger here than we would be there." I said, not daring to share with her all the doubts I secretly harbored about this certainly questionable idea that we would be better off in the country.

"Well, that settles it, then," she said, softly stroking the hair on my chest. "When do we leave?"

CHAPTER SEVEN

A State of Emergency

January 2016, Omaha

"Hope begins in the dark, the stubborn hope that if you just show up and try to do the right thing, the dawn will come. You wait and watch and work: You don't give up."

— Anne Lamott

The first official sign that we were under martial law came through the radio. Mom was listening to it in the kitchen and I walked in to hear the tail end of a news story. The sounds of tank engines were clearly audible over the radio.

"They're saying that we've lost sixty percent of our oil and about twenty percent of our natural gas," she told me. "The governor has called in the National Guard." She looked up, pointing at the radio. "Do you hear those tanks?"

"Yup, that will certainly help me sleep better at night." The idea of vehicles burning up gas or diesel in gallons per mile didn't convince me this was a step in the right direction. "What will martial law do to help us?"

"At least the riots are over," Mom replied.

I snorted in response. "No surprise there. What's left to steal? The stores are all empty or out of business anyway."

"Alex," she said gravely, "it's time to get out of here –"

She was interrupted by screams coming from down the street. I rushed out the door to see what the problem was.

Three houses down the street, a garage was on fire and people with buckets were trying to dowse the flames. Sean, Cameron, and

Mom and I quickly grabbed a container and ran toward the house. "Be careful!" Leslie called after us, balancing Hope on her hip.

As we approached, I saw that the fire was restricted to a detached garage adjacent to the house. A neighbor had turned on a hose and was doing his best to spray water on the roof to contain the flames.

Others helping with the fire were running to houses across the street and filling up pails of water to throw on the garage. If these flames spread to adjacent houses, the entire neighborhood might go up in flames.

"Has someone called the fire department?" I yelled.

"Yes, but the dispatcher wasn't sure an engine would be able to make it," someone replied.

"Damn it!" I yelled. Sean and Cameron began rushing to the hose across the street, waiting in line to fill their containers.

"Thank God there's water pressure today," one of the neighbors stated. "Half the time, we turn on the faucet and only a trickle comes out."

Our firefighting efforts, I noted, were like trying to bail out a large leaky boat with a beer can. I headed for the bucket line.

"Dad," Sean said, "why don't we string some more hoses together?"

I was struck by the simplicity of his idea. "Sean, that sounds great. Can you and Cameron round some hoses up? The closest two houses are the ones right behind this garage and the one next door."

They rushed around liberating hoses from a couple of houses, and within a few minutes we had the full water output from three different hoses dumping water on the garage. The flames were soon controlled. Just as we finished putting out the last hot spots, the water pressure died. We all looked at each other and shook our heads at our good fortune. Other neighbors looked up at the sky as if to thank God. This fire could have spread to their house.

No one was at home, and it wasn't clear to any of us whether or not this had been an accident or arson.

"Alex," called one of our neighbors. "Thanks for your assistance! We really dodged a bullet on this one!"

"It would seem so. I'm glad Sean had the good sense to string some more hoses together. Did everyone get their hoses back?"

"I'm sure they will. You guys seem to be doing well," commented a neighbor I didn't know. In a suspicious tone he continued, "I was so weak from lack of food that I could barely hold the hose on the fire."

"We've made a few trips to the soup kitchens!" I explained. "Luckily, they like kids."

"I'm glad to hear that." said a familiar voice.

I scanned the milling crowd for the associated face. Martin Anderson stood a few people away. "I sure wouldn't want your kids to go hungry."

I regarded him as if he had just risen up from hell. He seemed almost supernatural, and there was little doubt that he was about to tap us for more food.

"Guess we'd better be getting home, boys." I said. "We're all wet and it's cold out here."

"Yep, I'd guess we'd better head to your house," said Martin with an unappreciated wink as he followed us home.

Another blizzard swept in from the north late that week and by morning had buried the yard and driveway with more than a foot of snow. The flurries came down so thickly that we could barely see out of our windows to the street. We watched television as thousands were said to be stranded all over Nebraska and Iowa.

I told Sean and Cameron to keep an eye out the windows and the two of them served as look outs at both the front and back of the house.

I was becoming increasingly protective of our stash. The only thing that really mattered now was my family's health and preservation of the food we had stored away upstairs in Mom's room.

I had called us all together after the first visit from Martin Anderson and the neighbor's fire. My goal was to develop our security plans and figure out ways to protect ourselves. We had three weapons: my shotgun, Mom's handgun and the thief's weapon with the few rounds left in it when we took it. We had very little ammunition overall, and I thought it better to hold on to it in case things got worse. We all tried to imagine ways we could fortify our house from attack, but quickly realized there weren't any. Attackers could come through any window or door at will. Once in the house, we'd be hard pressed to stop anyone from doing whatever they were intent on, short of shooting them.

"Dad! Dad! Wake up!!" The urgency in Cameron's voice told me something was seriously wrong. I shook my head to clear away my grogginess. "I heard gun shots!" he whispered, trying not to wake Leslie and Hope.

"What?" My body was swinging out of bed before my brain had consciously registered the full significance of his statement. Adrenaline surged in an instinctive fight or flight response.

"Gun shots! From the house up the street. They woke me and Sean up. I think they're being robbed. Come see."

He raced back to his room on the other side of the house. I grabbed my robe and the shotgun from beside the headboard and followed. As soon as I turned down the hall, I could hear a muffled pop like a car backfiring in the distance. From the window in the boys' room I spotted a house up and across the street. I remembered that an elderly couple lived there, but I didn't recall if they were still in the home or had left recently. Lights were flickering all over the house and I could make out dark figures running in and out the front door. "Call 911" I told Cameron but he didn't move. "Cam, go call 911!"

He turned with a stricken expression. "I did, Dad. Before I came and got you. The cops should have been here by now, but I don't even hear sirens. What the fuck is going on?"

His language startled me. He'd never used it in my presence before, which indicated just how angry he was. "I don't know, son. I wish the cops were here." After another quick volley of shots, lights in an upstairs room went out. Two figures ran out of the house and the neighborhood became deathly quiet. The whole incident had taken less than fifteen minutes.

We watched this house for movement for another half hour, but saw none. Very early the next morning, I walked over to investigate. Most of the ground-floor windows had been knocked out. The front door was ajar and the snow on the ground served as a sound blanket that kept the noise down. The snow was heavily trampled going in and out of the house.

I called out "Is anyone home?" Receiving no answer, I cautiously entered the house with my handgun at the ready, both of my hands grasping the stock of the pistol like I had seen police do on TV shows. I moved from room to room slowly and deliberately. The temperature inside the house matched that outside, and I wished I had gloves on.

I discovered ample evidence of random destruction and vandalism. Smashed vases, shredded sofa pillows, and an overturned side table littered the living room. A TV set was clearly missing and someone had taken a knife to a large oil painting behind the sofa. Canvas curled down out of the frame in long, jagged strips. I could almost understand theft, but vandalism for destruction's sake alone had never made sense to me. With nothing else to note downstairs, I slowly made my way upstairs.

Two elderly bodies lay in the hallway in an embrace. The man had been unceremoniously shot through the forehead and the woman shot in the chest several times. She must have had time to join him before she died since they lay together in death. I stepped around them and peered into the closest room to be sure I was alone.

It was obvious what had been stolen up here. Empty jewelry boxes lay on the floor and a wallet was discarded empty on the bed. Clothes from the closet and drawers were dumped in piles, indicating a thorough search for valuables. The mirror on the dresser and in the bathroom had been smashed, and each of the bodies was missing an ear. I wondered if they were even dead before these invaders had collected their macabre trophies.

Whoever had done this had done it with a level of viciousness that was difficult to imagine. Just like that they had extinguished two lives that had never bothered anyone.

The police still hadn't showed up and I doubted whether they ever would. I wrapped the bodies in quilts and dragged them downstairs and into the backyard. The ground was frozen and too hard to dig into, so I placed a tarp from the garage over them and covered them in snow. Someone else would have to bury them in the spring, I decided, because it was time for us to leave.

We were heading to the Ark.

CHAPTER EIGHT

Planning

FEBRUARY 2016, OMAHA

"It is not the strongest of the species that survives, nor the most intelligent that survives. It is the one that is the most adaptable to change."

— CHARLES DARWIN

It was reality check day. We had made all our plans to leave town. Everything depended on whether we could obtain a full tank of gas. If so, we'd drive out of town in the middle of the night with a considerable load of necessities and belongings. We really didn't have a Plan B. Public transportation options – trains, planes and buses – had all been considered and discarded. None allowed us to carry all of the things we would need, and the personal shipping industry was pretty much out of business. Trains only went to select destinations, airline tickets were out of the question, and bus lines were booked into May. All these sectors faced the same high fuel prices, making their ticket prices prohibitive.

Still, we were at tremendous risk on any journey. A heavily loaded motor vehicle with a trailer would be a red flag to potential thieves. Cameron and I laid a false floor in the trailer that would hide some things, but I wasn't sure if it would even be worth the effort if we were hijacked on the highway.

Nevertheless, our immediate concern was fuel. Gas station owners no longer had any shame in pricing gasoline at whatever the market would bear. When gas prices initially soared, some gas station owners actually rationalized that it would be wrong to sell their existing gas at the new higher prices. I wondered where they had all gone in the last four months. Most gas stations now had

Planning

armed guards to protect the staff from angry motorists and gasoline thieves.

I pulled into one of the gas stations close to our house. This had once been a very busy station with four islands of dual-facing pumps. That allowed sixteen cars to fuel up simultaneously. There were three cars in the fuel area today and only one of them was actually refueling.

Leslie headed for the building, but I got only as far as a window next to the cashier. A badly attired guard with a shotgun looked up at me, trying to determine whether I was a security threat. I was cautious to do nothing to set off this rent a cop. He had a job and was probably pretty determined to keep it.

A well-dressed cashier spoke to me through the glass. "Sir, may I help you?" The designer quality of her clothes startled me, but then again, she was employed in a world where people were willing to give away everything they owned for a few gallons of gas. My bet is that she lived in the local area since I couldn't imagine they'd pay her enough to be able to drive to work.

"Yes, I'd like to buy some gas." I tried to state as casually as I could.

"Okay. How will you be paying, sir?" came the quick reply from behind the glass.

"Well, I've got a hundred dollars here in cash."

"Yes sir, is that your car at pump nine?" She responded.

"Yes, it is." I said as I shoved the bills through the window.

"That will be two gallons on pump nine." She hit a few switches and pointed back at my car.

Fifty dollars a gallon for regular! The price was a shock. Two gallons wouldn't take us far, but hopefully enough to travel to a pawn shop.

When I finished, I pulled the nozzle out of the gas tank and shook it carefully, trying to make sure that every drop made its way into our tank. After returning the nozzle and replacing our gas cap, we both got in and drove slowly up the street.

Driving around town was considerably more challenging than in the past. The good news was there were fewer cars. The bad news was that the cars on the road did not want to stop for any reason. A red light was simply considered advisory these days. A stop sign was a yield sign. Stopping the car's motion completely wasted gasoline and drivers would go to great lengths to slow their cars in advance so the light would change back to green before they got to it. If the light turned red, then many drivers would attempt to coast through the light if traffic allowed it.

We were both on the lookout for police cars and reckless drivers as I drove, and I feared both. Driving a car these days was almost probable cause for police officers to believe that you had money. Since the only way that the local police departments could keep their officers employed was to extract money from motorists, these police officers were reputed to be very aggressive in efforts that would generate revenue.

Leslie navigated me to the pawn shop where I pulled in and parked. I clutched one of Leslie's gold bracelets and our wedding bands in my pocket. I was hoping that we wouldn't need to barter the wedding bands, but getting gasoline was urgent and I didn't want to learn that we hadn't brought enough jewelry to accomplish our mission.

The store was crowded, and we took our place at the back of the line. The clerks ran furiously about trading goods for cash. For many people, this was the only game in town left for them. After the break-in the other night, I wondered how many of these goods now being pawned were actually stolen. In thirty minutes we made it to the front of the line.

"Hello." I said cheerily. The clerk was an older gentleman with an air of importance and he was busy. There were many others behind us. I carefully pulled our jewelry out of my pockets. Neither of us spoke as the clerk assessed the value.

He placed our wedding bands on a small scale and made a note. I glanced at Leslie and saw a tear silently roll down her cheek. I reached for her hand and squeezed it tightly. She sniffed and wiped her cheek. I was disturbed to watch something we held so dearly get weighed – as if its full value could be explained by its mineral content.

"I can offer you three hundred euros for the gold bracelet and one hundred euros for the wedding bands," the clerk stated in a bored tone. This practice of buying things in euros had taken us back when clerks first started doing it, but it was a perfectly rational response to a dollar whose value was careening all over the place, mostly downward. Leslie and I glanced at each other in hopeful surprise.

I did some quick mental math. At seven euros a gallon we could purchase about thirty gallons for 210 euros and still give us a cushion of ninety euros. This would allow us to fill up our tanks and also fill some spare cans for the trip. Since the value of gold had soared, I suspected that we were being ripped off by this offer, but at this juncture we could accept his offer or go wait in line at another pawn shop and hope they'd be more generous. "Just the bracelet," I replied. He handed the rings back and we ceremoniously put them on each other's finger – the way we had when we were first married. I kissed her, because it seemed like the appropriate thing to do, and we both breathed a sigh of relief.

I took the bills he passed through the window slot and shoved them deep into my pocket as we walked out of the store. The pawn shop's guard walked with us to our car and we headed home. A few minutes later, we purchased the extra gas along with several gas cans.

As we paid our gas bill in euros, Leslie came to a realization. "If our price for gas is seven euros a gallon, isn't that just a little bit more than what they've been paying for gas in Europe for quite a while?"

"Yep, I think so," I said. "Since the European governments have taxed gas at high levels for at least the last fifty years, they've seen fuel prices in this range for a long time now. Their pump prices may be a bit higher lately, but from their viewpoint, this level seems pretty normal. Their economies are already designed to operate on high oil prices by U.S. standards. My sister Katie says the public transit systems are more than adequate; I don't think she even drives a car anymore."

Somehow, affirming Europe wasn't inconvenienced by the current oil shortage didn't make Leslie or me feel any better. Our prospects were bleak here. Yet nothing could be gained by complaining about how unfair life was. The culprits were *our* trade deficit, *our* profligate borrowing habits, and *our* car and truck dependent culture that left us so vulnerable to the type of oil disruptions that Dad saw as inevitable.

As we left the station, a car started up and then started to follow us.

I made several turns on major roads and this car remained fixedly behind us. "Leslie, I think we're being followed."

She turned around sharply. "Shit, what do you think we should do?"

"I don't know, but I don't want to waste any more gas than I have to. This has got to end now."

I turned onto an unfamiliar side street and the car continued to follow us. I pulled the car to a stop and the car behind us passed us and then pulled to a stop in front of us several car lengths away.

To Leslie's dismay, I pulled out a gun from under the seat and handed it to her. "I'm going to turn around now in a three-point turn. When we're perpendicular to the curb, I want you to roll down your window and make a point of aiming at the car in front of us. I hope you don't have to shoot at them, but if so, simply aim over them to scare them off. If they return fire, start shooting directly at them and we'll head out as fast as we can." Leslie looked terrified, but she obediently nodded.

I swiftly started to turn, the window came down and Leslie immediately took a shot that splintered a wooden mailbox to the left side of the road. "Damn, I missed. Hold still so that I can blow their heads off." She screamed out the window. The car in front of us instantly hit the gas and headed off down the street.

We sped in the opposite direction and were able to get back on the main road and out of sight before they reappeared. Our ears were ringing from the concussion of the shot. She continued to watch carefully out the back window while she pressed against the side of her head trying to confirm that her ears were okay.

When we were almost home she said. "Alex, I can't live like this. It's like the Wild West! There's no law, no safety anymore."

"But you were so brave." I said. "You really scared the crap out of those guys."

Leslie's composure suddenly evaporated as we swung into our driveway. "Alex," she sobbed. "I want my life back!"

"Me too." I said. I took the gun out of her hand and held her until she stopped crying. We both knew that our lives had changed and they would never be the same again.

CHAPTER NINE

The Journey

MARCH 2016, OMAHA TO ARKANSAS

"A journey of a thousand miles begins with a single step."

— LAO TZU

Leslie, Mom and I pulled out all the maps we could find for roads between our neighborhood and the Ark. The mileage was just over 450 miles if we took the interstate. Any other route would add distance, but at most we were looking at 600 miles. We debated routes long into the night, the women wanting to take major interstates, while I wanted to take back roads. There were pros and cons to each route, as well as several unknown factors, including safety, food and the availability of gas along the way, if we needed it. I started to crunch some numbers.

My tank held twenty-five gallons, and I figured we could get twenty miles per gallon fully loaded and pulling a trailer if we drove under fifty mph. Therefore one tank might get us all the way and with the extra gas cans we ought to be able to make it for sure. The trip would take at least twelve hours of driving with additional time for breaks. While it might be possible to drive the whole distance in a day, it would be a long haul. It'd be better to simply plan on taking two days for this trip.

"Honey, which route will have more gas stations? Leslie asked.

"Gas stations? We've got gas!" I replied, annoyed at this pointless question "We need to find the safest route."

"Alex, I can't go twelve hours without a bathroom. And we will need food and water. Won't gas stations be the most convenient?"

Mom chimed in. "I agree, son. With a baby and two boys, we will need to make stops rather frequently. Besides, the highway patrol or local militia may be patrolling. Won't the freeways be our best choice?"

"Look, remote gas stations would not be safe. My bet is that they've already been attacked by desperate travelers or thieves. We need to avoid spots like that."

"But what if we break down?" Leslie asked. "Don't we need to be on a major road for safety?"

"I don't think so," I replied slowly. "I think we should head for the back roads, through the small towns and off the beaten path as much as possible. I think we'd have a better chance of finding safe places to stop for breaks if we go through farm country. That way we can hope for some small town hospitality."

We argued all these issues well into the night without coming to an agreement. The next day Mom suggested I call the highway patrol and AAA to get more information. What they told us was shocking. Both sources emphatically told us to stay off the interstates. Those roads were packed with people trying to go someplace else, most without any idea of where. Broken-down and out-of-gas vehicles littered the roads. Most gas stations had been shut down, as I had suspected. There were also incidents of pirates roaming these roads. We would head south to southeast on the back roads through the heartland.

The boys helped me move stuff around in the garage so we could pack both the trailer and our van inside with the garage door down. The attacks on well-to-do neighborhoods had continued, and we didn't want to give anyone reason to think we had more than anyone else on the block. Over the next few days we judiciously selected everything important to us. In the past, we would have just filled the car with toys and gadgets for our kids. Now we carefully picked everything we couldn't live without and packed deliberately.

"Yo, sons!" I called to the boys. "We need you to help us pack some of this gear. We've got to use every inch – so think Tetris." Sean laughed and scrambled inside the trailer to help fit everything in.

"It's a lot like we're going on a camping trip, huh, Dad?" Cameron said. "Look at this stuff, a camping stove with canisters of propane, a tent, tarps, a number of pots and pans, and sleeping bags and pillows for everyone."

"Yup, you can think of this as a grand adventure." Yet both he and I knew better. I surreptitiously placed a handgun under the driver's seat while Cameron laid my shotgun under the backseat along with several boxes of shells.

Leslie came out to the garage with our wedding album and several family videos. "Alex, can you find a safe spot for these?"

"Of course, babe." I placed them carefully in a plastic container that held our important papers and a few personal mementos along with my laptop so we could connect to the world – assuming that we could find a link and electricity. The rest of the car and trailer were gradually filled with the rationed remains of our food stash, work clothes, winter coats, a few essential items of furniture, some "how to" books, containers of water, our extra gas cans, the boys' bikes, and anything else we thought might be useful.

"Dad, do we have room for this?" Sean asked, holding up a box with their television game system with a dozen CD's.

We didn't, but I tried to couch my rejection in terms that seemed less harsh. "I really wish we could take it, son, but I don't think we'll have much electricity. It won't work without it, so it will just take up space. Why don't you leave it here for your friends? They will probably have electricity more often than we will."

"Okay," he sighed with disappointment. "Maybe when we come back, I'll play with it again."

I patted his shoulder but didn't have the heart to tell him that this would be a one-way trip.

With most of our food supplies packed up, I decided it would be easiest to have our last meal at one of the church-run soup kitchens in our area. For our last meal in the area I thought we should head north to a little church a mile away. We left Mom at home with some leftovers; she'd watch Hope and guard everything with my shotgun.

Twenty minutes later, we walked in the front door of an ancient, musty room that they used as their church hall. We contributed a large can of yams upon entry, a gift that was noted by many.

We found a table and sat through the blessing and short scripture reading. The food was sparse and the meat was a mystery. We didn't ask what it was, and they were not generous with the portions.

We sat quietly next to a table full of rough-looking men and a few women and overheard them bragging about some recent raid they'd been on. "That can of soup that I contributed," said one of the women, "will never be missed by the family that used to own it." There were several guffaws and we all just looked at each other.

One guy at that table noticed we were eavesdropping. He called over to me.

"Would you like to join the Co-op for Survival and feed your family real regular, mister? Your boys sure need more than this slop to stay healthy."

Sean quickly blurted out "This food isn't so bad! I've had worse – Dad burned oatmeal once!"

The group laughed and the man said "Real nice boys you got. Plenty smart, too. Our Co-op could use additional members."

"No thanks," I replied cautiously. "I think we'll take our chances with the food kitchens. I'm not much of a raider."

"A raider? What's that?" he said, and they all cracked up again.

"You know, mister," he said. I've been to a lot of food kitchens and I've never seen you guys before. You guys look a little too well fed if you ask me."

By now I had my answers to that remark all down. "Boy, I wish that were true. It's been the toughest diet I've ever been on, but the easiest to stick to. No food – no temptation!" I said, patting my gut. "Finally lost that extra thirty pounds my doc kept bugging me about." Several people laughed and nodded. One woman shook her head and muttered something about missing chocolate.

The man's interest persisted. "Well, tell you what, I've kind of taken a liking to your family. If you can tell us where you live, we'll bring by a care package for you."

"Well, that would be neighborly of you," I said. Without pause I gave him the address to Martin's house.

I flinched as Leslie kicked me under the table. We quickly gulped down the rest of the meal and headed home as fast as possible.

"Alex, that was stupid!" Leslie hissed as soon as we were out of earshot. "Now they know which neighborhood we live in!"

"Yeah, but we're all packed, and we can leave in a couple of hours. Besides, Martin was a problem and he deserves a payback."

"And just who do you think he'll finger when the raiders don't find anything at his house?" she snapped at me.

"Shit... I guess I wasn't thinking. Come on, boys. Mom and I will race you home."

We literally ran home. I was determined to get us on the road before everything went to hell. We didn't know if Martin would expose us if he was raided, but we didn't want to be around to find out.

While Mom and Leslie furiously finalized packing the car, I dashed over to our most trusted neighbor.

"Jim, we're heading out soon. I don't know if we'll be back. Here's the key to the house. Feel free to take whatever you need or want."

"I'm sad to hear that. Where are you going to?" he asked.

I lied to him. "My sister lives back east, so we're heading to her place." He seemed satisfied by this explanation.

As I came home, I heard shotgun blasts coming from the next street over. "Come on everyone! In the car! Right now!" I yelled as I hooked the trailer to the hitch. We quickly loaded everyone in. I dashed to the driver's seat and pulled forward enough to clear the trailer then pushed the remote button to close the garage door. I kept the van lights off and we eased down the road. We turned left at the far corner and coasted to the stop sign at the corner of Martin's street. Leslie and I glanced to the left. "Alex, I think those raiders hit Martin's house."

Far down the block I could just make out a large crowd of people. A fire had been lit in the road, and I could see a man with his hands up in the air. He kept trying to point over his shoulder toward the block where we lived.

I was shocked by the daring of these people. "I can't believe they found it so quickly. I thought they'd hit during the middle of the night, not at eight o'clock in the evening."

Suddenly, someone in the crowd started yelling and pointing down the street toward us. I immediately realized that the streetlight above us was working.

The mob came pouring down the block, heading toward us.

Why in the world had I told these guys anything about Martin? Couldn't we have simply left him alone? A shot rang out and we heard an impact strike our trailer behind us.

One bold yahoo came from nowhere and stepped out in front of our vehicle.

I hit the gas pedal, spinning the tires in the road debris. "Go!" Leslie screamed as more shots peppered the area around us. He dove to the side of the road as we roared over the spot where he had just stood.

The shots ringing off the metal of our tailgate startled Hope and she began to cry. In the distance, I could see most of the mob railing at us as they shrank in my rearview mirror. I suddenly noticed several vehicles emerge from their crowd and speed toward us.

I immediately turned down the next street and headed for some of the darker side streets in our area. We twisted in and out of a number of unlit neighborhoods with our headlights off. A vehicle with a trailer would not be hard to mistake if we inadvertently crossed paths with our pursuers.

We turned on to a main road and continued on for several miles. Finally at an abandoned strip mall I pulled in behind the building and stopped.

"Alex! What are you doing?" Leslie screeched at me. "We need to get out of here!".

"Well, we won't get far if there's a bullet in a tire." I snapped back at her. "I'm going to give us a once over to make sure we didn't take any serious hits. Just relax for a second and we'll be back on the road."

I was back in the car in under a minute. The trailer had a couple of bullet holes and a can of pears was oozing sticky nectar that dripped out of the trailer door, but otherwise I hadn't spotted any damage.

We were on our way heading southeast within five minutes.

"Well, another adventure on the road to marital bliss for the MacCasland family, eh, sport?" Leslie tried to joke, but there was a weakness in her tone that barely concealed the panic that she felt.

I grimaced and replied, "For better or for worse, babe – just like I promised."

"It doesn't get any better than this, does it?" she croaked "Fleeing from bandits in the dead of night? But hey, we're going to get to live on a farm."

If, I thought darkly, we ever get there.

CHAPTER TEN

On the Road

MARCH 2016, ARKANSAS

"I think that God in creating Man somewhat overestimated his ability."
— OSCAR WILDE

Once out of our immediate neighborhood we slowed down and resumed a more normal speed. The eastern horizon was barely visible from the moonlight shining through the leading edge of the storm clouds.

The drive out of Omaha shocked us. This city had changed remarkably in a short period of time. There were few trees anywhere in sight and garbage was strewn all over. The garbage usually indicated that people were still living nearby. Many neighborhoods stank of waste and backed-up sewers. Apparently trash service and sewage treatment had been additional casualties of recent events in parts of town. Lots of houses had broken or boarded-up windows, with piles of discarded furniture and toys bearing witness to other departures like ours. Beyond the residential areas were abandoned strip malls, closed gas stations, and vacant fast food joints. Here and there a pawnshop or bar had signs of activity, but mostly it felt like we were leaving a ghost town.

I drove carefully, trying to avoid numerous potholes, and kept checking the rearview mirror to watch the approaching storm. We crossed the Platte River and headed south, using our car's GPS to parallel Highway 75 on country roads. I didn't want to use any main roads if possible.

As our journey continued, abandoned vehicles, trucks, and farm equipment appeared everywhere just off the roads and on the sides of fields. In several places the desolation of a burned-out farm house kept the fear of encountering desperate people foremost in our minds. The bad weather was actually a relief when we realized fewer people might be traveling. The wind picked up and light snow began to drift across the road. The lack of traffic allowed me to drive down the center of the road most of the time. I kept the speed down just in case other traffic appeared.

Spotting taillights up ahead, I eased back into the right lane of the road. The car in front of us had a SLOW bumper sticker and glided along at 45 mph. The Society to Limit Oil Waste was an organization that Dad would have approved of. The whole purpose of their organization was to increase awareness of the conservation benefits of simply driving more slowly. I nodded to the driver approvingly and gave him a thumbs-up as we gently eased by them and returned to our normal speed.

"Why did you wave at him?" Leslie asked me.

"I don't know, I guess it reminds me of a topic that I used to discuss with my students."

"What do you mean?"

"Well, he had one of those SLOW stickers – you know, the group that made such a big deal out of driving slower and saving fuel," I said continuing to focus my attention on the road in front of me.

"And?" she asked.

"Well, I've just never personally been real excited about the potential of their movement."

"How so?" The kids were asleep in the back seat and it was something we could talk about to help pass the time.

I took a moment to collect my thoughts. "Okay. Here's my take on energy conservation in general. Let's say, for example, that instead of buying a vehicle that got twenty five miles to a gallon, you bought one that got fifty miles to a gallon. It certainly makes you feel better and you immediately cut your gas bills in half."

"That'd be great." Leslie said.

"Yeah, but here's my point. The difference in fuel usage between the two vehicles is roughly a hundred barrels of oil over the life of a typical car. If a million cars switched, then we'd save a hundred million barrels over a ten year period. That seems like a lot, but it's only enough to fuel the world's oil thirst for a little more than a day."

"You're kidding," she said settling back in her seat. "Only one day from all that effort?" She fell silent and sat looking out the window toward the dark skyline of trees along her side the road. A few minutes later she asked quietly, "Are we doomed?"

"Dad thought so – especially since we weren't doing anything to prepare for the long term when oil prices were cheap. Personally I still haven't seen enough efforts put into other energy solutions to give me much hope." When she didn't respond, I added belated encouragement. "I think we'll be okay."

Leslie's face contorted as if she were about to register an objection, but then, all sign of emotion drained from her features. She just sat there as if lost in a trance and returned to gazing out the side window in silence.

We drove slowly for a couple of hours that night, crossing into Kansas and then pulled off behind an abandoned building. I had wanted to drive at night only, but the weather and the adrenaline drain from our close escape had exhausted us. Plus I had discovered significant difficulty in navigating unfamiliar and largely unmarked country roads. We needed light to find our way.

When dawn lit the sky, we were back on the road, the boys scanning the fields and pastures for cattle, horses, or even sheep. The land was strangely empty as far as we could see. The farms and ranch houses we passed were mostly inhabited, if the smoking chimneys were any indication. Maybe farmers were just keeping their animals out of sight for added security from travelers, or maybe the weather was keeping them indoors. But this lack of activity disturbed me and did not seem to bode well for near term food production.

North of Topeka we started to angle southeast so we could head down between Topeka and Lawrence, Kansas. We got on Highway 16, then cut south on a country road. Mom and Leslie used maps to navigate a route away from cities and large towns. We passed under I-70 and skirted Clinton Lake moving southeast.

Approaching the town of Garnett around nine in the morning, the kids complained of being hungry. As we had not seen any traffic on the road, we decided to chance stopping. I pulled into a likely place, the Country Mart, for food and news from the area. Mom stayed in the car with a shotgun deliberately visible across her lap to guard our supplies while the rest of us entered the building.

There were a number of people shopping the almost bare shelves, but local chitchat stopped when we walked in. All eyes turned to watch us as Cameron got a basket and moved toward the produce department with Leslie. I walked to the deli counter. A lady stood behind the counter, flipping through an old farmer's almanac. Her shirt had "Rosie" embroidered above the pocket.

"Can I get some food to go?" I asked.

"Sure thing, but our 'take-out menu' is pretty thin these days." She cocked her thumb over her shoulder to the case behind her. It had a small selection of goods like fresh bread, butter and honey that, according to a small sign, were made by a local farmer's wife. I spent about sixty bucks on them, some cheese curds and hard-boiled eggs. I couldn't see any meat. Asking Rosie if they had any, she laughed and shook her head.

"We haven't had USDA meat in over a month. A government guy came by in early January and bought every cow, pig and goat the farmers would sell and confiscated some they wouldn't. Most farms have a bull and a cow left so they can breed, but there isn't much else in these parts."

"Anybody growing food?" I asked.

"Not much beyond big gardens for personal use. There isn't any fertilizer for the spring planting even if we had enough fuel to run the plows. We had a farmer's market twice a week where farmers could sell their silo stock, dairy stuff, and any excess garden produce from last fall, but that ended about six weeks ago because there wasn't anything left to sell. We've still got some seed potatoes, carrots and onions and canned stuff, but it's too early in the season for anything fresh yet." She stated matter-of-factly, "You all got relatives in the area?" Her question wasn't overtly suspicious, but I was pretty sure she wasn't giving us a full picture of the available food in the area.

"No, we're headed east to meet up with my sister's family," I lied. "There's some land in the family but we are going to have to learn a lot this year. You don't know if anyone is selling seeds for a garden, do you?" I replied, acting casual about the whole thing.

Just then Leslie, carrying Hope, came in with the boys tagging along behind. I saw Rosie relax a bit when she eyed the whole family. She seemed to make a quick decision.

"Head over to Garnett Siding and Lumber. It's just a couple of doors down," she said, jerking her head to the south. "Tell them I said you need a basic garden starter package. They'll know what that means. Might cost you a pretty penny these days, but..." She shrugged her shoulders and smiled at the baby. "You got a cute family, mister. Good luck to you folks."

"Thanks, Rosie. We really appreciate your kindness." Leslie reached over the counter and touched her arm, smiling with gratitude.

Rosie patted her hand and nodded. "You make sure that baby gets some good fresh mashed veggies next fall. Nothing like 'fresh from the garden' mashed peas and carrots for kids to grow up strong."

"Thanks again, Rosie," I said. She just smiled and waved as we left.

81

We walked a little farther down the road and went into the hardware store. Mom followed us in the van and parked lengthways across some parking spaces – just in case we needed to make a quick exit. The store was a marvel of a Midwest general store, with a wall of small drawers and an old-fashioned scale on the long counter. Leslie and I gazed around in delight, then asked if anyone knew Rosie from Country Mart. A young man approached us. "Rosie's my aunt. What can I do for you?"

I gave him her message and his eyes almost bugged out of his head.

"Wow! She must have taken a real liking to you all. Come with me." He walked down the aisle to a back room. Inside, he turned toward a large locked storage cabinet. Pulling a key out of his pocket, he unlocked the door and pulled it open. I peeked over his shoulder and saw several bundles wrapped in brown paper and tied with twine. I spotted marking on the packages, but nothing made sense to me. The kid shuffled through a few packages before pulling a large one from the back of one shelf. It was about the size of a twenty pound sack of dog food.

"Here's what you need." He said, tapping the package. "Be sure to pay attention to planting dates for the zone you are in. We haven't gotten any new shipments in a couple of months, and personally, I don't think we will get any before this season's planting. You ever had a garden before?" he asked, looking at my un-callused hands.

"Oh yeah!" I laughed, remembering our backyard garden in Texas growing up. "But it's been years."

A flicker of doubt crossed his face. "Okay, well, composted plants make great fertilizer. Use it and you'll have some nice vegetables later this summer."

"How many acres will this cover?" I asked.

"This seed package is designed to cover about two acres with about twenty different plants, which should help feed your family and give you a start on a marketable crop – assuming that you don't have any animals to feed."

"Sounds perfect. How much do we owe you?" I asked, expecting the worst.

"It'll be a hundred bucks." The kid said. "Little more than the price of a few gallons of gasoline."

"A hundred bucks! Are you sure?" I exclaimed at this pleasant surprise.

The kid grinned. "Like I said, mister, my aunt must have really liked you. We've never sold a packet to a stranger since things went crazy with the fuel. I hope you know enough to make this pay off."

"I promise to honor your aunt's faith in us. Thank you so much." I handed him the money and we took the package and headed back to the car.

As I started to strap the seed package on the roof, the young man hollered down the street at us. "Hey, Mister! Make sure you keep that dry! If it gets wet it will be useless!"

I pulled it off the roof and threw it onto the back bench seat and made the kids sit on it. "Don't spill any drinks on that," I warned.

Leslie waved and yelled back, "Thank you!" as we drove off again.

The farther south and east we moved, the better the weather got, but the fewer open stores we saw in the tiny towns we passed through. Sometimes a stall was set up in a parking lot with a family selling preserved garden produce or what looked like all their worldly possessions. We also passed a few horse-drawn wagons and people pushing or pulling carts loaded with household goods. I was reminded of photos from the Dust Bowl days of the 1930s.

I kept to back roads as much as possible, but when we approached a town, I kept an eye out for anyone who might have ulterior motives if we had to stop at a light. We bypassed towns unless there was no easy way around, then we passed directly through. For the frequent bathroom breaks, we pulled over by bushes or other concealing cover. I was too suspicious of the few places with "open" signs posted – mostly bars and honky-tonk dives where locals still gathered. It was slow going. We were only averaging about thirty miles per hour.

As we drove through Oklahoma, we could see large fields of pale green shoots on both sides of us, though here too there were signs of neglect. No trespassing signs were clearly posted along the properties with warnings of grave consequences for violations.

Hope had been sleeping or quietly watching her brothers up until this point. Whether confinement in her car seat, a wet diaper, or hunger finally got to her, we didn't know, but her whimpering quickly built into a crescendo of screaming. I pulled over near a lake past a spot in the road called Turkey Ford. We were near an eastern arm of a huge lake called the Grand Lake of the Cherokees. We were about fifteen miles northwest of South West City, Missouri. This small town was in the corner of the state just north of where Arkansas, Missouri and Oklahoma came together. We were getting close.

Leslie got out while Mom unhooked Hope from her seat. As it was early afternoon and much warmer than we were used to, the boys immediately asked to go down to the water. We had been riding for hours and I was tired. Maybe a short break to eat and stretch was in order.

"Okay, but do not get wet or…" The boys were gone before I could finish my threat of having them ride naked.

Mom and Leslie were changing Hope, who was still pitching a fit. I noticed a growing wet spot on Leslie's blouse.

"You're leaking."

"Ya think? We should have stopped an hour ago for me to feed her."

"So why didn't you say so?" I snapped back at her.

"Because I fell asleep. Didn't you notice?"

"I was driving!" I stomped down the slope toward the boys, upset by the undisguised irritation in her voice.

I yelled at Sean every now and then to stay out of the water. Mom wandered down to the water's edge as well. I tensed, waiting for her rebuke of my behavior toward Leslie, but she kept her thoughts to herself. I took a long, deep breath and called out.

"Come on guys! We need to hit the road. We still have some ways to go."

"Alex, wait," Mom said and I tensed again. "I found a secluded spot back there. I think it might be smart and safe to just camp here tonight. You're already beat and Leslie's exhausted. A fresh start in the morning would do us all good."

She was right. We didn't need to arrive at the Ark at night. "Yeah, okay. I'll go set up the tent and move the van."

Dinner was a Spartan affair of sliced egg sandwiches, white bread, peanut butter and honey, and some water that had been kept in gallon milk containers for a few days. The kids weren't very impressed, but being able to play outside sufficiently distracted them from the meager meal.

The sky was moonless and cloudless, and the stars seemed much brighter than I had ever remembered. The most memorable part of the evening was an orchestra of wood frogs that must have recently emerged from hibernation and were eagerly seeking mates. Their love croak chorus welcomed us to the area and seemed to have a calming effect on Hope, but didn't ease the simmering anger between Leslie and me.

We spent a strained, chilly night huddling Hope between us. Mom groaned every so often as Sean squirmed and kicked in his sleep. Cameron was sacked out in the car. Dawn came early, but was bright and sunny in that pale, washed out blue of a late winter, early spring morning. Today we would see our new home. Packing up and getting back on the road only took a few minutes as everyone seemed to be anxious to move on.

A half hour later, we entered Arkansas. Sean noticed the sign first and got excited. "Mom, is this the Ark?"

Leslie said "No, sugar, we've just entered the state."

"You mean we are going to live at The Ark, Arkansas?" he laughed.

Sean and Cameron cracked up and tried to name all the words that they could rhyme with Ark. "Park, shark, dark, bark, hark, stark, spark, lark, Ozark…" they rambled on. They then found other words to try to rhyme. Mom quickly cut them off when Sean suggested they find things that rhymed with "duck." Next was the old game about going to the fair and taking along something that started with some letter of the alphabet. Leslie kept them on task, for a while, until the boys grew tired of this exercise. They chattered back and forth as we headed closer to our new home.

We had a map to the property Dad had bought. Mom had safeguarded it for many years and had made regular mortgage payments on it. We had never visited it and I doubted that she understood just how he planned to renovate and prepare the place for living. I didn't have any idea what he had done to the place in the years before his death.

Many times I had thought this idea of moving to Arkansas was ridiculous. Given our lack of farming know-how and the dangers of the trip, it seemed like such a desperate thing to do. Sure, Dad had insisted that we grow stuff as kids, but that was little more than a home garden. Here we were throwing our fates to the wind in a strange place with no contacts or much knowledge about how to get by. Would anyone even miss us if we just drove off into one of the ditches along the highway?

We arrived at the gate just as our tank approached empty. We had expected the gate to be locked, but the lock was nowhere in sight and the gate was ajar. Tree stumps dotted the fence boundary. The route into the property had once been a reasonably kept gravel road, since taken over by weeds, but ruts in the weeds suggested recent activity. We pulled into the property and stopped short of coming into clear view of the cabin. I was cautious and wanted to learn more about our new home before everyone disembarked.

"Leslie, can you and Mom make sure the boys stay close while I check things out?"

She nodded.

I saw no signs of telephone poles or electrical lines in the area. The soil appeared dark, and lots of natural vegetation covered the ground with trees in thick growth around the property. There was a slight chill in the air, but at least it was dry. I could hear the burbling of the creek running behind the cabin. I remembered Dad's enthusiasm about the place and wished I had been mature enough to discuss his vision instead of just bitching. Could I make his concept a reality? God I hope so, I prayed. My family's survival depended on it. I got out with my pistol in hand, and headed around the bend in the path.

I quickly scanned the property. It seemed more remote than I remembered and more overgrown.

The cabin was still standing, located at the north edge of the lot. Dad had apparently had some basic work done, including an addition off the back, a large shed behind the cabin, and what looked like a larger, more functional outhouse. The upper part of the chimney had collapsed, and an additional stovepipe popped out of the roof where the rain barrel had been. A modern cistern was now anchored securely to a small platform tower just to the side of the cabin. A small wind turbine had been erected behind the cabin, but it wasn't turning. I could make out the handle of a pump sticking up through the weeds. The bushes and weeds had grown up so high, the front porch was obscured. I had no idea what had been done to the interior but was grateful that Dad had managed to get some work done before he died. There didn't appear to be any fruit trees on the property, and there was no recognizable evidence of either a garden or crops. We apparently would be starting from scratch on food production here. "Home, sweet, home," I murmured to myself drearily.

Spring was just starting to bloom, and the creek flowed forcefully behind the cabin and down the hill to the east. I was just starting to warm up to the rustic beauty of the property when I noticed well-defined trails leading from the cabin to the shed behind the cabin. It looked like we had company.

I clicked the safety off the pistol, felt for the extra clip in my pocket, and started to creep toward the cabin.

I quietly edged off the road and into the woods left of the cabin and headed slowly to a large tree adjacent to the main structure. I listened closely, but could hear no noise. I moved toward the window and continued to listen. A bird darted out of the tree startling me. I approached the window very slowly and kept the gun pointed up and slightly tilted toward the cabin.

The cabin was even smaller than I remembered and unlit. It took a while for my eyes to get accustomed to peering into the interior gloom. There didn't appear to be any activity inside, and I slowly moved around the back of the cabin and stealthily tested the handle to the back door.

The door was unlocked and it opened outward. A strong smell permeated the area, and I wondered if a skunk had moved in. I opened the door slightly to peer inside – there a loud creak of the hinges announced my arrival.

"Drop it or you're dead," a large voice boomed out of the house. I recoiled from the door and planted myself flat against the back porch of the cabin.

"Crap!" I thought to myself.

"Who are you and what are you doing here on my property?" the booming voice challenged. This was followed by an audible click of what sounded like a shotgun being cocked.

CHAPTER ELEVEN

Home Sweet Home

MARCH 2016, ARKANSAS

"I think a hero is an ordinary individual who finds strength to persevere and endure in spite of overwhelming obstacles."

— CHRISTOPHER REEVE

Your property! I don't think so. But I'm not arguing with a gun. I bolted for the woods. My immediate thought was to rejoin my family and make sure they were safe from whoever was in the cabin. We weren't about to relinquish our claim to the property, but it appeared that we might be in for a fight. I carefully circled back to our vehicle trying to stay out of sight of the cabin.

I spotted Mom about fifty yards away near the front gate with the boys, who were trying out a slingshot on some unlucky squirrels up in the trees. Their aim left a lot to be desired, and she was trying to coach them in marksmanship. Leslie was leaning up against the car nursing Hope.

"Leslie, could you come here for a second?" I tried to keep my voice calm as I arrived breathless back at our vehicle.

She sighed, shifted Hope to her hip and closed up her blouse. "What's up?" She yawned, shaking her head to stay alert. "Can we unload now?" She was worried by this move to the wilderness. The ongoing tension with her mother-in-law, traveling with energetic boys and a cranky baby, and being crammed into a packed vehicle for a slow trip on potentially dangerous, unknown country roads had visibly shaken her. Arriving at this weed-choked property with a small rundown cabin and primitive outhouse had been an even worse shock.

"Uh, there's someone in the cabin." I said, trying to appear calm and hoping that neither Mom nor the boys would hear. "I think he has a gun."

"Damn it, Alex." Her face transformed from exhaustion into anxiety, then anger. "What the hell? Could we possibly have any other nasty surprises? I can't believe we left Omaha for this! Just who the hell is in there, because I want them out!" She was fed up and about to walk up to the cabin and take the vagrant apart herself.

"I don't know," I replied. "But I think we need to take things slowly."

"Is there a cop in that pissant town we just passed through?" Leslie snarled.

"Beats me," I said. "But I don't want to go looking for help that might not be there. Maybe we can talk to the neighbors." I wasn't sure Jasper was big enough to have any local law enforcement, but a neighbor might be of assistance, especially if they knew our squatter.

"I saw a couple of houses down the road on our way in. Let's try them," she growled, her fatigue burned away by anger and frustration.

"Okay," I agreed. "Let's load up and go see if we can find anyone at home."

In a couple of minutes we had the kids and Mom back in the car. We slowly backed out the gate and turned down the road to look for a local we could safely approach.

"Hello," I greeted the man standing on the porch of the closest house to the Ark. We had pulled up and parked right in front of a sturdy two-story log home with a rustic appearance, much like its owner. The kids, Leslie and Mom looked curiously out of the windows. I studied the man as I walked closer to the front steps. He was lean, standing close to six feet, and looked about sixty, but his weathered wrinkles had a deep sun baked color that could easily mask his true age by ten or fifteen years either way. His hair was either gray or bleached blonde; I couldn't tell from his position in the shade.

"Howdy," he said. "You all lost?"

"No sir, I'm Alex MacCasland, and that's my family," I said as I pointed back at everyone in the van. "We're here to move into the fenced-in area just down the road and I wanted to introduce myself."

"The fenced-in area?" He looked at me incredulously. I could have just landed from Mars. He glanced suspiciously at our vehicles as if we were going to ask him to take us to his leader. "No owner has even visited that place in almost twenty years. Where have you been, son?"

"Omaha, mostly. My dad bought the place as investment property, but now... Well, times are tough, so we're moving in."

"Wonder what Floyd will have to say about that," he snickered, the laugh lines at his eyes deepening.

"Umm... who's Floyd?" I asked.

"Well, Floyd's been living in your cabin for years. He figured no one was ever going to move in. Guess he'll be surprised." His face betrayed some amusement at our predicament. "I'm Will Kingston, by the way."

"Pleased to meet you, Mr. Kingston," I extended a hand and asked, "What do I do about Floyd?"

"Oh, yeah, Floyd," he frowned. "Best I can remember, Floyd has lived there for almost ten years now. We kept telling him the owners would come someday, but he always told us he'd be ready for them."

This last comment sounded ominous. In rough times, actual occupation of a piece of property wasn't to be taken lightly, even if we did have a deed proving it was legally ours. I hoped Mr. Kingston would assist us in encouraging Floyd to leave. "Would you mind introducing Floyd to us?" I asked.

He spat a wad of tobacco off the porch and then looked me over, sizing me up. "Floyd's never been quite the same since he came back from the first Gulf War in Iraq. His unit killed a lot of Iraqis and may have been exposed to some type of chemicals in the air. Whatever happened to him, he came back a different man."

"He was a soldier?" I was very glad that I had not tried to be more aggressive with him earlier. "Since you know him, could you come with us?" I asked again, now very concerned.

"No problem," he said. "Want to go now?"

I readily accepted and we loaded Mr. Kingston in next to Mom and headed back to our property. We parked as close to the cabin as the weeds would allow.

Our neighbor jumped out of the van and gave a howl like a wild coyote. From inside the cabin a voice echoed his howl. Out of the cabin came a massive man in his late forties. His grin dropped to a scowl when he noticed our vehicle.

"What the hell are you doing here?" he demanded as he looked testily from Mr. Kingston to us.

Floyd was a huge, long-haired bear of a man with dirty clothes, a receding hair line and a stink that could be smelled across the property. Unfortunately, we weren't across the property, and at this short distance, the smell was almost intolerable.

"Meet the property owners, you smelly bastard," Will barked with obvious enjoyment.

Floyd's jaw dropped and his face sagged. He seemed to acknowledge us but also looked vacantly past us. "Where have you been?" His gruff tone was filled with considerable disappointment.

I explained the history of the place; then briefly described our latest challenges in Omaha and our trip here.

Floyd listened, but seemed very distracted by the time I ended my rambling. When I finished, he nodded and raised his hand as if he were saluting something. He then walked into the cabin and rummaged for a few seconds.

Leslie and I looked at each other; then looked at Mom as if asking what had just happened.

Floyd reemerged from the door with a badly faded duffel bag and briskly walked by us on his way down the road toward the front gate.

Leslie's face was a mixture of amazed shock and subtle satisfaction, but some untapped instinct surfaced, and before I knew what I was doing, I asked, "Floyd, where are you going?"

He stopped, lowered his bag and turned around. "What do you mean? I'm leaving," he said. "She's yours."

I blinked at this complete reversal of our situation. My mind was in a whirl. I lifted my hand toward him. "Can you give us a second?"

He looked blankly like I had just asked for money. I motioned for Leslie and Mom to join me. "Look, I'm going to need help around here. I think we ought to ask for Floyd to stay for a while to show us the ropes. What do you think?"

"Are you out of your mind?" Leslie choked out then proceeded to point out his resemblance to Big Foot. Mom bristled as well and crossed her arms.

"It's not like I'm asking you to adopt him."

"Son!" she responded. "We know nothing about this... this person, who obviously has been squatting on *my* property and has made himself at home for the past decade or more. Not to be indelicate, dear, but you are half his size, he stinks to high heaven, he is armed and we have kids to think about."

She ended in a crescendo and snapped her mouth closed when she realized how far her voice had carried. Mr. Kingston covered his mouth, hiding his smile over on the other side of the van. Floyd had gone rigid and was beet red.

Oh shoot, now she's done it, I thought. He is never going to want to stay and I need another man until Ace comes. I quickly weighed the odds and pressed on.

"Mom, calm down," I replied. "These are strange times, and we're pretty ignorant about this wilderness stuff. We've stumbled upon Grizzly Adams and he's been able to live here off the land for years. My bet is that he'd be one heck of a guide for showing us the ropes. It wouldn't have to be forever, just long enough for us to figure out what to do."

"You call that behemoth harmless? His smell alone will kill us!" she snapped. "Mom, be reasonable," I pleaded with her. "I'm not Superman. We've got to plow some ground for crops and a garden, find an immediate source of food, get that windmill working – there's a million things to do, and if or until Ace gets here, it's you, me, Leslie and Cameron to do all the work, most of which we are novices at. We need help and he is huge."

All of my reasons caused a change of heart. "Well, I guess we do need help. But Alex, good God," she said glancing toward Floyd. I could see I had won my point, but I could tell that she was still trying to work through the living arrangements in her mind.

"Don't worry. We'll get him cleaned up some and have him stay in the shed. It can be his 'apartment' for now. Besides, if he was willing to leave immediately, he'll be fine with a week's notice. It won't be forever." She nodded but crossed her arms over her chest and pinched her lips tight.

"Leslie?" I looked at her and sensed pros and cons bouncing through her mind like ping pong balls. "Well?"

She sighed. "Crap, I guess so. Just as long as he gets cleaned up some." She gave me a resigned and somewhat disgusted look. She obviously did not agree with what I was doing and was putting me on notice that whatever happened would be my responsibility.

I nodded and quickly walked up to Floyd, looking at him eye to Adam's apple. I hadn't realized just how big he was until I was standing right in front of him.

"Floyd, we've talked it over among ourselves, and we'd like to know if you could stay with us here awhile." I tried to keep it as simple and clear as I could, but there was a bit of a plea in my voice.

Floyd looked at me, and then looked slowly from Mom, to Leslie, to the boys, to the baby, back at Mom who was starting to fidget like a teenager, and then back at me. "You've got to be kidding me," Floyd chuckled in astonishment. "You'd have me stay?" He let go a laugh that rattled the windows of the cabin. "For years I've had my takin' leave speech in my mind. For years I've kept most of my gear in this duffel bag by the door so's to say good-bye without taking much time. And, just like that, you ask me to stay?"

I wasn't sure he was even willing to stay. He seemed more taken by the irony of the situation. Floyd was probably a hermit and not particularly comfortable around either women or kids. Afraid that he would decline our offer, I added some context to my previous offer. "Floyd, we don't mind that you've been here for a few years, and I suspect that you've had a lot of peacefulness around here all alone. But, we're city folk and we've come a long way. We are tired and our food won't last much past summer. I don't know much about farming or hunting and even less about surviving without the basics. You seem to have that part down and, man to man, I need some help. What do you say, will you stay?"

Mr. Kingston, enjoying the humor in this situation, was following the discussion with obvious interest.

"Okay," Floyd thundered back at me finally, like a big overgrown kid. "I'll stay for a little while – just to make sure that you folks get settled in okay."

Mr. Kingston was still smiling curiously, which was starting to bother me. Starting to feel some buyer's remorse over my just-completed transaction with Floyd, I asked Will if he wanted a ride back to his property. "No, thanks," he said airily, "save your gas. I'll walk. You all come by if you need anything else."

That night, Leslie, Hope and I slept in the tent while the boys and Mom stayed in the van. For one last night Floyd had the cabin to himself, which saved us from figuring out our sleeping arrangements inside the cabin. It was probably just as well. From the sound of things, Floyd was doing a little cleaning up, or at least shoving stuff around in the cabin; even going so far as to move some of his junk outside. That night, however, there wasn't an audible owl, cricket or frog orchestra, as Floyd's snoring drowned out all other night music and kept us in a state of sleepless irritation.

I guess it was close to three am when Leslie rolled toward me. "Honey, don't we have a pistol somewhere?" she mumbled in my ear. "Because I'm going to use it on either Floyd or myself, and right now I'm not sure which of us goes first. This just isn't working for me."

I stared up at the canvas above my head. What had I done? Getting used to Floyd was only a minor challenge. I had brought my family out in the woods to survive.

CHAPTER TWELVE

Breaking Ground

MARCH 2016, ARKANSAS

"Every day is a new beginning. Listen my heart to the glad refrain, and, spite of old sorrows and older sinning, troubles forecasted, and possible pain, take heart with the day and begin again."

— SUSAN COOLIDGE

Leslie, Mom, and I were slow to adjust to our drastically new situation, but the boys took to our new life like early pioneers establishing a homestead. While we spent the first week unloading the trailer and van and setting up house, the boys explored the property, fished in the creek with sticks and string, and climbed trees. Hope was entertained with a set of metal measuring spoons and her toy duck in the safety of the now empty trailer.

Floyd set up living quarters in the shed, which he referred to as a bunkhouse. Mom managed to add some soundproofing by way of hanging all our extra quilts and spreads against the shed walls. It wasn't much, but it would do until we could insulate the small building. I got Floyd cleaned up a little by innocently asking about a pond, or swimming hole, anywhere close by for the boys to have some fun. All four of us guys took off on a small adventure exploring a place at the river a few hundred yards away. Floyd showed us how to swing out over the water and cannonball into a deep spot.

"Now, you boys need to get a running start or you won't swing out far enough." Floyd pointed up the river bank and handed Cameron the knotted rope someone, presumably Floyd, had tied up in a large pine. "You just run down the bank and keep a grip on that knot. I'll yell for you to let go."

I waded out into the river to make sure the drop zone was deep enough. Cameron came careening down the bank, flew out over the water and let go when Floyd yelled. He dropped about six feet and disappeared under the water with a big splash.

"Hey, that was awesome!" he yelled as soon as he surfaced. "Come on, Sean! You're gonna love it!"

An hour of physical fun and daring flew by, with all of us managing to soak off a week or more of grime. Floyd had been particularly ripe when we arrived, but there was no hint of "Eau de Floyd" after the first couple of dunks. He did present a rather unexpected anatomy lesson for the boys, however.

The sight of Floyd naked was beyond words or full comprehension. Both Cameron and Sean asked me numerous shy questions about hair, anatomy, and especially about male endowment for several days afterward.

Mom and Leslie were just grateful we could all breathe fresh air once again – at least away from the outhouse.

We had everything to set up a basic kitchen, including our camping gear, several cookbooks, some pots and pans, utensils, and all the food we had left in our cabinets and garage cache. As Leslie unpacked each box, she made notes on a piece of paper and shook her head, trying to figure out where to put things. Mom rattled around, scanning the unpacked items and muttering to herself. Her half-overheard comments finally ticked Leslie off.

"Janine, do you have some problem?" she snapped.

"Yes! Who packed this stuff? What will we do with jars of chutney, Greek peppercorns, and a can of artichoke hearts? I can't make meals with these odds and ends."

"Well, look over in that box. We have a decent supply of basic ingredients." Leslie pointed to a large plastic bin. "And for the record, I packed that stuff – better to have odds and ends than nothing at all." She threw down her pen and paper and stomped out of the house.

"Humph," snorted Mom, as she started to work her way into the contents of the indicated bin. "This is more like it. How about some stew and biscuits for dinner?" She asked me.

"Mom, don't you think a little cooperation would go further?" I was annoyed at her feigned obliviousness to Leslie's anger. "We've only been here a few days and I'd like to think Dad's little survival project might actually work for us. But you've got to see how this all seems to Leslie. She has no idea how to live in these circumstances. You had the benefit of living with Dad for thirty some years."

The gleam in her eye told me that she considered herself better in the kitchen anyway. "Yeah, I guess you have a point," she conceded. "But I don't intend to mollycoddle her, and you shouldn't either. We're just going to have to do the best with what we've got." She turned back to the box and started placing the contents up on the shelves.

The next morning Leslie was back in the kitchen, unloading boxes and attempting to get things organized for cooking. Mom was nowhere to be seen and I was grateful for her absence. Yesterday, Leslie had been out by the creek crying when I had found her. She had made light of the argument with Mom, but I knew it still rankled her. It hadn't occurred to me how domestic chores were going to be divvied up between Mom and Leslie. The cabin was basically Mom's, but she had moved in with us in Omaha. Now that Leslie didn't have a job to go to, I wondered if she would want to take charge in the kitchen. I knew she wasn't really sure how to cook without her microwave, stove, oven, blender or mixer. She wasn't even sure she could mix by hand, although she had found an ancient heavy-duty hand beater at a flea market before we left Omaha, similar to one her grandmother had owned. "I guess women have baked for centuries without much more than a spoon.

Maybe it will build up some arm strength," she said, smiling tentatively as she put the beater in a drawer.

The "kitchen" consisted of a sink, without running water, some drawers and shelves and a laminate counter surface that Dad had put in to replace the plywood surfaces. We had no fridge and no electricity, nor anything to keep food cool. Leslie sighed deeply and turned toward the fireplace across the large central room with a cast iron pot. We walked over to the fireplace together.

Several hinged iron arms had been installed in the side walls. Leslie swung one out and hung the pot on the arm. "I guess you swing it over the fire and heat water or soup – if I have anything to make soup with!" she added.

"Not until we get the chimney fixed," I said.

Her jaw dropped at this revelation. "What?"

"You didn't notice the stones have collapsed on the outside?" I asked. "Cameron and I will need to find some concrete or mortar to rebuild it."

Leslie dropped down on her knees and stuck her head in the fireplace to look up the open flue. "I can see daylight. It should be pretty easy to fix. Think Floyd or Will would know where we can get fire bricks?"

"We can ask. Meanwhile I can set up a tripod for the pot outside. Think you could cook over an open fire?"

"Oh geez, Alex! How the hell would I know?" She closed her eyes tight, "I'm sure your mother can. She seems to know how to do everything else. I guess I need to rethink my function in life now."

I hastened to reply. "Leslie, this may be Mom's house, but you're my wife. If you want to cook, you can cook. If you want to be in charge of the garden, it's yours. You get to decide what you want now. I'll talk to Mom to ensure that she understands this.

Of course, that was a fine lot of talk. How I'd ever convince my mother was another question altogether.

Mom had placed the last of the spices on a shelf the day before and she had carefully unsealed the cardboard box and folded it flat for storage. We now had a growing pile of cardboard by the fireplace. We would use it for fire starter or perhaps sound insulation for Floyd's shed.

I was beginning to understand why my great-grandmother, who had lived through the Depression in the 1930s, had saved everything, rarely made unnecessary purchases or threw away leftovers. The past few months had taught me almost everything had value when you had no guarantee of ever getting more.

Cameron came in, carrying the last kitchen box from our move. He set it down and opened it up. "Boring," he said with youthful disdain, "It's just a pot and a bunch of jars."

"Oh, hallelujah! I was worried we'd left these behind!" Mom said as she hurried over to the box. She knew how to preserve food and was thrilled when we located two cases of canning jars on the bottom shelf in Wal-Mart before it closed after Christmas. "You'll be happy we found these." Mom snapped, shaking her finger in Cameron's face. "They should help us get through next winter."

Cameron's eyes got big and he quickly stepped back.

"I can put all the veggies we grow or any berries you find in these glass jars, clear to the top, mind you! Then we seal the jar with this flat piece and screw it on tight with these rings." She remembered another step and added. "But most important is putting the jars in the pot of boiling water to kill the bacteria. That way we won't get food poisoning."

As I watched her carefully put the little jars and other canning paraphernalia up on the shelf, I wondered how much use they'd really get. As we became real farmers and gardeners, we'd need to preserve what we couldn't immediately eat. I hoped we'd have something to can by August.

"What kind of berries?" Cameron asked Mom.

"Hey, Come on and I'll show you," said Leslie, showing up at that moment. "Go find your brother and we'll scout out the berry brambles."

Leslie took the boys out along the fence and showed them what berry bushes looked like. They found a handful with new shoots and then sent the boys to hunt for wild raspberry or blackberry vines along the roads and pasture areas. If they could locate enough we might have fresh fruit by late June and jam year round.

"Mom, I want you to understand how much we appreciate all that you've done for us," I said after Leslie and the boys left.

"Oh Alex, you don't have to say anything."

"Actually, I do. There's a problem that I think we need to address at the outset."

Her eyes began to narrow. "Go on," she said warily.

"Mom, don't take this the wrong way, but we're in real tight quarters at this point, and we need to clarify some responsibilities to assist everyone in understanding who is responsible for what around here."

Her suspicion instantly died away. "Alex, look, I understand that this is my house, but I have no intentions of running it. Please rest assured that you should simply consider this house yours and treat me as your guest."

That was easy. "Mom, you're the best." I sighed with relief. "But I hope you're a working guest. We need your understanding on how to do so much around here."

"I'm at your disposal." Coming closer, she turned my collar down. I hadn't even realized that it was sticking up. I instinctively turned my neck away as if to resist her touch to my clothing. I loved my mother, but I had never planned on living in such tight quarters with her after all these years. No, Leslie was not the only one that was starting to feel defensive as our cramped living space began to encroach on our personal boundaries.

With the kitchen set up, we turned our attention to the rest of the house. Our furniture consisted of the card table, several folding chairs, Hope's crib and the few mattresses we had brought with us. In addition, the cabin was "furnished" with a rocking chair, a couple of dressers, a badly worn sofa, a worn wooden picnic table, and the bed Floyd had been using, minus the mattress that we had dragged out to the bunkhouse – after giving it a good airing. We moved the bed frame into the back room behind the kitchen and laid one of our mattresses on it. Leslie, Hope and I would sleep in there. We set up the crib on my side of the room, with the rocker close by. The boxes of our clothing went on the other side of the room. Mom took the smaller room Dad had added in back of the living room. Our important papers and books were stored in a low dresser that doubled as a low table, so we shoved it in front of the living room window and set plants on it.

The boys slept in the living room close to the fireplace, until they discovered the pull-down ladder to the attic. I climbed up first to make sure the flooring was sturdy and they wouldn't fall through. Dad had installed insulation and floor planking and, in addition, had drywall put up. But the real surprise was the beds built in under the eaves.

"Hey, Mom?" I stuck my head out of the access hole. "Did you know there are beds up here?"

"Really?" she asked. "How many?"

"Six – all built-in, with lots of open floor space in the middle."

"Sounds like Aiden expected there to be grandkids here with us. He would have been so thrilled."

Ecstatic, the boys promptly hauled their bedding and possessions up the steep ladder to make the area their own.

That evening, after Leslie put the kids to bed and Floyd had retired to his "bunkhouse," I turned to Mom hesitantly, "Do you think Ace will come and join us?"

"I've been wondering that myself, Alex." She closed the book she had been reading. "He knows how to find us, but wouldn't you stay in school if you could? He's had an internship for the past two summers. I told him what we were doing, but if he could find work and finish school, we wouldn't expect him to show up yet. UCLA may not have had the same kinds of attendance problems as your community college" Her face clouded over as she thought of something else. "My bigger worry is food. Do you think the big cities are getting enough?"

"I'm sure they are. I heard food from the San Joaquin Valley is mostly going to Los Angeles and San Francisco. Besides, Ace says Californians are all about green living and conservation. He's probably already rooming with someone who's got a garden. Plus, fish and seafood should be available. He'll be fine." I tried to sound positive, as I could see the deeply etched lines in her face.

"I hope so, Alex. I just have this nagging suspicion that he's not safe. I wish I could get in touch with him." She sighed and went back to her reading.

A couple of days later I noticed Leslie standing at the counter with a rumpled piece of paper.

"Whatcha doin, babe?" I asked.

"We need to inventory our food. Would you see if you can get Floyd to bring all of his cans in? I think his daily serving of beans is, ah… a contributor to the… ah… " Leslie looked resolved on the issue of controlling Floyd's odors.

I caught her drift and laughed. "Oh yeah! We could do with more fuel and less gas. Let me go talk to him and see where we stand. Do you want me to ask Mom to come help you? I think she went down to the creek."

"I don't know," she said, "It's nice having her out of the house. Sometimes she really gets on my nerves, but there is so much work to be done." She sighed, "Let's just let her enjoy the creek, okay?"

"We could have some private time ourselves." I suggested, moving behind her and curving her into my arms. She leaned back and took a deep breath and suddenly stiffened up, sniffing. "Uh, maybe we could go down to the swimming hole and clean ourselves up a bit."

I realized she had caught a whiff of body odor. Whether mine or hers didn't really matter, because the mood was broken. I looked at all the boxes, recognizing how much work was waiting for all of us and deferred to my better judgment. "I wish, but look at all of this. Let's just enjoy the break from Mom. I'll help you unpack. Okay?"

I turned when I heard a noise behind me.

Floyd appeared in the doorway with a big box in his arms. "Where you want me to put this, Mrs. Mac Junior?" he asked in his deep rolling bass voice. "It's my empties."

"Your empties? I don't know what you mean," Leslie grumbled. "Can you translate that into English?"

We kept telling ourselves that Floyd's lack of social graces was not his fault. He had lived here alone for more than a decade and just didn't care much what others thought. His reply surprised us.

"You know, my empty food cans. Mr. Mac said you needed to know what I get from the store each month – well, what I used to get. Nowadays it's slim pickings. But I keep the cans so I know what I ate. I got about a million yonder." He placed the box on a card table and started to unload it.

"You have a million empty cans somewhere?" Leslie's eyes scanned his face to see if he was kidding us.

He replied in all seriousness. "Well, come to think on it, I don't know as if I actually ever counted all of them. But there's sure a pot load down my hidey hole. You need more than a month's selection?" He glanced over at me, so I snapped my mouth closed. "I was thinking that would give you the gist of my order each month. I never did much cooking, just heat and eat, but if you need some cans in exchange for real meals, it'd make me no never mind. I'd sure like some home cooking for a change."

Mom came back in, ambled over to the table and began looking at the labels. "Lots of beans here, Floyd" she observed dryly. "Doesn't that get a little boring?"

"Nah, but they sure do give me farts something fierce." His candid reply made me laugh, but Mom winkled her nose, frowning in distaste. She was still very uncertain about Floyd's usefulness, canned food not withstanding. Floyd continued, "I just told Mrs. Mac Junior that I'd switch anything for some home cooking and I bet Mrs. Big Mac is a right fine cook, too," He gave Mom a big smile. In response, Mom quickly moved closer to me.

With a glance at Mom, Leslie took charge of the planning. "Okay, everybody, if we've got to feed seven of us – eight, once Ace arrives – we need a meal plan. We have a Dutch oven, several pots, but no real stove. Baking will be limited unless we can find an old fashioned stove for the kitchen or find material to build a little solar oven. We also don't have much ability to keep things cool except the creek and we don't know how that is in late summer."

Floyd interrupted. "There's my hidey hole where I keep all my empties."

"And why did you keep all the empty cans?" Mom asked. "Did you have a plan for them?"

"I'd like to do something useful with 'em," Floyd said vaguely, "I just ain't yet had a project where I needed 'em."

I could see the gears turning in Mom's mind. "Where are all these cans, Floyd?"

"In my hidey hole."

Mom rolled her eyes at me out of Floyd's sight and I coughed to mask a laugh.

"Where is that?" I asked with an admonishing look at Leslie and Mom. "We might find a good use for some of them."

"Well, it's back yonder in the cave."

Floyd's nonchalant pronouncement stopped us all in our tracks. It was Mom's turn to show her surprise. "Cave, what cave? There's a cave here? Don't let the boys hear that!" All three of us again began to speak at once with Floyd switching his glance back and forth among us. He had no idea what we were excited about.

Cameron walked in just in time to hear the last comment. "What am I not supposed to hear?"

Mom and Leslie groaned. I sent Cameron back out to fill some water jugs and took Floyd over to the table to look at our property map.

"It's right here, Mr. Mac." He pointed at a small hillside on the northwest edge of the property. "You have to know right where the hole is or you'd never see it. Every week I take my cans in there. And when the delivery guy brings the food, I put the new stuff on my shelf, in the shed now, and I deliver the empty cans to the hole."

"I guess you'd better show me," I said. "Leslie can look at your empties and decide if you need to change your monthly grocery order."

"Okay, as long as I can have my peaches. Gotta have my peaches!"

Mom was already scanning through his empties. "Must be twenty peach cans in here. And even more beans – that's going to change!"

Leslie laughed and turned back to Floyd and me. "You go on and find this cave, but make sure the boys aren't following you. I don't want them exploring any caves until you've checked it out. Oh yeah, do you know which box has the food list in it?"

"I think it's the one marked 'kitchen books and papers'" I said. "Come on, Floyd, show me this cave of yours."

I wasn't sure what to expect from Floyd's cave, but when we reached the hillside, I saw the limestone outcroppings and wondered if we had an extensive cave system running under the property. Floyd pushed aside the long branches of a bush, revealing an opening in the rock face. He squeezed through and I followed him in.

107

The cave was small, more like a large den for a bear with a huge mound of debris to the left. In the dim light from the opening I couldn't see any openings or formations farther back. Suddenly a light clinked on and I realized Floyd had a big flashlight. The debris mound turned out to be an enormous pile of empty tin cans. As Floyd pointed the light around the area, I could see it was just one big chamber. There was a large chest freezer at the back of the cave and Floyd headed straight for it.

"What the heck is that?" I asked, half afraid of what he was likely to hold in the large container at the rear of the cave. I could see the prongs of an electric cord suggesting that this had once been a standard freezer. More trash, no doubt.

"A freezer," he shared rather casually.

"Yes, I know what it used to be, but what's in it now?" I queried.

"Mostly Popsicles and milk, I reckon," Floyd responded.

This answer sent me reeling. "You have a functional freezer?" I stammered. "But how?"

"I put ice and snow in it in the winter and try to keep it shut up tight most of the time. I only open it every other day or so. The ice lasts through most of the summer." He started to open the lid and I felt cold air emerge from it. I pushed the lid back down.

"Oh my God, do you know what this means? It means we don't have to bottle all of our produce and fruits in order to preserve them for more than a few days. We might not have to salt all of our meat or make jerky out of it," I exclaimed excitedly. "This is huge! I've got to share this with Leslie right now."

I left his cave in a flash and headed down the hill to where Leslie was hanging some clothes on the line.

"Leslie, we've got a freezer in Floyd's cave."

She looked at me as if I was joking. "A freezer?" She paused to look at me again. "Really?" When I nodded my head I could see her excitement building. "Show me."

I hurried back to the cave with Leslie in close pursuit. Floyd was standing at the opening, not sure if he was in trouble or had done something good.

"Floyd, can you show Leslie the freezer?"

Floyd reentered the cave with his flashlight. Leslie suddenly looked less excited about the freezer as she realized she needed to go into this dark, dirty place that was probably creature infested. Nevertheless, the promise of getting access to an appliance that she once considered just a normal part of her life was much too alluring.

When Floyd reached the chest, he carefully lifted the lid again and moved aside a large piece of heavy duty Styrofoam. Leslie and I moved closer and peered inside.

The chest was lined in big bubble wrap and bricks of ice. The right side had a maze of small openings in what looked like a solid block of ice. I could see sticks poking up out of many of the openings. On the other side, a couple of quarts of milk surrounded in bubble wrap were set deep in a larger cavity of ice.

"I have to wrap the milk or it can freeze solid, but my Popsicles do just fine in their little holes" He reached in and gave a stick a quick twist and held out an orange Popsicle. "You want one?"

Leslie accepted the Popsicle, not to eat it, but to just feel the cold on the skin of her hand.

Her eyes widened as she finally realized that it was true that there was a source for cold storage on site.

"Floyd, how long have you had this?"

He looked away, scuffing his toe. "I dunno. I guess I got it a few years after I moved in. It's a pain not having electricity sometimes."

Leslie nodded in amused agreement. I could tell her mind was racing through the various options on how to best incorporate this new discovery into our lives.

I studied the design of his freezer. I could see how the bubble wrap allowed the water to drain away from the items in the freezer as the ice melted. I glanced to the exterior of the chest and saw a drain hole had been drilled and stopped with a cork.

"How long does the ice stay?" I asked.

"Usually until September if I'm not too greedy. Sometimes I'll get someone to drop off a bag of ice for it if it gets too low. The more I open the chest the faster the ice melts. I try not to open it often. Probably should shut it up now." He carefully replaced the Styrofoam interior covering and shut the freezer lid. Leslie stayed by the freezer and started wiping dirt off the freezer lid with a rag that had been lying nearby.

I wandered over to his pile of empty cans. There was a box of round lids and another with flat rectangles of tin. "What did you plan to do with these?"

"Don't rightly know. Just seemed a waste of good metal to pitch them. Maybe shingle the cabin roof if it had holes. But I never did make a ladder to climb up there, so…" He shrugged and picked up a can. "You have to cut off the other end and clip up one side, then flatten it out and weight it for a while. I didn't have a plan for the ends."

A flash of memory lit my mind and I wondered if it would work. "Hey, Floyd, is there a way to punch a hole in the ends and string them on wire or twine? They might be useful for scaring away birds in our garden or in a crop field."

"You just hit a screwdriver with a hammer. Pops right through," he said shrugging. Don't know about twine or crops. Never had a garden, but you are welcome to all this."

My mind was already setting Sean and Cameron to work on this project while I envisioned Floyd and me figuring out where to plant crops and start plowing.

"Alex, could we do like Floyd said and use these to shingle the outhouse?" Leslie was holding a couple of the flattened tins. "It's leaky and the flies get in. If we re-roofed and sealed the cracks…"

I didn't hear the rest of what she was saying. I was already halfway down the hill calling for the boys. We had work to do, and it was time the four men of the Ark got busy.

CHAPTER THIRTEEN

The Grasshopper and the Ants

MARCH 2016, ARKANSAS

"Farming looks mighty easy when your plow is a pencil, and you're a thousand miles from the corn field."

— DWIGHT D. EISENHOWER

There is an old proverb about a grasshopper that plays all summer while the ants toil. When winter comes, the grasshopper has no food saved up and the ants are prepared. In some versions of the story, the ants feed the grasshopper in exchange for his playing songs. In other versions, the grasshopper simply starves or freezes to death.

I recalled this parable while watching Floyd sleep under a tree while Leslie, Cameron and I tried to plow the field by hand. Floyd was a grasshopper.

Our neighbor Will revealed that Floyd had a psychological military disability, some sort of post traumatic stress disorder. His war experiences had left him emotionally scarred and apathetic about almost everything, and work in particular. He never said exactly what had happened to leave him in this condition, but some nights his snores were interrupted by agitated, but mostly unintelligible, speech or screams from his nightmares. I once witnessed him diving to the ground after a loud, sharp sound.

As a disabled veteran Floyd received a check every month. My hasty assumption that he was a Grizzly Adams living off the land with a wealth of knowledge about survival was dead wrong. His survival skills seemed to be limited to retrieving said check from the mail box and exchanging this money for supplies and food that he stocked the cabin with. He had the exchange process down to a science; the check would show up around the first of the month and the food delivery would arrive a few days later. He would sign the check over to the delivery guy and that was that.

When Will commented that Floyd had changed, what he really meant was that Floyd was either unwilling or unable to work in any meaningful way. Unwilling was the family consensus. Mom would give me that "I told you so" glance several times a week. I doubted if anything would ever improve Floyd's standing in her opinion.

Floyd wasn't totally useless to our farming efforts. He had shown the boys how to use tin snips to cut through the side of cans once they had used a can opener to remove the bottom. Sean was "in charge of" pounding holes through the tin disks, a job he enjoyed for about twenty minutes a day. We didn't bug him. By the time we got a field plowed, he'd have enough disks punched to cover a field.

Will, on the other hand, was a godsend. He looked at our seed packet and advised us on what we could easily grow in our garden and what probably needed to be stored until we learned more about farming. He shared local seeds with us, loaned us some of his extra tools, and pretty much checked in every few days to see how we were doing. He wasn't quite the perfect expert, since his farming techniques had relied upon diesel tractors and mechanical devices. Without the use of fuel he had to rethink some of his methods. Even so, he always had an idea on how we might tackle a particular problem. He had one small tractor with a tiller that he ran occasionally. I figured he couldn't have much fuel and I didn't ask to borrow it.

Our most pressing problem was planting a garden for food. Mom and Leslie had laid out an area following the advice of Will's wife, Judy. It was about half the size of a football field, which seemed huge to us, but once the rows and borders were laid out, we could see why so much space was needed. Pumpkins, squash, and zucchini all needed vine growing room. Corn needed almost a foot between stalks, and since we wanted some chickens, we would need lots of corn over the winter, not to mention seed for next year and enough for us to eat.

We hadn't understood why marigolds, poppies, yarrow, foxglove and some other flowers had been put in the garden seed packet we had purchased. Judy explained that certain flowers, herbs and plants could be grown around the boundary of a garden to discourage bugs, deer, rabbits and other creatures from eating the rest of the garden. She also recommended we plant certain herbs next to crop plants to enhance the vegetable taste, like lemon basil near tomatoes. Other flowers and herbs, such as daisies, sunflowers, and thyme, would attract beneficial insects that would eat the pests. Since we had no commercial fertilizer or pesticides, these techniques were especially useful. Leslie had picked up an old book on medicinal herbs and was glad to see we had some of them in the seed packet as well.

"This will all make more sense if we just sit down and map it out." Judy suggested, gesturing to her kitchen table. "Would you like some water?" The ladies sat down with a piece of paper. "First you draw out your boundaries," Judy said, mapping out a large rectangle to represent the whole garden. "Now we plant the stuff animals don't much care for all along this perimeter," she said and wrote in the names of the various plants she had been telling us about. "Some areas need mounds or ridges, others just need the soil turned and hoed." She sketched in those requirements, too. "The weather is warming up, so you'll need to work fast to get everything planted." We thanked Judy and Will and left feeling much better about our proposed garden.

The garden prep work was given to the boys. "Here's how this is going to work, guys," I said after dinner. "This is the area we are going to use for the garden," showing them a grid map I had drawn up. "You will get a shovel, and if you dig down about a foot you might find some useful treasure!"

Cameron rolled his eyes. "Are you serious?" he groaned. Sean missed his remarks and let out a whoop of excitement

"Oh, cool!" he yelled. "Do we get to keep the treasure we find?"

"Sure do!" I said, running with his enthusiasm and ignoring Cameron's reasonably perceptive view. "You can keep what you find and use it."

Floyd had an old box of tools that he generously donated to the game. Each night I took a couple of tools and, using a slender spade, opened up a couple of holes and buried them. The boys eagerly or reluctantly dug their grid looking for the treasure. We managed to turn most of the soil in a week. And both boys had the makings of a basic tool set to use as they pleased.

Once the ground was turned and the clods broken up, we laid out the garden according to the map. The boys found sticks in the woods that served as stakes for the boundaries and row markers. We each took an area and the appropriate seed packets; the boys worked together. I gave the boys sticks that were marked with the right depth and separation for the corn they were planting, and off they went. Sean was about halfway down a row when I realized he had reversed his sticks.

"Sean! Shallow hole, long space!" I shouted, trying to constrain my anger, but not being able to do so. I was hot and dirty and disgusted with farming.

"Oops." Sean ducked his head down into his shoulders like a turtle trying to retract into the safety of his shell. "Sorry Dad."

"Sorry isn't going to cut it! Go back and dig up the seeds and do it right. We need all the corn we can get this year."

Cameron was laughing at his brother, and I turned my ire on him, "Okay Cameron, since you think this is so funny, you can help him replant his rows."

"Ah, Dad, that's not fair. I didn't screw up."

"No, you didn't, but Sean is learning like the rest of us. You are supposed to be a team, but you didn't catch his mistake, did you?"

He shook his head and kicked at a clod of dirt.

"Then you get to show you understand what team means."

Sean had been busily digging up his mistakes as I lectured Cameron. He was almost to the end of his row and yelled back at me. "I think I got them all, Dad. Long space and short hole, right?"

Cameron cheered up significantly at this development and answered for me. "Yeah, that's right. Why don't we work side by side and check each other? We don't want short corn crowded together."

The boys really wanted to be useful, and increasingly they were.

Watering the garden was a chore. We got the pump to work, but short of hauling individual buckets over to the rows, we hadn't figured out how to irrigate or channel the water over. Sean came to our rescue.

"Dad!" he whispered early one morning. "Dad! Wake up! Come see how this works." I rolled over and tried to focus, my mind slowly decoding his words. "Wake up" wasn't converting to "Get up" yet.

"Come on. It's im-por-tant!" His emphasis on each syllable roused me sufficiently to get up and follow him outside.

He stopped on the front porch, pivoted with the precision of a military guard and gestured to a pile of cans and twine tied to a short piece of one by four. "Isn't it great?" he announced proudly.

"Uh, yeah... wow!" I scrambled for something to say except: "What is it?" My still drowsy brain finally grasped the obvious. "Hey, sport, why don't you give me a demo?"

"Good idea, dad." He picked up the board and started explaining his contraption.

The hours of punching holes in tin can lids gave him the idea, he said.

"I found several large cans in Floyd's pile. So I took six of them and punched a couple of holes through the sides near the top here." He carefully pointed out the holes and showed me how he had threaded a double twist of twine through them, then up to a notched stick. "Then I tied three cans to each side of the sticks and looped them up on the board so I can carry it all. See?" He stood up with the plank across his shoulders with the two rows of three cans dangled about knee level and just about the width of our garden rows. "Now watch," he directed as he walked over to our water trough.

Dipping each side in the trough under the pump filled each can with water in a couple of seconds. The yoke and sticks supported the full cans until Sean slipped the yoke off and deliberately tipped the cans over. The immediate area under each can was well watered. "See how easy this is?" He asked.

"You are a genius, kiddo," I said, genuinely impressed. "Think you can make more so we can all water?"

"You bet, Dad!" he grinned. "I'll get right on it."

He made four more of these contraptions, and we worked as a team to water the garden twice a day. It took about thirty minutes with all five of us hauling. We looked like ants scurrying back and forth from pump to garden, but Sean was thrilled with his ingenuity.

"Dad, Dad! Wake up! You gotta come see!" Sean was pulling on my arm to rouse me from sleep.

Not again. "Sean, stop yanking my arm. What is it?"

"You gotta come see for yourself. It's important."

Leslie groaned and covered her head with the covers, muttering into the pillow. I let her sleep.

"Dad!"

"Okay, okay, I'm coming. Just let me grab some clothes." I reached for my T-shirt and robe, slipped my flip-flops on and followed Sean out the door. He dashed around the side of the house and headed toward our garden.

Bright flashes of light sparkled in front of me as I rounded the corner. I stopped dead in my tracks, trying to figure out what I was seeing. Slowly it began to register and I could see why Sean had been so excited. Strung over the various rows of herbs and vegetables were hundreds of shiny can lids. Below the spinning disks were hundreds of tiny green shoots. Our garden was growing!

"Sean, you strung all the lids?"

"Yeah, me and Floyd did it last night. It was my secret mission."

"Floyd helped?"

"Well, sort of," he amended. "He tied the strings to the top of the stakes for me 'cause my knots aren't good."

"I'm amazed. Good job, son! And can you see all the little green shoots coming out of the ground? Our plants are growing!"

"Yeah, I saw them yesterday so I had to finish my mission. I don't want the birds and bunnies eating our food."

"You did a great job. I'm very proud of you. Now how about some breakfast?"

"Can we have pancakes? I miss pancakes."

I wanted to say yes, but I couldn't promise. "I don't know that we can make pancakes. Let's go tell your mom we have something worth celebrating with a special breakfast. Maybe she can make us something yummy." My sense of accomplishment and confidence rose a few notches. Our garden was growing! Mom and Leslie made old fashioned flapjacks with some honey drizzled over them.

Besides his somewhat limited willingness to help Sean and Cameron with whatever they asked, we eventually learned a little more about our big grasshopper. To be fair, Floyd contributed in a number of small ways. He loved to play the banjo and sing, thereby providing entertainment and music lessons for the kids. Floyd occasionally introduced us to some neighbor he knew when we needed something. And, he did know something about the woods.

He knew where to sit to listen to woodpeckers or owls or to watch deer walk by. He knew which berries were edible and which trees were which. In the beginning, we tried not to work on Sunday, and Floyd would take us on nature walks through the woods, teaching us about the plants and the wildlife in the area. This was also his major exertion during the week. He continued to take the boys swimming, and by default Sunday night became the compound's bath and shower night. Once the guys got out of the water, the deep spot was turned over to the girls.

Hope took to the water with glee once she adjusted to the cool temperature. She would splash and churn her little legs while Leslie supported her belly. Once in a while, Leslie would hold her face to face, blow air at her nose and quickly bob under the water. Since babies instinctively hold their breath when someone blows air in their face, it was a quick way to get her used to having her face underwater and not risk drowning. Eventually she learned to associate the one, two, three bounce as a preliminary to the dunk and would hold her breath by herself. One day she just put her face in the water and started to wriggle. We had a mermaid in training.

Sunday evenings were the best part of our hardscrabble life. Everyone was clean, relaxed and feeling good about the workweek. After dinner, Mom would read a story from one of the books we had kept. We would listen to the story and on clear nights watch the stars pop out like someone poking holes in backlit navy velvet. The evening critter chorus would start up, sometimes joined by the baritone of a barn owl, or yapping of dogs and coyotes. We were beginning to feel less like exiles and more like homesteaders. It was on one of these Sunday nights that we had our first new arrivals.

CHAPTER FOURTEEN

Company

APRIL 2016, ARKANSAS

"Be cautious with whom you associate, and never give your company or your confidence to persons of whose good principles you are not certain."
— WILLIAM HART COLERIDGE

Everyone was so intent on the story Mom was reading that we didn't notice the small cluster of people walking up our path until they were almost to the cabin. A couple of women followed a man pulling a cart and several children walked behind the women with another one riding on the cart. I guessed that one woman was in her mid twenties, and the man and other woman appeared to be in their mid thirties. All of the children were young, and none appeared to be over the age of ten. The younger woman was strikingly attractive. She had long, wavy dark hair, deep brown eyes, a clear complexion and an alluring figure; she was beautiful even in the worn, stained clothing she wore. I caught myself staring at her before I realized the new comers might pose a danger to us.

"Hello," I said gruffly, trying to sound challenging. I was wearing only a pair of shorts and my hair was wet. I wasn't exactly in a state that would intimidate anyone, and I wasn't armed.

The man stopped and his whole flock halted with him. "Hi, I'm Richard," he said. "Mind if we stay here for the night?"

There were numerous sad and tired eyes behind him that didn't look like they could go anywhere else that night. I wasn't sure what we should do. One night might become two, which might extend to an indefinite stay. We had plenty of people already, and we didn't need to more than double our occupancy.

"Okay," I said, "but you'll have to leave tomorrow."

Cameron and Sean came running out of the shadows, excited to have other kids to play with. They ran up to one of the boys in the group and introduced themselves and ran off together while my condition for staying hung in the air.

"Yep," he said. "No problem. Where do you want us?"

I guided him over to a clearing along the path and showed them an area they could use to sleep and prepare themselves for the night. I didn't like the idea of them going to the bathroom just anywhere on our property, so I ran a thin rope from this area to the outhouse – so they could find their way in the dark.

The women appeared to be exhausted as they slowly started to organize the bedding arrangements and unload items from the pull cart. Some of the kids were whining about dinner, but the women were noticeably avoiding this question. Leslie astutely figured out the problem and motioned Floyd over. He had been standing outside his bunkhouse looking at the newcomers.

"Floyd, can you bring some fresh water over in plastic containers?" she asked, "These folks need some water, and I bet they don't have enough for dinner."

"I'll go get the water right now," he said, eyeing the beautiful brunette. He returned a few minutes later with two large jugs of water and a sack of cans from his stash. He walked over to the beauty.

"Here's some canned goods you can have... Uh, in case you haven't been eatin' good. Or... well, to round out your meal." The kids and other women crowded around and stared at the bag of canned goods. I thought he had just handed her diamond earrings the way she gently took the food sack and thanked him. She immediately handed out the cans to the others, retaining a sole can of beans for her own needs.

Before leaving, Floyd handed the younger woman a can that he had brought especially for her. "I thought you might like some peaches," Floyd said shyly.

"Thank you so much," she said. "My kids will love these." She impulsively gave him a warm hug. Based on the pleased look on his face, I half expected Floyd to run back to his shed to get more food.

Floyd had little else to say, but didn't seem to want to leave the group. The curious thought that he might leave with them and the young woman crossed my mind. I wondered when, if ever, he had any kind of relationship with a woman.

I hesitated to get friendlier with the travelers, fearing it might encourage them to stay. I turned as Leslie approached.

"Alex," she whispered, "we need to be hospitable. A few cans from Floyd's stash won't break us. We don't have to sit and visit with them if you don't think it wise, but we should be kind."

I nodded, but tried to look tough and imposing. "I hope they keep their word and leave tomorrow. I don't think we could handle a regular flow of folks through here."

"Fine," Leslie sighed "but let's make sure they are settled."

"By the way, Floyd seems to be particularly concerned about the welfare of one of the ladies."

"You mean the real pretty one?" Leslie queried.

"Yes, that would be the one," I said with just a wisp of a smile. Shortly afterward we disappeared into the cabin, making it clear we weren't interested in socializing with them.

I awoke alone the next morning. Leslie, with Hope on her hip, had gone out to the group with Mom to visit, bringing the travelers some homemade bread and preserves. I watched from one of the windows in the cabin but couldn't see much. Mom was talking to just one woman and there seemed to be fewer children running around. I washed up in the sink and scrounged up some breakfast.

A half hour later, Leslie came back in the cabin and found me.

"Is everything okay?" I asked.

"You're not going to believe this," she said, "but Richard's family is gone. The other woman – you know, the really pretty one

– is named Teresa, and she's been left behind with her two kids, Jason and Stephanie. She is really worried. The kids are only seven and five. She doesn't own anything more than the clothes on their backs."

I was immediately concerned. These were hard times for a single mother on her own. "What's her story? Did she tell you anything?"

"Yeah. It's absolutely horrific. She said her husband was an older man. I'm sure she was a second wife. Anyway, he worked at one of the casinos on the river in Shreveport. When the prices all shot up, fewer people gambled and he lost his job. The stress gave him an emotional breakdown, and they decided to move to the Kansas City area where he had some friends. They made it up to Fort Smith and were on I-540 when they got hijacked. A gang of people stopped their car, shot her husband, gang-raped her and then left her and the kids by the road. She was just wandering down the road in torn clothes when she came upon Richard and his family. They didn't really accept her, especially Richard's wife, but let her travel with them for a while."

"Jesus! What's she going to do now?" I asked, assuming she'd move on to some other friend or relation somewhere. I was totally unprepared for Leslie's answer.

"She will be staying with us now," Leslie replied, arching her eyebrow at me as if challenging any negative reaction.

My jaw dropped open and I began sputtering with a mix of outrage and surprise.

"She has nowhere to go, Alex," Leslie said firmly.

I briefly thought about it – three more mouths to feed without a strong worker to help me. But then I thought what I would want for Leslie and the kids if the situation had been reversed. Who would have taken my wife and kids in? I accepted these new additions stoically. I also wondered how tight our food supplies would be during the next winter and where beautiful Teresa and her kids would sleep. The Ark was filling up.

CHAPTER FIFTEEN

Reality Sets In

SUMMER 2016, ARKANSAS

"Trade increases the wealth and glory of a country; but its real strength and stamina are to be looked for among the cultivators of the land."

— WILLIAM PITT, EARL OF CHATHAM

I sat down under one of the last few trees bordering the field we were struggling to clear and took a sip of water from the jug Leslie had brought out to me earlier. The sun was hot, but cumulus clouds were building, providing much needed breaks from the burning rays. We might have a thunderstorm later I thought, watching the build-up of darker clouds to the west. Rain would be good I thought wearily as I lay back on the mossy coolness.

God I hurt, every muscle throbbing from exertion, but I didn't dare let on how much pain I was in. Everyone looked to me for assurance that we were going to be okay. I needed to be strong and show leadership, but frankly I was overwhelmed. We were all stunned by how much work there was to do and how little there was to show for it most days. I considered what we had managed over the past month.

Clearing our fields for a cash crop was a perfect example of something not easily accomplished without diesel equipment. First, we had cut trees down with a saw we borrowed. We had to keep it sharp using a file, which we did have, thanks to Floyd's habit of picking up odd tools here and there. Then each tree was cut into smaller portions so we could safely move it to a storage pile until we needed it. Each cut took a half hour of effort or more and a great deal of energy. Then we had slowly, painfully dug out the stump and roots embedded deep in the earth. This required a shovel, axe, and sometimes a chain wrapped around the stump so we could all haul on the chain and pull it out. No wonder pioneer families were large. It took an army to get things done.

I scanned the fruits of our labor from my spot under the tree. After several weeks of effort we had finally cleared a couple acres of land to be cultivated. It was uneven terrain, given toward dips and depressions where we'd pulled out stumps and stones. But the soil looked good – a nice rich brown. We were as ready as we could be for the next phase. I groaned with the thought. Now even more work followed.

My first choice for plowing and seeding would have been a tractor, naturally. My second choice would have been a horse and plow and let the animal do all the work. We didn't have either. Will had a tractor, but we didn't have any means to pay for renting it, or to pay for fuel. There might have been horses and plows in the area, but we didn't know of any that we could borrow. Our only choice was to do it the hard way. We would need a leather strap to pull some sort of rudimentary plow through the soil. I got up and headed back to the cabin. Maybe the women would have some ideas for the harness we would need to pull a plow. It had been a long day already.

We didn't have leather for the harness strap, and we had no idea what a manual plow ought to look like. We approached our neighbors and finally located an old horse collar that we could adapt for our purposes. For the plow itself, we must have tried a dozen different discarded farm tools before we finally came up with something we could use. It was made from an old V-nosed wheelbarrow and a couple of tiller blades. We pounded the nose into an anvil shape and turned it upside down. I moved the wheels to an outrigger beam and we put the tiller blades under the back end of the barrow. In trial runs the blades helped toe in the nose and turn the plow ridges out, but the ridges looked like a boat wake.

125

"Damn it!" I complained. "I can't go up and down a row like that. It will just uncover the previous row."

"Let's reverse one blade," Leslie suggested. "They will both turn the soil the same direction if we slant the blades to just one side."

As always she had clever ideas. "I think that will work." I quickly switched out one blade and made another trial run. The soil was split and turned in two uniform rows.

"You know, hon, it's nice having a wife with brains." I smiled at her.

"Thanks, but we still have to rig a means to pull it."

"Rope, but we'll need the boys to make it." I said. "Can you get the boys on it?"

Leslie showed them how to braid several lengths of twine into four equal lengths of rope. We attached the rope to the old horse collar and pulled. It wasn't easy but it worked.

The latest additions to our Ark clan couldn't contribute much to these early efforts. While Teresa and her children were useful in helping us weed the garden, water plants by hand, and perhaps help to harvest them in the future, they didn't have the strength to clear or plow.

This left most of the work to me and the boys, and they were still too young to provide much raw horsepower. Floyd was too apathetic to throw his weight behind this effort, though from time to time we would be able to convince him to assist us in moving a particularly heavy boulder or log.

We did plant some of the seeds early in a cleared acre, but it took us until the late part of June to clear another acre. This was too late in the year to plant corn, so we planted some lentil packets. We didn't have much choice but to try them. It was looking increasingly likely that we weren't going to make much cash from our crops this season.

Much about our new life was difficult to get accustomed to. Before the crash, the temperature of our lives could be measured between sixty-five and eighty degrees. We had heaters in our houses and cars when the temperature fell below this range. We had air conditioners that cranked on when it got too warm. This gentle range just seemed normal. We now paid close attention to the weather and felt whipsawed by the changes and temperature extremes. When it was hot, we were hot; when it was cold, we were cold. When it rained, we were wet. We lived our lives on a temperature roller coaster with little predictability and considerable discomfort by cheap oil standards.

We weren't the only ones suffering from the reduced access to air conditioning. We frequently watched small groups of drifters heading north away from the sultry south, though we suspected that winter would make many of them regret their trip. Most were just passing through, on the way to someplace else and were often desperate for food or anything else of value they could find. There had been a number of incidents, and Will suggested we make sure our gate was locked all the time.

We fixed our gate, and the boys and I routinely walked the perimeter of our little compound to make sure it was still secure. Will stopped by periodically to pass on news from town, and we occasionally walked down to his place to save him the trip.

"What do you hear in town, Will?" I asked one day in late June when he stopped by.

"It's not good," he said, shaking his head. "The radio was talking about an epidemic out in LA. Something's spreading in the water – cholera, maybe. They warned the people to boil the water, but the electricity is too inconsistent, so that didn't work out. Hospitals can't handle the sick. People are dying."

"Damn, my brother lives in Los Angeles."

"Well, you can't always believe all these crazy rumors," he added with unconvincing sincerity.

Will had just confirmed what I could have projected. People were leaving the old American West in droves. Much of Southern California had been a desert before water was artificially brought to the area from other parts of the region. Cheap oil had allowed us to fool ourselves regarding the sustainability of certain parts of the country – especially for larger municipal populations in these areas. The epidemic in Los Angeles would push more people out of the big cities, and I worried for my brother's safety.

Will interrupted my ruminations. "Hey, you want to join us for the big Fourth of July festival in Jasper? There will be lots of bartering and trading and even fireworks. I'm going to hook up a wagon with hay to haul folks into town. You want a ride?"

I jumped at the idea, then paused. I didn't want to take advantage of him. "Just as long as it doesn't cost too much. How are you going to pull the wagon?"

"With my truck. I have a still and make my own ethanol. I went to that a few years ago when fuel prices started heading up." Will glanced over at our vehicle, which was surrounded by weeds.

"You make your own fuel?" I asked.

"Yeah. Saves me a ton of money, too. Takes care of my crop waste and pays me in fuel. By the way, when is the last time you ran your vehicle?"

I too looked over at the forlorn vehicle. "We start it up for a few minutes every few weeks just to keep the battery charged. What did the still cost you, if you don't mind my asking?" I said.

He started ticking off on his fingers. "The first one was about a grand. It was pretty small. But I bought three more, each one a little bigger. I can now run one tractor and my truck on occasion. I did some calculations. A pair of horses would cost more in the long run." Will looked up toward the west where some flashes of lightning were looking ominous. "Sorry, I need to be going." He turned to start walking home.

"Will! We need to talk." I caught up with him as he started walking back towards his property. "I've got at least twenty acres I want to plant eventually. We managed to hand-plow about four acres and a half this year. It's part corn and part lentils, so I'll have some crop waste. Let me ask you, can we process our waste for a split of the fuel?"

He smiled easily. "You got a deal – I'll just process it alongside ours. Just let me know when you want to haul your waste over. We can plow eight acres in about an hour." He picked up pace and the wind started to blow strongly.

"Oh, hallelujah! After hand plowing the little we did this year, we didn't think we'd ever get the bulk tilled. This will be great." I said.

"Glad to help," He said then jerked a thumb behind us. You might think about heading back home. That storm looks pretty nasty. See you on the Fourth."

"Thanks, I sure will." I was heading back toward the cabin when a torrent of rain arrived and poured down on me. Lighting and thunder shook the property, but I was feeling a whole lot better. "Let it rain!" I shouted to the trees.

Our physical labor demands were unrelenting, and much more difficult than any of us had ever imagined. We were engaged in a low-tech, labor-intensive form of primitive agriculture.

Washing clothes was unbelievably hard. Sometimes we just made the boys go in the creek with their clothes on and rub sand over the dirtiest spots. It worked, sort of, but the abrasion was very hard on the fabric. The adult clothes we took in bundles to the creek. First they were soaked and then touched up with small dabs of soap on the dirty spots. The fabric would be bundled up around the soap bit and rubbed together vigorously to get the stain out. This was repeated for each spot. Finally the whole garment was rinsed out several times. Two people would twist the dripping cloth in opposite directions between them, wringing out most of the water. Then the still wet item was hung out on a line or tree branch to dry. Washing took most of the day for two people.

Hope's diapers were another obstacle altogether. They were the personal job of Mom or Leslie, and they had to be done twice a week to keep her in dry nether wear. The wet diapers were rinsed out as quickly as possible and soaked in a pail of water and diluted bleach that we had brought with us. These could then be rinsed and dried. But we couldn't rinse them directly into the creek. Floyd had told us where some old fifty-five gallon drums were stored back in his cave. We rolled one out and used it for the diaper rinse water.

    The dirty diapers needed much more work. The contents had to be shaken out over the outhouse pit. Then each diaper was placed in an old coffee can with a little detergent. The lid was placed on the can and it was shaken vigorously for several minutes or until our arms got tired. The diaper was checked for overall cleanliness and the process repeated if necessary. The wash water was poured into the pit when all the diapers were washed. We still needed to rinse them in the big drum. Once the diapers were rinsed out thoroughly, they were given a final rinse in a plastic bucket of clean water that Mom had steeped in flower petals. This added a fresh smell and helped soften the fabric slightly. We dried the diapers in direct sunlight as much as possible. The gray water was used on a special corner of the garden that Mom had planted flowers in. She said since we weren't going to eat them, it wouldn't matter if the water was less than pure. She would also mutter that since there had to be a silver lining somewhere in the whole diaper chore it might as well be her flowers!

    Other nasty problems came to life. In our previous life, bugs, mostly flies, spiders and mosquitoes, were an occasional annoyance, handled with Raid, special candles, or a bug zapper on those rare occasions when we elected to be outside. Now we fought bugs both inside and outside and generally lost. Without pesticides they extracted a horrific toll on our bodies, food, and crops. Chiggers fed upon us constantly, and we spent a lot of time trying to kill horseflies, bees, wasps, ticks, and lice. We tried a number of home remedies for itchy bites, stings, and infestations, but nothing seemed to work very well. Our surviving vegetables were often blemished and pockmarked, forcing us to stew much of our food before we ate it. Cockroaches, ants and spiders weren't content merely to visit our cabin; much to Mom and Leslie's dismay, they moved in and wouldn't let us evict them. Mosquitoes, flies and gnats infested the outhouse, which partly explained why the smell of feces and urine began to emanate from the woods nearby. The children weren't the only ones avoiding this facility.

We used the outhouse "night soil" to fertilize our fields, but this effort was clumsy and nauseating. It was one of those duties I personally took on out of necessity, since no amount of wishing would allow me to delegate this task. In time we built a long-handled bucket and pulley system to accomplish this requirement in a more tolerable manner, but initially it consisted of pulling up the outhouse "seat," climbing down into the pit in my underwear and shoveling the crap into buckets used to haul it to our field. Primitive didn't begin to describe how I felt about that job.

Hygiene became a critical issue on top of everything else going on. This single outhouse was not designed for daily use for ten people. It began to stink even worse as we continued to load it up. We decided we needed to turn it into a compost pit with a cover and dig another latrine pit. Cameron had helped haul "fertilizer" to the fields only under severe duress. He asked if we couldn't come up with a better system to treat the sewage before we hauled it out. Leslie, Mom and I gave it some thought and scoped out potential pit sites. Leslie took my laptop over to Will and Judy's to hook up to their electricity and do some research on the subject. She came home very excited.

"Sweetheart, you won't believe what helps with both the smell and speeds up decomposition. We can throw our fire ashes down the hole. And I have a sketch for a possible design."

"Good news," I said, heartened by the idea of cutting down the stinking. Any other info?"

"There are real composting toilets for cabins. Some are self-contained; others need a basement collection pit. I looked at several designs and think I can modify one to work for us."

Leslie's design had a pit with a trough to a holding area that we could position on a slope. We found an area not far from the current outhouse location, but with a downhill slope behind where the seat could be placed. We would need to dig the pit out of the side of the hill and then build wall braces for a trough to a lower pit. By adding ashes every day to the lower pit we could reduce the smell. As Teresa and Sean had complained the most about the stink, Leslie put them to work digging. After they had dug one of the holes, they stopped complaining about the smell.

We all pitched in to complete the new design and had a true sense of accomplishment when the facility was up and running. Mom suggested that we pour some gray water down the pit each day to ensure the flow down to the lower pit. The kids would take a bucket of ash every other day and sprinkle it over the contents. It wasn't exactly indoor plumbing, but it was a big improvement over our first outhouse.

Inch by inch we slowly improved the way we lived. We had been working continuously and relentlessly since our arrival, and we needed a break. I sent Cameron over to confirm that Will and Judy's invitation still stood for the Fourth of July celebration. It did and the Ark was soon abuzz with excitement and preparation.

CHAPTER SIXTEEN

The Celebration

July 2016, Arkansas

"When humans participate in ceremony, they enter a sacred space. Everything outside of that space shrivels in importance. Time takes on a different dimension. Emotions flow more freely. The bodies of participants become filled with the energy of life, and this energy reaches out and blesses the creation around them. All is made new; everything becomes sacred."

— Sun Bear

Before we knew it, the Fourth of July was only a day away and every one was focused on getting ready.

Will and Judy had told us to bring crafts, produce and junk that we could trade. We'd be bartering for things we might want. Leslie gathered Hope's outgrown baby clothes, a couple of cooking pots we never used, a few party dress outfits, complete with jewelry, and several pairs of her high heels. *What on earth was she thinking when she brought these?* I thought. Maybe some lady in town would trade them for a sturdy pair of rubber boots.

Cameron rummaged through a box of his stuff but ended up taking only a couple of things out.

"Cam, isn't there more stuff in there you can take and trade?" Leslie asked.

He laughed. "Mom, I'm taking the box. These are the only things I want to keep." He pointed at the model plane and a couple of small toys.

"Oh, I see. Is there something special you are hoping to barter for?" Leslie chuckled.

He dropped his gaze and mumbled something about a telescope or maybe a microscope.

Leslie gave me that quick tilt of the head indicating she'd made a mental note of that suggestion. Cameron's fourteenth birthday was less than two months away.

Sean had a pile of shoes and pants he had outgrown in the past three months. I was surprised that he was growing so fast even with our restricted diet, but then it occurred to me that perhaps he had been eating fairly well. No junk food, no sodas, little sugar, lots of fresh vegetables, limited meat and more exercise than he had ever had on a daily basis.

"Anything special you hope to find in town?" I asked him.

"I want a basketball and hoop." His announcement caught me off guard.

"Sean, we don't have any pavement around here." I said.

"Yeah, I know, Dad, but I have a plan." I nodded waiting. My younger son was becoming an inventor. "It's pretty easy to make concrete. My friend Jamie back in Nebraska helped his dad make a pad and I watched. If I can get a bag of concrete mix, we can set up boards for a frame and mix water and sand in, then smooth it out and let it dry."

I debated with Floyd over his old tool set. He never used any of the tools we borrowed, and the items we had duplicates of would be useful for bartering with in town. Floyd had decided to stay at the Ark, on "guard duty," while the rest of us went into town. We assured him that locking the gate would work fine for one day, but he was insistent and I was actually glad that he was staying. He would guard the compound and make sure no passersby rifled through our things while we were gone.

Teresa had almost nothing and was in desperate need of some clothing for her self and the kids. We had very little to spare but gave her a few items she could barter for. Floyd, who was normally oblivious to such concerns, found Teresa before we loaded up.

"I've got something for you." He ambled back into the shed and came back a few minutes later with a small opaque plastic bag. He handed it to her. "I thought you could use this."

"Floyd, what is it?" she asked, and I found myself staring at her beautiful face, backlit by a lamp. Floyd wasn't the only one mesmerized by her. Luckily, I never had time to think about it.

"Don't open it. Just give it to Joe at the Jasper mercantile." Floyd said, seeming to take note of the way that I was looking at Teresa.

"Okay," she said. "Is there anything else you'd like?"

Floyd thought a moment, turned beet red and walked over to me. He whispered a request, turned over several of the tools in his box to me, and hustled off toward the woods. Teresa stared at me in confusion.

"What did he ask you for that I couldn't get for him?"

"Ah, he wanted some – personal items – guy stuff. I guess he was too embarrassed to ask you," I said. "What did he give you?" I gestured toward the bag in her hand.

"I don't know, but you probably heard him telling me to give it to someone in Jasper."

"Well, I hope Joe thinks it's worth something."

"I do too. My kids need clothes to wear."

Teresa put the bag into the large purse she was carrying and called her kids to get ready for bed.

Mom had knitted a number of things for all of us, but also had extra hats, mufflers and mittens. We could take some of them as well. She came out of her room with a small list of things she thought we might look for. Canning jars and supplies were first on the list, followed by salt, chickens, chicken wire and a goat.

I looked at the list and cracked up. "A goat!! You want a goat?"

She interrupted pertly, "Of course I do. We can build a pen so the garden survives." She sniffed and went back to her room.

135

Obviously her knowledge of barnyard creatures far exceeded my own.

"When is Will picking us up?" Leslie asked.

"He said he'd be by about eight in the morning."

Sean and Cameron were the first up, indicative of their level of excitement. They hadn't been off the compound except to go over to Will's in three months. Teresa's children, Stephanie and Jason, were too young for Sean and Cameron's expeditions into the "back country." All the kids would hopefully meet others their own age in town.

By seven-thirty everyone was ready, loaded with a bag, bucket, or box of something we needed to take with us. We walked down to the gate with Floyd following to lock up behind us. He kept giving Teresa quick glances as if he wanted to tell her something, but never spoke to her.

"You won't forget, now?" Floyd asked me. "I'm really hoping you'll find me a good one. And don't fret yourself if you can't find just the right size. Bigger is okay. I don't care what color. Just try an' find one. And a little bouncy one, if there are any."

"Don't give it a second thought, Floyd. I'm sure there will be a good selection." I tried to reassure the big guy, but it was as if I was talking to the wind. Floyd kept on insisting I not worry if I couldn't find just what he wanted.

Soon Will's truck appeared and rumbled down the gravel road that passed our compound. The wagon behind the truck had his kids, a crate of ducks, several bags and boxes and some hay bales spread around to sit on.

"Howdy, Will!" I called as Will rolled down his window and spat out a stream of tobacco juice. "We sure appreciate your giving us a lift."

"That's what neighbors are for – especially now. I expect you'd do the same if you could." He motioned toward the rear. "You all climb up in the back there and make sure the kids are sitting down. Don't want to lose someone before we get there."

I wondered what made Will and his wife Judy so helpful to us. Was it just heartland hospitality? They were honest, hardworking and earthy. Mostly, they were just good people.

The kids all scrambled into the back of the wagon, while I helped Leslie, Mom, and Teresa climb up and handed them our stuff. We settled in for a rather jolting ride into town. Will passed back a small bottle of his homemade ethanol.

"Take a sip!" he suggested. "Newton is a dry county, so white lightning has always been home brewed. We just use it a little differently now."

It was too early to have a drink, but my curiosity got the better of me. I tilted the bottle back and had a small swig. It burned, but left me feeling warm and flush.

"So that's what moonshine tastes like," I commented. "Not as bad as I expected. Too bad engines don't have taste buds."

Will laughed. "Well, if they did I'm not sure how much work they'd do."

I saw Leslie eyeing the two of us with a frown. "It's a little early to be swigging moonshine, don't you think?"

"I wasn't going to drink any more," I replied. "We might just need it in the gas tank to drive home."

"Whatever," she sighed and turned away from me.

The closer we got to town, the more people we saw on the road. Very few had cars or trucks. Most were walking or riding bikes or horses, with a few on motorcycles. I caught Mom's expression as one roared past us and realized she was worried about Ace. We hadn't heard from him and had no telephone at the cabin yet. I had already decided I'd look for a pay phone in town.

Will pulled the truck and wagon into a parking spot behind the courthouse hall. It was the designated headquarters of the day's activities. Teresa asked for directions to the Jasper Mercantile and headed directly there. She would meet us back here once the bag mystery was resolved.

We walked into a large hall and looked around in astonishment. Booths were set up all around the room and formed several rows in the middle. It looked like a craft fair and garage sale combined.

"Hi folks. Welcome to the celebration!" A man greeted us at the entrance to the hall. He held a stack of papers in his hand and offered one to us. I quickly scanned my copy. It was a list of activities, times and locations with a map of the town and little stars by various businesses. "As you can notice on the map we have different items grouped together," I couldn't see that on my copy, but maybe he'd explain it better.

"We've got homemade jams, preserves and bottled honey over at the café, and the ladies from the Methodist church are selling pies there too. The produce is all at the farmer's market just to the south – figured people would check on food there anyway. We don't have any meat to speak of, but live animals are out in the parking lot, and I believe whatever dairy that's coming in from the farms will be there too." He paused to take a breath and covered the next portion of his directions.

"Home crafts like furniture are displayed out on the back lawn; tools and such are at Emma's Museum of Junk. She should really think about changing the name now," he added in an aside. "Homemade clothing, art, and quilts are over at the Old Carriage House."

"Excuse me, but how do you know where everything is? My map doesn't show anything but stars –" Leslie asked.

Mom interrupted, "There's a list at the bottom of the page."

"Not on mine," Leslie said.

"Or mine," I added.

"Oh, well, you must have some first runs – shoot!" he said as he flipped through his pile and then dropped them on the counter in disgust. "Let me get you the right run copy. I'll be right back."

As he disappeared into a back room, I wandered over to a table displaying books. The man standing at the table had various self-help books on counseling, coaching football and passing college algebra, but none of the books that I wanted on low-tech farming techniques, animal husbandry, or mechanical system designs. I wandered back to Leslie.

"This is a cash or barter setup," I related to her. "Mostly it's barter. He's looking for copper wiring in exchange for his books, or he'll take cash."

"We should look for some books for the boys. They'll be needing some home schooling pretty soon," Leslie said, then asked, "Was there a particular subject you were looking for?"

"Yeah, I hoped there was a book on farming and building things. You know, one of those 'How things are made' type books. There's so much I don't know."

"No luck finding anything, huh?" Leslie asked.

"Nah, but he said there's another setup like this outside the town library," I replied. "I'll have to check it out."

That prospect turned her thoughts in another direction. "We should talk to Will and Judy and agree on a meeting spot and time," she suggested. "I don't want to lose our ride home or inconvenience the Kingstons."

"Oh right. It would take a while to round up all the kids once we turn them loose," I agreed. Life without cell phones required some old-fashioned verbal coordination.

The greeter came back to the desk with a different handout, this one showing the list and locations. "This should make sense to you now. And we have a potluck starting at five o'clock down at the school. If you have something to share, please drop it off fifteen minutes earlier so they can start serving."

We thanked him, gave the children the time and spot to meet us for supper, and then sent them off in pairs to explore the town. Leslie and I kept Hope with us and advanced into the hall to look around. Teresa reappeared and rushed over with a big warm smile.

139

"Oh, Alex, just look!" she exclaimed, opening her purse and showing me a small roll of cash.

"So," I said, "I guess Joe liked what you brought him?"

"Yeah, it was medicine of some sort. Apparently Floyd provides him a bag like that every few months. Joe gave me almost $300! I know I owe you and Leslie all of it for taking us in…" Her voice trailed off, but her large brown eyes stared up into mine. I stared back, lost in her excitement. I was jerked back to reality when I heard a soft cough behind me and saw Leslie had joined us. I turned back to Teresa.

"No – no, Floyd gave that to you. We have very little to help you with anyway, just this bag of Hope's outgrown baby clothes."

She peeled off a few twenty dollar bills and handed them to me. "Well take this and get him what he asked for with it. That way we are both helping Floyd." Delighted with how the day was turning out, Teresa took the bag of Hope's baby clothes from me and headed for the dress shop with Stephanie, while Jason wandered off with Sean and Cameron.

"You know," Leslie said. "having her stay was my idea. But it seems that you're liking the idea better all the time."

I coughed to cover my confusion. "What? Oh, Floyd and I are just trying to assist her in getting settled." I put the emphasis on "Floyd".

"Well, you know what they say," she said sarcastically. "No good deed goes unpunished."

I wasn't pursuing this line of conversation. "It's nice to be able to assist her, I said. "That's all."

We started to wander through the tables.

Much of what was on display was really trash, but Leslie spotted a few items that would make cooking over an outdoor fire easier. Mom joined in as we looked at a nifty metal tripod with hooks for supporting pots. "We could sure use something like that," she whispered.

"I know. Wonder what they want for it?"

"You two walk on and I'll see." We kept browsing, and a few minutes later Mom caught up with us. She had the tripod tied together in twine and a big smile on her face.

"That was quick," Leslie said. "What did he want?"

Mom giggled like a girl and said, "My earrings."

"Those little diamond hoops?" Leslie said.

"No, they were cubic zirconium. I told him they weren't diamonds, but he wanted them anyway. Anniversary coming up and not much available for his wife. I thought I'd go put these items in the truck, but I wanted to let you know we got it," Mom said.

"That's great, Mom," Leslie said turning toward me. "I need to change Hope, so we'll meet up with you where?"

"I'm heading down to the mercantile store. Meet me there when Mom gets back."

Okay," Leslie replied, heading to the restroom "See ya in a few minutes."

Ha! I thought. It'll be at least an hour! She was shopping for the first time in months and was in her element.

Will and Judy had headed straight for Emma's Museum of Junk, and I caught up with them as they were finishing their shopping.

"Where's the good stuff?" I whispered to Will.

"Check the back left aisle, and there's some decent tools out front in a bin. Just look deep," he replied.

"Thanks, I'll do that." I headed inside to see what I could find before the women caught up to me.

By the time the three of them strolled up almost an hour later, I was out front bartering for a saw. I was already carrying a box and I could tell that Leslie was really curious what I'd gotten. I shook hands with the man, exchanged something for the saw, and caught sight of Leslie walking up.

"Hi, sweetheart." Leslie struggled to keep the baby in her arms as Hope reached for me. "Here, give me 'little Miss Squirm-a-lot'. How's my princess doing?"

Leslie handed me Hope and she threw her arms around my neck.

"So what did you give him for the saw?" Leslie asked, tipping her head back toward the other man.

"You remember those cell phones we had brought with us?" She nodded.

"Well, I threw them in when we left Nebraska, thinking maybe someday we might need them. But I figured they are almost obsolete now, so why not exchange them for something we can really use? He said he still has money to activate them. He was so happy that he gave me a box of nails, too."

"You gave away our cell phones?" she asked outraged. "Wasn't there any chance we'll get to activate them again at some point?"

"Nah, that would be too expensive for us and besides, we're living in such tight quarters at home, what would we need with a cell phone?"

"Yes, times have changed," She said sadly. "So what's in the box?"

"Take a look!" I held out the box and Leslie opened up it up. She looked inside then arched an eyebrow.

"Alex, what is this?" she asked. "Handles, rollers, a weird piece of wood and a shoe brush?"

"The mechanical piece goes on a wash bucket. It's a wringer to squeeze out all the water before you hang up clothes. The wood panel is a genuine washboard with a scrub brush for the clothes."

"What do you do with it?" she asked dubiously. "I've never seen one before,"

"You put the wet dirty clothes on the board, add some detergent if needed and scrub with the brush. It is much easier than rubbing the cloth with sand like the boys do or by hand like we've been doing." I had a grin that went from ear to ear. Leslie seemed skeptical that this would be an improvement in our wash day, and she frowned at the device. "What's wrong?" I asked her.

"Well, it does look like it would make washing a one-person job, but I was starting to enjoy talking with Teresa and Mom as we worked. Sort of diminishing the drudgery, you know?"

"Hmm, I guess you could take turns while you washed clothes and still talk?"

Leslie rolled her eyes at the idea.

"No really, I'm hoping this will save you some time." I suggested optimistically.

"I guess we'll find out. How'd you know what they were?" Leslie asked.

"Mom found it."

"Of course. Mom to the rescue again." Leslie said in a bitter tone right before Mom walked up.

Mom was carrying something covered with an old cloth flour sack.

"What is that?" Leslie asked, distrusting another old fashioned gadget.

Mom laughed. "I'll tell you in a second, but first you have to understand why I know what this is. Aiden used to show the kids pictures of 'turn-of-the-century' conveniences. He'd tell the children that their children might have to go back to these hand-powered appliances, and he wanted them to know what they were. He even educated me on a few details. Did your parents ever go to Disneyland?" Mom asked her.

"Yeah, of course – didn't everyone?"

"Well up until the early seventies there was a round building in Tomorrow Land – I think GE sponsored it – the carousel of progress. The same family kitchen and living room updated for each quarter century or something."

"Uh-huh." Leslie said.

"While the future rooms were interesting, the past room had a bunch of stuff like this, and Aiden made me sit through that dumb ride a hundred times pointing out all of this old stuff to me. That's how I know what this is." With a flourish, she removed the flour sack and exposed something that looked like a stone bundt cake coming up out of a wooden box. She handed it to me and took a small dowel out of her purse. The dowel stuck into a small hole in the top of the stone. "Ta-da!"

"Cool, Mom! Now we just need grain!" I said.

Leslie looked at me and Mom in disbelief. "You both know what that is?"

We looked at each other and laughed. "You tell her." Mom just smiled a sheepish grin and said, "Come on, there's more to see around here."

"Wait! Isn't someone going to explain?" Leslie shifted Hope to the other hip.

"Okay," I said. "It's a home mill. You drop grain down this center hole and use the dowel to turn the grinding stone. Once the grain is milled into flour, it gets pushed out the edge and drops down into the box. You can lift the stone out and you have home stone-ground flour."

"Okay, I think I get the idea. Guess I'll figure it out when we get home." Leslie started to move off. "But Mom, as nice as that little gadget probably is, do you think you can confer with me before you buy anything else for *my* kitchen? We just don't have that much room."

"Alright dear, whatever you say." Mom said disappointed that Leslie wasn't more enthusiastic about her discovery.

The next couple of hours passed quickly as we all hunted for the items we deemed essential. The day began to take on a festive air as neighbors greeted each other, figured out how to swap skills and share knowledge or supplies.

Will and Judy were gracious in introducing Leslie and me to all the people they knew and advised us who we might want to trade some corn for wheat, or canned tomatoes for empty mason jars.

We quickly found that much of what we needed was available, but not always for the "coin" we had. Leslie and I found two quilts she really liked in very untraditional designs and colors. They were bright and bold with a pattern of stars on one in deep blues, purples and greens, almost like aurora borealis on cloth, and the autumn green, gold and red of a New England forest on the other. "These are gorgeous," she said, running her hand over the soft cushiony fluff of one quilt.

I thought them nice but excessive. We simply needed blankets to keep us warm, and these were works of art.

"Are you selling or can I barter?" Leslie asked.

The woman behind the table was in her forties with long dark hair and deep green eyes. She was piecing another design as she waited for people to come by. "Either, depending on what you have in exchange."

"Well, I have some shoes, dresses, a little jewelry – not valuable but good quality department store stuff."

"Hum, don't have much use for shoes or jewelry. Got cotton dresses?"

"No, actually they are party dresses." Leslie pulled pictures of her in the dresses out of her purse to show her.

She flipped through them quickly, then again a little slower, lingering over an emerald green satin, silk and chiffon gown. "Do you have this one with you?"

"It's in our neighbor's truck. Shall I go get it?"

The woman bit her lip. "Yes, I'd like to see it, please."

Leslie spotted Cameron pulling a cart with another boy. "That's my son. Let me get him to bring it back for you. Hey Cameron!" she yelled.

145

The Celebration

He came over to see what we wanted. Leslie quickly explained, telling him to bring the silver shoes and the purse with the jewelry in it too. Then she asked him, "What are you doing, anyway?" She pointed her chin toward the other boy and the cart.

"Oh, we are running a hauling service. People have too much stuff to carry around, so we load it up and take it to their wagon, vehicle or house. It's fun and I've met loads of kids."

"Are you getting paid to haul?" Leslie asked.

"Sort of. They give us little tips like books or pocket knives, but it's food mostly. This is the first day in a long time I haven't felt hungry. Those church ladies make some great blueberry cobbler! I'll go get your stuff and be right back." He dashed off after stopping for a second to tell his new friend what he was doing. The boy nodded and started pulling the wagon down the street.

While Leslie and I waited, she looked at the other quilts, but none were as vivid or bold in design. It didn't even look like the same work. "Are these other quilts your work also?" Leslie asked.

She smiled softly. "No, they are my sister's work. She is very much a traditionalist."

"It's lovely. Your work is stunning. Who are you?" Leslie asked.

"Call me Raina. My sister is Sunni. And you are?"

"Leslie MacCasland and this is my husband, Alex. Pleased to meet you, Raina. Why are your quilts so different?"

Raina basked in the praise. "I like to think I'm an artist and cloth is my medium. I prefer to preserve what I see in fabric."

"It's beautiful... it's very effective. I see nature in these," Leslie observed.

She smiled at Leslie. "Then I have succeeded in my endeavors."

Cameron was back with a large bag in a few minutes. Mom came by too, having found chicken wire and an odd assortment of canning jars. She spoke with Cameron and loaded her stuff into his friend's wagon.

Meanwhile, Leslie had opened the bag and pulled out the shoes and purse. The dress slid out of the bag with a whisper and pooled like molten emerald lava on the table. Raina stared at the fabric, her hand poised, ready to caress but hesitating. Leslie placed a silver and malachite necklace on the dress with the silver shoes. "It's a beautiful outfit. It's a size ten. I think it will fit you."

She glanced at the shoes and necklace, then pushed them back toward Leslie. "Just the material," she said, taking it in her hands and turning it so the shimmer of the silk and shine of satin caught the light. "Yes, I can do something with this."

To Leslie's amazement she began measuring the hem seamstress style, then the length from waist to hem. She smiled to herself and nodded. "For this I will barter, and if you have more like it too." She waved a hand not taking her eyes off the fabric. "The quilts are yours. Come back before winter and see my spring time quilts."

"Thank you, Raina. I will do that."

By four o'clock, everyone except Cameron had come to the designated meeting spot and sat down. We compared notes on our bartering experiences.

Leslie had a bag of various items for the boys and her new quilt. Leslie also had purchased Hope a number of outfits that would fit her for the next couple of years.

Sean had a basketball and a number of bags of concrete. Sean and I were going to learn some new project tricks over the next few weeks. It sure didn't seem like much concrete to do what Sean wanted.

Teresa had exchanged Hope's old baby clothes for several outfits for her two children and had gotten herself a winter coat, some jeans, and a pair of rain boots. She also complained that she had been unable to find the underwear that she had been looking for and had to settle for a pair of remarkably sheer bras and panties. While I never saw the items that she spoke about, I noticed that Leslie grimaced when she heard these last remarks.

Mom had taken orders for several hat, mitten, and scarf sets in exchange for a crate of young chickens, several skeins of homespun yarn and a basket of machined yarn, the canning supplies, and chicken wire. Also, there were two newly weaned goats, one of which was currently curled up in her lap, sleeping; the other was tied to the tree behind her, watching everything around her. "Are they siblings?" I asked her.

"No, I think we should consider breeding them, so I got them from different families. We can get a male for stud, but they recommended we not own one. Apparently, they smell once they mature." She stroked the head of the little doe in her lap, whose long pink tongue emerged to lick her fingers. "Sweet now, aren't they?"

Sean had snuggled up next to her and was stroking the kid's body. "Do they bite, Grandma?"

"They can, but they don't do it on purpose. Usually, they are hungry and your fingers get in the way."

"Can I name them?"

She regarded the kid with fondness. "I think you and Cam could do that."

"By the way, where is Cam?" I asked.

"He's making some hauling trips for people. He said he'd meet us for the potluck," Sean replied.

"And I'm getting hungry. When is this potluck? What did we bring to share?" I asked.

"We brought some fresh corn on the cob, early tomatoes, and I have a vegetable casserole from things Floyd didn't want. And that reminds me, Alex. What did Floyd want you to get him?"

I grinned and glanced at Teresa. "He wanted some new underwear, but don't tell him I told you. Plus, he wanted a puppy."

"A puppy!" Leslie and Mom laughed in unison. Sean perked up

"That would be cool, Dad! Did you get him one?"

Leslie asked "Why?"

"Well, he thought if he got the dog, then the boys could have a pet without it being an issue for us, because Floyd would be the official owner. And he said the bugs aren't much company in his bunkhouse, so a dog might be nice."

"Dad! Did you get him one? Does anyone have any puppies here?"

"Nope. Didn't see a single puppy anywhere, but I asked around. If anyone knows of any, we'll hear about it."

"What about the underwear?" Mom asked dryly.

"Yes, I found him some and a red set of long johns too. Figured he'd need something warm in winter."

"Now there's a visual I didn't need," Mom said. Leslie and I laughed.

"I guess we should load up everything and get our food to the potluck. Will the goats be okay tied up in the wagon?" I asked, since I didn't want them getting loose and running off.

"There's a holding pen for them up by the town hall," Mom said pointing that way. "The town planned this event out really well." Mom said.

"Okay, everybody, gather up your stuff and let's take it to the truck."

Will and Judy had introduced us to several of the key townspeople – the mayor, the police chief, and some Chamber of Commerce folks who all knew him by both name and reputation. Everyone was friendly and we were given considerable respect, as if we were part of Will's extended family. I had the distinct impression that Will could have been elected mayor of this community were he so inclined.

The potluck down at the school was amazing. Four long tables were loaded with more food than we had seen in months. One of the local farmers had donated a steer, so there were hamburgers for everyone. We loaded up plates with potato salad, fresh corn on the cob, deviled eggs, three-bean salad, macaroni and cheese, and

149

several dishes we didn't recognize. It was such a shock to realize that a year ago we would have taken all this for granted and been unhappy that we didn't have fried chicken, hot dogs and various sausages. A year ago we would have taken whatever we wanted but not eaten it all, tossing paper, plastic and food in the garbage. This time I knew everything would be eaten, and there would be little trash generated.

Some of the people who were joining us for this feast were obviously transients. They had hollow looks and seemed a bit skittish. Complete families sat away from everyone else and returned repeatedly to the food line. I was glad to see them enjoying our community's celebration, but I was wary that the encouragement might induce them to stay in the area.

Will approached me as we were devouring some raspberry pie. "Alex, I've been telling some people about your economics background. The mayor wondered if you'd be willing to give the folks here a simple explanation of what happened. Most folks around here are just farmers or shopkeepers. We've never had much background in world affairs, but ..."

I nodded. "Does he want me to talk here or somewhere else?" I was a bit hesitant to oblige. While most of the attendees had limited access to college professors, I hadn't had access to much information over the past six months and felt out of touch with the world.

"If you don't mind, right here."

"Sure." I went with Will to the head table. The mayor stood and shook my hand, and the three of us huddled for a few minutes. Then the mayor mounted the stage steps with me following. The mayor flipped on the microphone at the podium and tapped it to make sure it was on. This also served to quiet everyone down. Chairs scooted on the floor as bodies turned toward the stage to hear.

"Hi, folks! We're glad you all made it for our Fourth of July celebration. We've got more fun later this evening, so stick around for that. Right now I'd like to introduce Alex MacCasland, economics instructor from Nebraska, who moved here this spring. He's agreed to explain in very simple terms what has happened. So please give him a warm welcome and a ready ear."

Everyone clapped politely as I moved up to the podium.

"Thank you, Mayor, new friends and neighbors. As His Honor mentioned, I taught economics in Nebraska. My father, Aiden MacCasland, was an energy guru of sorts and bought some property in this area just in case we were going to have problems like we've recently experienced."

Heads were nodding in the audience and I went on.

"What may surprise you is the fact that our current problems come as much from our financial problems as they do from the lack of oil. Over the past quarter of a century, investors in both developed and developing countries were accustomed to loan us their savings. They bought our company stocks and bonds and also held our government debt in various forms. In addition, they held dollar currency or deposits for transactions or simply as foreign currency reserves. The dollar was accepted around the world as if it was the world's currency. Heck, even South American drug dealers wanted to be paid in U.S. dollars.

"Meanwhile, the world was moving along nicely and there was considerable development happening all over the world. While those of us in the United States were all wallowing in cheap oil, a lot of our manufacturing operations quietly moved overseas. Countries like India and China and a whole host of other countries were bettering themselves as a result, and in the process, they fell in love with the automobile too.

"This all worked fine until one day when oil prices started to soar and a large number of these investors came to the conclusion that the U.S. as a country was not such a good investment anymore. After all, we only produced about a third of our crude oil and had to import the rest. The smart money simply decided to hold other currencies instead of dollars, and to reduce the numbers of dollars they were already holding. As more dollars were freed up and became available to be traded, the value of the dollar started to head south, and this panicked other investors who wanted to get out while the getting was good."

Most of the attendees in the audience were looking a little vacant by this point. I noticed my own kids looking at each other as if I were speaking a foreign language. This explanation wasn't working for this audience. I stopped and tried to think of a better example to share.

"Okay, here's another way to think about it. We were all in the same economic boat together, and when some of the investors decided to move to one side of the boat, everyone moved to that side of the boat. When this weight shifted, the boat flipped. Does that help?" I looked around and suddenly everyone was nodding their heads.

"Usually when you flip the boat, you can turn it back over and bail it out. This time we couldn't turn it back over because when the dollar's value fell considerably, we couldn't buy enough crude oil to run our economy. So our boat is still upside down in the water.

"We're pretty tapped out as a nation, trying to use whatever energy or funds are available simply to get by. We will probably never go back to the way life was. We will each have to figure out new or very old ways of getting things done. We will have to continue to adjust and learn to live with much less crude oil.

"For those of you that are old enough to remember the cold war, think back on how quickly the collapse of the Soviet Union came. One day our soldiers were huddled in fox holes on training exercises along the Iron Curtain waiting for a massive invasion, and the next thing we knew, they were tearing down the Berlin Wall and abandoning communism. Historians later claimed that the Russians essentially had learned that their economic system could not compete with ours, and they threw in the towel.

"Our economic system with its central and pervasive demand for oil – a product we no longer produced in sufficient volumes to meet our own needs – was no more sustainable than the planned economies of the Former Soviet Union – given that we ignored our growing oil dependence. We had a great run, but in the end we were more vulnerable than we realized. Our lives are different, but, as we learned today, we can barter, trade, share and continue living. The United States is still a great place to live.

"So I'd like to thank the mayor and all the folks who made today possible. I think our Founding Fathers would be proud of all of us today. Have a happy Fourth, everyone!" I raised a hand and nodded to the crowd, acknowledging the polite applause.

The Mayor came back up, thanked me and made an announcement that the high school gym was open for music and refreshments, and we would have a small sparkler, bottle rocket fireworks display once it got dark. All the kids clapped and a shiver of general excitement rippled through the gathering. Fireworks!

As it turned out, the celebration was muted. About nine o'clock the DJ announced an intermission for the fireworks, and we all trooped out to the field. Some patriotic overture suddenly blasted out of the speakers, making everyone jump and signaling the fire marshal to ignite the fireworks. The fireworks were sparse, most likely leftovers from previous years. Even so the kids were excited. It was quaint and cool and the best possible holiday in a small town. Hope's eyes were like saucers and her expression was of pure joy. This was a Fourth to remember.

CHAPTER SEVENTEEN

Summer Time, and the Livin' Ain't Easy

August 2016, Arkansas

"*Our lands produce all the fine things of paradise, except innocence.*"
— William Byrd

Reality came back in full measure the following day. I let everyone sleep in a little, since we were all exhausted from the excitement of the holiday, but the goats and chickens would all want to be fed, Hope was wet and fussing, and Floyd was already rumbling around in his bunkhouse. I could tell he was awake by the relative silence in his general vicinity. In other words, no snoring meant he was awake. He would be anxious for his underwear, and I hoped he would like the long johns. They were a far cry from the puppy he wanted, but secretly I was relieved that no one had had any puppies to give away or sell. I suspected that the lack of food for pets was causing a significant reduction in their population. That's not to mention the darker side of that food equation. People were hungry enough to eat anything.

I changed Hope to let Leslie sleep in and the two of us went out to check on the new animals. The chicks were scratching around in their box looking for something to eat. Join the crowd, I thought and opened the small bag of grain that had come with them. After I scattered a handful into the box, I sat Hope down and she watched them scratch through it to select the morsels they wanted.

Hope crawled toward them as if they were toys that she could play with. Okay, a chicken coop that she can't get into, I thought. All I needed is for Mom to come out and find Hope holding strangled chicks in her little fists.

Sean came out looking for the goats, and he wandered over to us. "Hi, Daddy, how are the chickens?"

"They're fine." I said. "I just fed them."

"Where are the goats, Dad?" he said watching Hope crawl through the dirt toward the chickens.

I picked her up again and tried to brush off the soil. "We put them in Floyd's cave with a barricade for safety. Do you want to go feed them?"

His face lit up. "Can I?"

"Absolutely. Go get a small flake of alfalfa from that box on the porch and take it down to the cave. Their leads are on the wall next to the barrier, so you can bring them back up here if you want after they've eaten. You and Cam get to help me build a shelter and pen for them today."

He hopped up on the porch and picked up a compressed chunk of green and dashed off to feed the goats.

After a full day of celebrating, it was hard to return to our regular chores and to what remained an almost suffocating work load. Before we could get back on schedule, however, we needed to take care of a few animal related details. Cameron and Sean helped me build a small shed for the goats, while Mom and Leslie worked on a chicken coop. It would be pretty basic for the time being but we would need to add nesting shelves for eight soon. We had six red chicks, nine white and two a mottled brown. Mom said she had a rooster for the white layers and a rooster for the red fryers, with one rooster for a free-ranging spare.

"Don't roosters fight each other?" I asked, trying to remember. "How are we going to keep them both?"

"Two houses in one yard should be okay. The layers and their rooster get a nesting house and the fryers with their rooster or roosters just get a perching house. I don't think the red and whites will fight too much."

"Don't think or don't know, Mom?" I raised an eyebrow at her, amused by her abashed look.

"Well, the chicken people said these all get along. They are just different colors of the same overall breed – comets or rockets, she called them – so I think they'll be fine."

"I hope so."

The next few weeks of summer were the hardest of my life. The days were filled with an endless series of weeding, watering, walking down rows to check on ripening vegetables, washing clothes, fixing buildings, designing, scrounging and bartering with neighbors. Real problems began to appear, and they nearly took me down.

Water treatment was an issue we hadn't put much thought into and we paid a price for it. We were blessed with fresh water flowing across the property so we didn't think we needed to spend much effort disinfecting it in the spring and early summer. We didn't have any means of testing the water we pumped out into the trough so we decreed it safe for all uses except drinking. As the summer dragged on, though, the water flowed less and less, and most of the feeder creeks dried up. The pump still worked, but the water was increasingly brown. What little water we could extract from the stream contained minerals and bugs; the quality diminished rapidly in color and taste. While we had rarely thought about the possibility of chemical and bacterial pollutants before, our concerns increased as our water appearance worsened. We had to hike over the far ridge and down to the main river to get sufficient drinking water. Periodic thunderstorms would fill our cistern and water the fields and gardens, but the kids were used to scooping up a handful of water from the creek without thinking twice about it.

The first indicator that we had a serious problem was a bout of diarrhea that we all got in mid July. The children whimpered and ran, often not making it to the outhouse before their bowels discharged. Stinking piles of shit-crusted clothes were stuffed in another fifty-five gallon drum, as we had insufficient water to wash them. Without toilet paper we had to use some of the available water to wash off after going to the bathroom. The adults seemed to understand how to do this, but the kids had to be closely watched and checked. Even so, almost all of the kids developed a form of diaper rash that chafed and rubbed them raw and made for lots of tears.

Mom caught a ride into town and stopped by to see the local doctor. She explained our troubles and asked what we could do. She came back with a laundry list of good advice. We could use a plant called lamb's ear for toilet paper. It was soft and velvety so the kids' privates would not be irritated further. He suggested that we could use an oatmeal paste, olive oil, or a chamomile wash for the rash, and we set aside one of the olive oil bottles in our stash for this purpose. Dr. Mitchell also recommended letting the kids air out thoroughly after each trip to the toilet. Skinny-dipping for the kids and then laying butt up on the rocks to dry off would help, and in the warm weather this was a popular solution. Hope could just crawl around diaper-less for a couple of days. Best of all, he told her we could put our drinking water into clear plastic containers in the sun and it would purify the water sufficiently to allow us to drink it.

This recommendation resulted in warm drinking water and the kids avoided it when possible. Floyd let us put some jugs in his ice box, but this made the ice melt much faster and we had to stop. Several of the kids became dehydrated and listless. Teresa's little girl, Stephanie, got so sick we thought we were going to lose her. This time Judy came to our rescue with a small jar of honey.

"Add a tablespoon to each glass of water. It improves the taste and adds a little something she can keep down. Keep her resting and let her soak in a tub of water – doesn't have to be real clean – just wet, if it gets too hot."

"How do you know all this?" Teresa asked.

"Had a son who wouldn't drink enough water before we got a well drilled. He ran too hot one summer and got sick like Stephanie. A neighbor told me what to do then and it worked."

We started her on the honey water therapy immediately. She was up and eating again in three days, much to everyone's relief.

No sooner had we cleared this hurdle, though, when Leslie got sick.

I woke in the middle of the night hearing her groan beside me in bed. The sheet suddenly flipped back and she dashed out of the room. I heard the door to the outhouse creak open and slam shut. She came back to bed a few minutes later.

"Are you okay?" I asked.

"Just the runs like everyone else. Don't worry about it," she replied.

She made four more runs before dawn. As light gradually brightened the room, I could see the dark circles under her eyes and the paleness of her complexion. I got up quietly, gathering Hope out of her crib and slipping out to the living room.

Mom was up and heating water for breakfast. "You're up early."

"I think Leslie's really sick. She had to go to the john several times last night and she looks bad now."

"We've all been sick," Mom said. "She'll get better, just like we have."

"We had diarrhea, but we didn't turn gray," I retorted. "She looks pale and waxy." Just then Leslie staggered out of the bedroom. She was bent double, holding her gut and panting with the effort of standing up.

"My God," Mom exclaimed. "Give me Hope and help her, son."

It was her last trip to the outhouse. Mom took one of our buckets and set it up in the bedroom. We tag-teamed her with fluids and food, but she was listless and had no appetite. She tried to drink purified water, but was so nauseated that she could keep only a few sips down. Food was almost out of the question in the early days of her illness. She tried to eat and drink to keep up her milk for Hope, but kept throwing up. I felt increasingly desperate.

"I don't know what to do, Mom. Hope is getting less and less when she nurses and Leslie is afraid whatever she has is going to be passed through her milk."

"Has Hope gotten sick?"

"She had some diarrhea and a bout of diaper rash, but nothing else. She seems to be okay; just a little fussy because she's hungry."

"If Leslie is still nursing and Hope hasn't gotten worse, then she probably won't get worse from Leslie's milk. Regardless, you probably need to get her started on some cereal or oatmeal. You'll need to get into the food cache and pull out some of the baby food."

"Ok, but what about Leslie?" I asked. "She's sicker than we were."

"She could just have some other bug. Let's see how she does in the next twenty-four hours. After that maybe Dr. Mitchell can come see her."

Leslie got worse. She could barely get out of bed to use the bucket we set up as a chamber pot. She wasn't eating or drinking enough to even use it much.

"Babe, here's some honey tea like we gave Stephanie. Can you try a few sips?" I asked her.

Her eyes flickered open and she strained to raise her head. She swallowed a few sips then sank back onto her pillow. "No more. Makes me sick," she rasped. "So sleepy."

Mom hiked over to the Kingstons' to see if they could bring Dr. Mitchell or any medical help out to check on Leslie. They wrote down her history and said they'd see what they could do.

A few hours later Dr. Mitchell showed up. "How's Leslie?" he asked.

"Not good. We don't know why she's so much worse than the rest of us were," Mom said as she walked him over to the bedroom.

He went into the bedroom with me to take her vitals and see what he could do. Leslie was lying on our bed. She had tossed the sheet off. She was wearing one of my old T-shirts and light blue panties. Her exposed skin had a damp sheen to it. Dr. Mitchell took her pulse, then her temperature. He checked her eyes, ears and felt for swollen lymph nodes. Leslie didn't say anything other than yes or no. She rolled on her side and closed her eyes. Her color was grayish and her usually shining hair lay flat and dull down her back. I had never seen her so sick. Dr. Mitchell signaled to me and we left the room.

Mom joined us and offered us some tea. We sat at the table and looked for his answer. "She's been vomiting?" he asked.

"Yeah, she can hardly keep water down," I replied. "Do you know what's wrong with her?"

"I can't make a specific diagnosis, but I recognize the symptoms. She's had contaminated food or water and has either a parasite or E. Coli."

"E. Coli! Isn't that fatal?" Mom had gone pale and gripped my arm.

"It can be in children and weak adults. Generally, it's not serious in stronger adults, but complications can lead to kidney failure if you get enough of the bacteria in your system or if your immune system is weak," he explained gravely. "But she was probably in fairly good health, nursing moms usually are, and she probably got just enough to make her really sick for a while. If she has E. Coli, and her fever indicates that, I think she'll recover. It will take a while for her to be back to normal, but she'll probably be okay."

"Is there any medicine she should take?" I asked, at the same time wondering if we could afford anything.

"At this point, let's just get a firm diagnosis. I'll need a stool sample to take to the lab."

"Uh, she's been using a pot in our room…"

"Sorry, needs to be in this, and fresh." He handed me a container and a couple of tongue depressors.

I stared at the tongue depressors. "Will I even need these if she's got diarrhea?"

"Well, we only need a sample, not a full container. It's up to you to figure out how to get it," He replied nonchalantly.

"I guess this counts as the 'for better or worse, in sickness and in health' part of marriage." I sighed, wondering how to gracefully explain all this to Leslie.

A few days later, Judy stopped by with an envelope from the Regional Medical Center in Harrison. Leslie did in fact have E. Coli and the medical advice was to keep her hydrated with lightly salted water.

Over the next few weeks she recovered slowly, but something about this illness changed her. She didn't smile very often and was significantly subdued.

"Leslie? How are you feeling?" I asked her each morning.

"Tired, I guess," she'd reply and turn away.

"Do you want to rework the chores? Maybe have Mom cook and you do laundry? The fresh air will be good for you."

"No," she muttered. "Just leave me alone."

This went on for several days, until my frustration regrettably boiled over.

"Leslie, you need to talk to me. Are you feeling better or what? You haven't laughed at Hope or even played with her for days. She needs you. We all need you. Can't you just snap out of this?"

"Okay, sure," she said, "Whatever you want."

She shut me out completely. When she needed a rest, she retreated into the woods. She'd return with her eyes and nose red. I knew she had been crying, but she never said a word. I was living with a very familiar stranger.

"Honey?" I walked over to Leslie one afternoon as she stood staring at the small fire under our makeshift cooking area. I had watched her for several minutes, but she hadn't stirred the bubbling pot of bean soup, or attempted to spoon the biscuit dough out onto the cast iron griddle. "Are you all right? The beans are sticking," I said as I stirred the soup. "Do you need to sit down and rest? I can do the cooking tonight. Why don't you go inside and lie down for a bit?" She turned wordlessly and walked into the cabin.

Leslie had done most of our cooking before she got sick. Mom and Teresa stepped in while Leslie recovered but the shortage of an adult worker hampered all our efforts to stay on top of the endless work.

Food preparation was still a complicated time-consuming operation. The cabin had been set up with a gas stove, but we had no gas. We needed a wood stove, but there was none to be found. The local stores had sold out quickly without any expectation of further deliveries. Those who owned stoves in the area weren't selling. Our meals essentially were campfire affairs where we built a small fire and cooked over it day in and day out. We had learned very quickly that we needed an overhead cover for the cooking area since rain and wind would put out the fire and wreak havoc on our food prep operations. Building cover was a time-consuming effort hampered by our lack of a simple tarp or ground cloth. We finally adapted the tent for this overhead protection. Unfortunately, it didn't provide any protection from the insects and flies that seemed to find the nearby outhouse a perfect nursery and breeding establishment. Mom kept swearing about how much she would give for fly paper. She had plenty of experience with camp meals and she had shown Leslie, then Teresa, how to make things flavorful with just a few herbs and seasonings. Teresa picked up on things quickly, but Leslie seemed to resent her expertise and showed total indifference to her suggestions.

Much of our early food supplies were in cans and needed little more preparation than heating. But, as our numbers increased, we realized we needed to conserve the cans for winter when we'd have no fresh produce. Our garden began to supply much of our menus. Mom made suggestions from the available vegetables in the garden. Though Leslie ignored her, Mom generally got her way, even though Leslie was technically in charge of the "kitchen." It wasn't that Leslie's opinion didn't matter, but Mom had a way of not taking no for an answer and Leslie reached a point where she seemed to just stop caring about anything.

"Alex, I think Leslie is depressed," Mom told me one afternoon. "She just seems so out of it lately."

"She's still doing her chores, isn't she?" I asked defensively.

"Yes and no – she's just going through the motions. You saw her with the bean soup the other day."

I let out a long sigh, discouraged by her listlessness. I knew what was getting her down. "Do you think she'll eventually warm up to our new circumstances?"

"In a perfect world, yes," Mom replied. "But we haven't got that anymore. And I think Leslie is well aware of it. We can't even cook in the house, for Pete's sake. She was a corporate executive and now she's stirring beans over a campfire in a ragged pair of jeans we have to beat with a rock in a creek to clean. I think she's giving up."

Those words scared me. "You mean in trying to cook?"

"No, Alex. I mean in trying to live." she said darkly.

I went out to the kitchen area to check on Leslie. She was standing at the campfire, staring into the distance. The wind was changing directions and periodically bathed her in smoke; she stank like a burnt log. I looked at her closely for the first time in weeks. The skin on her hands had grown rough and coarse from the manual labor, heat, and the sun. For a woman who had enjoyed regular manicures, it was shocking to see her hands beginning to resemble claws. Her face suffered with crow's feet emerging

163

around her eyes, and gray hair appearing in the outgrowing roots of her hair. She had seemed to age several years in just the past few months.

"Hey babe, how are you doing?"

She turned with a sullen glare. "What's it to you?"

"Wow, that smells good," I said, trying to muster up some cheer.

"Do you need something?" she asked blankly.

"No, I just wanted to know if I could give you a break so that you could go enjoy a dip in the creek, or something."

She made a vague motion to sniff herself. "Yeah, I guess I do stink, don't I?" She picked up some carrots and threw them in a pot.

"That's not what I meant," I said. "I just know that things have been tough on you. This hasn't exactly been the life of an executive lately."

"You think?" she said flatly.

My efforts were not succeeding at all. "Well, you've been such a trooper in doing such physically demanding tasks for us." I tried to brush her hair away from her face, but a blast of smoke caught me by surprise and made me cough.

Tears streamed down her face, I started to panic.

"Leslie, this has got to be the worst duty on site. Can we have Teresa or Mom take over these responsibilities for a while?"

"What," she said sharply. "You don't think I can handle even this?"

"That's not what I meant," I said, not understanding why she was getting defensive about my offer.

"Just leave me alone!" she hissed in a low voice.

I instantly backed off. Whatever I was doing, I wasn't helping. "Okay, it's all yours. Just let me know when you need a break." With that I turned and headed back to the field where Sean and

Cameron were weeding. If she didn't want to talk, I wasn't going to press the issue.

We had to get up early in the morning to accomplish everything that needed to be done, and we worked until after dark every day. My fatigue was so pervasive I generally had little interest in anything other than sleep at the end of the day. One morning, though, I awoke earlier than normal and in the natural state common to men. I was rested and suddenly felt an equally normal cave man urge coming over me. I moved closer to Leslie, hoping to satisfy needs that had gone unmet for both of us for weeks, only to be put off by the rather unpleasant odor of her smoky, unwashed body. I rolled away from her but it was too late. She had felt my movement and seemed to want what I wanted. Her hands reached toward my face and she looked up with an imploring look.

The vast reservoir of built-up testosterone should have allowed me to ignore the issue and press ahead. Unfortunately, my body no longer took a firm stand. I hugged her and fondled her, but there was no response below.

"What's wrong?" she asked.

"I'm sorry, there is just too much on my mind." I lied. I kissed her and felt her withdraw from my kiss. Then I realized my own smell must have been overpowering to her as well. We were like two porcupines interested in making love, but were being put off by the quills.

I got up, trying to keep the noise down so no one else would wake up, and went out to the privy. Leslie followed me to the outhouse, and I allowed her to go first while I waited outside. It was a crisp but dry morning. The birds were just beginning to stir and call. A rabbit eyed me from the edge of the corn field. I bet he'd been eating the lentil plants again – little bastard! I watched the clouds morph from blue to pink and crimson, then streak with the golden rays of the sun that would be coming up shortly. It would be hot again today.

Leslie finished using the privy and I went in. At least you're good for something still, I thought, eyeing my brainless extremity, and sighing deeply. When I came out Leslie was standing there with nothing on. The first rays of sunshine backlit her and turned her hair to an auburn fire floating around her shoulders. A soft breeze wafted a sweet flowery odor toward me. Her nude body surrounded by glowing light was enticing. She was Venus, and Mars was rising in welcomed response. She motioned me to be quiet and I followed her to the woods. We would have to get everyone moving shortly, but for now, we were intently focused on other matters.

Our need was such that we made short work of our mission. Collapsed in the clasp of release and satisfaction, we were suddenly jolted as Stephanie's screams rose from the direction of the cabin. I jerked on my shorts and chased Leslie back to the house. I could hear the boys yelling, then Mom started screaming, and she was joined by a chorus of panicked shrieks.

CHAPTER EIGHTEEN

An Invader

AUGUST 2016, ARKANSAS

"It is easy to be brave from a safe distance."

— AESOP

We burst into the cabin to confront utter chaos. Hope and Stephanie were screaming while Teresa and Mom were trying to hold them up while standing on chairs. Mom was yelling at the boys to move back. Teresa was screaming at Jason to get out of the way, but he was shoulder to shoulder with Sean, ignoring her repeated demands. Jason, Sean and Cameron formed a semicircle to the side of the fireplace, each holding something and yelling excitedly. Jason had a broom, Sean had a hoe and Cameron was wielding a shovel. I couldn't see what they had cornered, so I hurried over to the small locked box under the front window where I kept the pistol. Leslie moved toward the women. I got the gun out and advanced toward the boys.

A huge snake was coiled in the corner of the cabin and appeared terrified. It was poised to strike and the boys were holding it at bay. The women were desperately trying to keep the little kids out of the way. Cameron was holding his shovel like a lance in front of the snake's head.

My immediate fear was that it was a rattlesnake. In the darkness the snake seemed to have a triangular head and slanted eyes. Had there been more light there might have been less confusion. A small rattling sound could be heard. When I returned, I braced to take aim at what must have been the largest rattlesnake in these parts. I took the broom from Jason, who was more than happy to give it to me. He fled to his mother by the table on the far side of the room and climbed up on the chair with her.

"Boys, I want you to back away and get behind me. Don't turn. Just back off."

"Dad, it's huge! What if you miss?" Cameron asked nervous and excited. He was also scared and was trying not to show it.

"I'll get him. Now do what I say!"

Sean and Cameron slowly backed up. A snake this size was the most exciting thing to happen in weeks. Neither boy wanted to miss any move I would make. I took a step closer to the snake, the broom pushed out in front with my left hand as a distraction. I held the pistol steady and took careful aim.

I was sucking in a deep breath before to squeeze off a round when a bellowing roar echoed off the walls, "No! Stop!"

Floyd, awakened by all the screaming, had come to the backdoor of the cabin and peered in. His thundering cry brought abrupt silence to the cabin as all eyes turned toward him.

I held back the shot that would have ended this snake's life and probably landed him on our dinner table.

"What are you doing to my snake?" Floyd yelled. He ran past me and made sure his body blocked a clear shot.

"Your snake?" I yelled back. "What the hell are you doing with a rattlesnake?"

Floyd pointed at the creature. "That's no rattlesnake, that's a python." Then he heard the rattling sound we had all heard and started laughing like a hyena. We glanced around at each other, wondering what was going on with the big guy. I kept the gun up in Floyd's general direction as he continued to laugh like a lunatic. When he finally caught his breath, he pointed out the cabin window toward a number of bugs that were flittering around.

"You see them bugs? They're grasshoppers and they make that noise. This snake don't even have diamond markings or a rattle." He walked over, reached down and picked up the snake, which immediately coiled around Floyd's upper body in a casual and familiar way.

"Meet Thelma," Floyd said. "She usually hangs out in my hidey hole, but occasionally she comes down to the cabin. She does a good job of keeping the rodents and other snakes away from here."

"Perfect! Just friggin' perfect!" Mom exploded in a post adrenaline meltdown. "A damn snake! Well, it's not staying in here, terrorizing little kids and women! Thelma can just go out to the bunkhouse with you!" she yelled, shaking her finger at Floyd. Yet he had a dazed expression on his face. He wasn't looking at Mom at all. The sun had come up just enough to fully light the cabin. Only then did I realize Floyd was staring at Leslie who, until this point, had been invisible in the darkness. I glanced over at her; she looked down, suddenly remembering she was naked, and tried to cover herself. I instantly saw the humorous side of this situation and asked: "Eve! What were you doing with the snake?"

Her face turned a bright red as the rest of her body flushed a lovely shade of pink. She bolted for our bedroom. She reappeared briefly wrapped in an old robe.

"I am going down to the creek for a sponge bath, and no one had better bother me!" she announced in no uncertain terms as she disappeared out the door.

Cameron, Sean and Jason had a range of age-appropriate expressions on their faces. This quickly passed and the boys hurried out the door hollering for Floyd.

"Hey, Floyd, wait up! We want to meet Thelma!"

Later that day, Leslie was wearing one of the better dresses that she still owned. It was nothing fancy, just a red cotton, mid-length outfit that she saved for special occasions. It made her look younger and I caught myself doing a double take when I saw her on the back porch.

"Wow, you look great."

"Oh sure, you get lucky, and suddenly I start getting compliments," she said, though she was flattered by my remarks.

"Well, if you think I'm complimentary, you should have heard what the boys had to say."

Her mouth dropped in feigned surprise at my reminder of her recent exposure. She did this in a playful way and I took advantage of her upbeat mood to give her a hug and a kiss. Responding, she brushed against the outside wall of the cabin.

I heard cloth rip as the back of her dress snagged on a nail.

"Oh no, not my dress!" she wailed. Tears came instantly to her eyes.

"Can't you fix it?" I asked.

She looked down over her shoulder. "It will never be the same," she lamented. "I'm going to take this off before the tear gets any worse." She ran inside and left me on the porch.

Just like that the high that Leslie had been feeling was gone again. She had been catapulted back into the darkness. The loss was irreplaceable.

If we wanted something we had to make it and that was part of the problem. The quality of things we used in our life had dropped off sharply.

The problem extended far beyond Leslie. We had the benefit of used clothes and shoes, but we were wearing these out quickly. The boys had already outgrown everything that we had brought with us and Sean had inherited all of Cameron's clothes. Cameron was now sharing my clothes with me. Once we ran through all the used clothes that could be bartered for in the next few years, what would we do? Leslie didn't even own a sewing machine, and even if she had, we didn't have electricity to run it or the material to use for clothes. As the reality of our situation sank in, it was clear that we were a long way from really being self sufficient.

I didn't know what I could do about it. While I'd never really known fear when I lived in a world with cash and grocery stores, I did now. And this fear was real, not the vague uneasiness of walking in the city at night. My fears now were for sufficient food, adequate shelter, safety from diseases and injury. We lived close to the edge all the time.

Prayer and meditation became a tonic for all of us. While I didn't have a belief system that fit in a box, Teresa was Roman Catholic and she took the lead on our religious ceremonies. She had erected a small altar along the sheltered side of the cabin and placed a hand-made cross on this altar. I walked by when she was praying one day and removed my hat and knelt behind her. A brisk wind blew from our right and sent the trees dancing back and forth on both sides of us and most likely masked the noise of my arrival. I wasn't sure that Teresa knew I was behind her, and I stayed very still while trying to make out what she was saying. She seemed almost angelic and this atmosphere communicated both devoutness and sincerity.

Her prayers were somewhat audible and what I couldn't actually hear, I filled in the gaps with what I might have wanted to hear her say. "God bless Richard and his family for bringing me to this place. Bless Leslie and Alex for allowing me to stay. Look after Floyd and his crops and Janine and her health, and please keep an eye on all the children. Forgive all those bandits that killed Pedro and molested me. Help me to do useful work and please provide for all of our needs and desires. Amen."

When she concluded, I quickly closed my eyes and started pretending that I too was immersed in prayers.

She walked quickly by me, and when I opened my eyes, she was no longer visible in front of me. I stood up and turned around and she sat on a plank that served as a pew in the very back of her little worship area.

"Alex, I had no idea that you were a man of the book," she said.

"Well, every now and then I need to visit with the Lord and ask for his assistance." This was a long way from the truth, but Teresa bought it.

"Me too," she said. "It is so good to have you join in worship."

An Invader

From that point on, I insisted that all of us have a weekly service of about thirty minutes each Sunday morning. At first Teresa led our services. They consisted of basic prayers for survival and thanksgiving that we'd made it this far, a home made sermon and some singing before we all rushed back to work. Leslie, surprised by my newfound enthusiasm for religious expression, volunteered to lead the service every other week when she was up to it. Had we been able to honor the entire Sabbath, a day of rest would have been welcomed. But there was simply too much work to do before the growing season ended. We found ourselves working dawn to dusk, seven days a week.

We also discovered the joys of singing. It started as a joke one day. Sean was complaining that he felt like a slave to the crops. Mom sang out the opening words to an old gospel spiritual to suggest that he actually was a slave to those chores. "Swing low, Sweet chariot" came drifting back across the field from Teresa, and we all started singing together. It felt good and we didn't sound bad. Before we knew it, songs became part of our daily ritual. On a good day we might sing a dozen songs. Anything from a religious hymn, like "Amazing Grace", to old Journey songs and current songs we had heard on the radio just before the crash. The kids didn't know most of the words initially, but as we sang these songs together they learned them. The singing helped the chores pass more quickly and lightened our spirits.

"Dad, can you help me make our basketball pad?" Sean asked me one day.

"You mean with those two bags of concrete mix that we got at the Fourth of July celebration?"

"Yes, we need to do something with the concrete soon before it hardens up and I really want to play some basketball."

"Okay, we'll tackle it this evening."

I had never poured any concrete, but he instructed me like a pro. We hammered together two by fours to make a frame on a leveled area beside the house. He had measured where a basketball backboard and hoop could fit on the cabin. He had measured out an area and used twine to stake it out. We excavated along the staked lines. Then Sean hauled up buckets of sand from the creek bank, which he used to create a base surface. We dumped a mix of sand, rocks and water into our hole and mixed it in place.

"Dad, take this board and lay it across the top of the form and level the concrete," Sean said.

"Like this?"

"Not quite. You need to saw it back and forth to force the concrete to level off."

"Like this?" I asked again.

"Better," Sean said. "It's a lot like the way that Mom levels the flour on her measuring spoon."

"How did you learn all this?"

"I watched Timmy's dad pour a concrete driveway in Nebraska. It was pretty cool." It was a fairly simple procedure and when the pad dried and we removed the frame, we were the proud owners of a smooth, level basketball pad. Unfortunately, it was only about sixteen square feet and only two inches deep, but he had the start of his basketball court and some place where he could bounce a basketball. Unfortunately, it was located right outside of our bedroom window.

Sean began to dribble the basketball for what seemed like hours a day. The noise of a bouncing basketball that started almost at dawn and continued almost any time that Sean wasn't working managed to reach Leslie the way that Floyd's snoring once had. The peaceful quiet of the country was replaced with a thump, thump, thump that seemed to reverberate all over the property.

"Alex, can you please make him stop?" Leslie pleaded one morning. "It's only six am."

"Leslie, it's good to see him passionate about something."

"It's a basketball, for God's sake. Can't he take up fishing?"

"Leslie, I don't want to tell him to stop. He enjoys it so much."

"If you won't, I will," she said with determination. She reached in the dresser besides our bed and pulled out a gun. As she stood up, though, she swooned back onto the bed in a cold sweat.

I removed the gun from our bedroom and let her stay in bed. It didn't look she would be getting out of bed again today.

Teresa saw me exit the room with the pistol in my hand. "Why the gun?"

"I think Leslie meant to shoot the basketball before she collapsed back onto her bed."

"Really, that's an interesting idea. Can I borrow your weapon?" she asked. She gave me a slightly amused look and then looked out the window toward Sean, who was still bouncing his basketball back and forth, using both hands.

"Not yet," I said "Let me go have a word with him. Will you be here when I get back?"

"Should I be?" she asked, moving toward me ever so slightly.

"That's up to you," I said, backing away toward the door, a little startled by the overtones in this conversation.

The Ark often seemed cut off from the rest of the world. We were mostly limited to walking these days, except for rare exceptions, and most of our time was devoted to getting through our chores. The net result was that almost all of our days were spent within a square mile of this farm and we spent a lot of time with each other.

At wishful moments I saw myself as the chief of a small tribe. My leadership was what kept this whole operation working. So, the distance between our farm and other available mates for Teresa meant that I gradually became the recipient of her unsolicited attention.

Her attention was a boost to my ego, because Leslie had been sick a lot lately. We had been good to Teresa and she was an appreciative woman by nature. She found ways to show her gratitude through doing little things, which I pretended not to notice but nevertheless relished.

Mom soon let me know that I was on treacherous ground. She approached me after a meal where Teresa had covertly served me extra portions of food from a meal she had mostly prepared herself.

"Alex, keep your eye on that one," she cautioned. "She seems to have some designs for you that may not be appropriate."

"What are you talking about?" I asked as if I had not noticed the growing interest that had been cast my way.

"This is too small a place to allow even the appearance of interest," Mom cautioned.

I shrugged off her thoughts, but frankly it set me to thinking.

The next day, I was working in the field under a hot sun trying to remove some slugs and other pests from our plants. Maybe I need a second wife, I murmured to myself. As I thought about this crazy idea, it actually started to grab a foothold in my reason. Here was an obviously fertile woman, judging by the kids she brought with her. If our farm had to provide for everyone who lives here, could we afford to allow her to have more children? What if she met other men at a town festival like on the Fourth of July? What if she got pregnant again? None of us had birth control other than abstinence and the rhythm method. If she were sexually active, we'd have more kids.

That would not be a problem if I was the mate. After she got pregnant with our third child, Leslie made it clear that she wanted to limit our children to just three so we could give them all a better chance. A few months before Hope was born, I had been "neutered," the term I generally chose to use to describe a vasectomy that had not been my first choice in our collective child prevention solution. After all, what if I were the only male on a desert island with a thousand women, and it were up to me to help repopulate the world... this argument was wasted on Leslie and I got snipped. So, since Leslie had insisted on my not being able to procreate any more children, wouldn't it be ironic if that was the very reason that I ended up with – or even deserved – a second wife. Wouldn't that be a just revenge to Leslie on some level? After all, as a male that could no longer reproduce, I could satisfy Teresa's sexual needs without any risk. My thoughts drifted toward more erotic possibilities, and I felt myself begin to respond physically.

All at once, I snapped out of my daydream, appalled at my thinking. I stopped to get a drink from my canteen and struggled to put my brain back into a rational orbit. Finally I was able to put this strange thought to bed. In an ironic twist of fate, a half hour later I was walking along the river looking for Floyd and the boys when I heard a noise. I peeked through a dense bush.

Teresa had been bathing and stood naked and wet on the shore after a quick dip in the cool water. She was only about ten feet away, and I stood frozen in place, too afraid to move and alert her that I was there. As I remained motionless, Teresa dried off her light brown skin in a bewitching way that seemed to accentuate every feature of her shapely body and her ample, firm breasts in particular. I could not have asked for a better view of her, and I now remained magnetically in place as if I no longer controlled the use of my limbs. I pulled gently on another branch to improve the view.

She finished drying, slowly put on her clothes and headed back to the cabin. As she walked down the path back toward the house, Teresa looked back at the bush that I stood behind and smiled curiously. I don't think she saw me, or if she had, I'm not sure she would have realized that it was me. God, she was beautiful.

When she was gone, I slumped to the ground and put my head in my hands. Why did I have to see what I just saw! Her image was playing over and over in my mind's eye, and I kept hitting the replay button.

Finally, my thoughts turned to Leslie. She had become so emotionally and sexually unavailable to me lately. When I reached for her in bed, she generally just turned away. Yet I couldn't do anything to hurt her. My erection quickly subsided and I returned to my search for the boys.

CHAPTER NINETEEN

A Harvest Hunt

Fall 2016, Arkansas

"I slew you; my bearing must not shame your quitting life. My conduct forever onward must become your death."

— William Faulkner

After all our long and hot days the garden was reasonably fruitful. Mom suggested we set up an assembly line for harvesting each vegetable as it ripened.

The tomatoes came in first. The children were shown which tomatoes were ripe to pick. They weren't terribly skilled as fruit pickers, and for each useable red tomato that ended up in their baskets at least a small green one was also added.

"Stop!" I said. "Has anyone showed you how to pick tomatoes?"

The kids all froze in place and just kind of looked at me as if I were from Mars. They then stared at the ground, concerned that they had done something wrong.

"Hmmm. Tell you what. The first thing that I want you to do is for each of you to find the best looking tomato in your basket. It should be red and should be a little soft to the touch."

Little Stephanie pulled out a rotten one, and I gently took it from her and handed her one from my basket. "Here, try this instead."

She took it and turned it over in her hand.

"Okay, see what this looks like?" I said. "Now, take a bite."

They all took a small nibble and their eyes grew wide from the pleasant taste. They proceeded to take another bite, and Stephanie finished her entire tomato.

"Now, grab one of those little green tomatoes – you know, the really cute ones."

The kids all grabbed one and held it just like they had the red ones.

"Okay, now take a big bite." I ordered.

They eagerly complied and then started spitting out the tomato as fast as they could. Stephanie started throwing a choking fit, and Teresa came rushing over.

"Are you okay?" she asked.

"Mr. Mac just told me to eat this green tomato," she said in an accusing tone, holding the offending half eaten orb in front of her.

"Alex, is that true?" Teresa demanded.

"Yes, but I did it for a reason." I started to feel a little embarrassed by my ingenious experiment. I picked up Stephanie's basket. "See all these green tomatoes?" I picked through them showing that half the tomatoes were still green. "Not only are they not ripe, but they're too small."

"I thought the best way to teach them to pick only the tasty tomatoes was to have them taste each."

"So, you think a little *taste* is going to make things better?" she asked in a sly tone.

"Well, it should certainly stop them from picking green tomatoes," I said.

"Maybe," she said with the same suggestive tone she had just used. "I guess that all depends on if they *like* them." She gave me a wanton look that took my breath away. There was no mistaking her meaning. Turning to Stephanie, she handed the basket back and said, "Don't pick the green tomatoes, okay?"

179

A Harvest Hunt

When the picking was over, Leslie and Teresa washed and separated the lesser quality specimens for processing; some were diced, some crushed and the rest were sauce. Mom cooked and canned. Twelve hours later we had almost sixty jars "put up." They would only last for about twenty meals with all the people we needed to feed, but it was a start. I was called in to lift boxes of jars onto a couple of shelves so that we could store them for later use. Teresa worked to help me and I couldn't help noticing the beads of sweat that ran down her neck and slid into the valley between her breasts. She seemed to be aware of my interest and casually brushed against my back as we maneuvered around each other. I kept my head down –afraid I might glance up and find Leslie watching us.

We would have repeated the process every other day for the next month with carrots, peas, corn, zucchini, and beans, had we had enough bottles or mason jars. Instead we stored what we could, anyway that we could, ate fresh as long as we could and tried to trade our fresh produce for cans and bottles of food with our neighbors. The open cabinets in the kitchen were full of vegetables. "Yucky vegetables," according to Stephanie, who at five, certainly would have preferred junk food. Out of mistaken sympathy, someone once gave Stephanie a box of cereal from our food stash and she proceeded to cry out for "Captain Crunch" cereal almost every morning.

When Sean, Jason and Cameron all started asking about meat, I knew it was time to hunt. The surrounding valleys of the Buffalo River and its tributary creeks supported a large elk herd. I knew poaching an elk was against the law, but one nice buck could feed the whole clan for the winter and maybe longer if we could dry enough meat into jerky. Or maybe I'd get lucky with a deer instead and not risk the law issue. But the real problem was much more basic. I'd never shot an animal in my life, and I had no idea what to do if I managed to hunt one down.

Oil Dusk

One crisp, just short of frosty, morning, a strange bugle sound woke us up. The nearby sound was deep and restless. Leslie and I got up cautiously. Hope was still sound asleep, but she had always been a deep sleeper. The sound blasted again, this time answered with a more distant note. We moved to the front window but saw nothing out of the ordinary.

Mom came out and excitedly asked, "Can you see him?"

"See who?"

"The bull."

"Bull? What bull? Didn't you hear that weird noise?"

"Alex, for Pete's sake! That's a bull elk bugling his harem and warning off other males. Must be rutting season."

My mouth dropped open. "What?"

Mom rolled her eyes at Leslie, who snorted back a strangled laugh and added, "You know, honey – horny male season?"

I was about to reply when the front door banged open and Floyd and the boys burst in, absolutely breathless and panting. Sean bent over and put his hands on his knees. Cameron was trying to slow his breathing enough to talk, while Floyd scanned the cabin, looking for something.

"Floyd! What is it?"

"Gun, need your gun! Now! No – wait, it's a shotgun, right?"

I nodded in reply.

"Shit!" Floyd screamed as he picked up a box and threw it to the side.

"Floyd, Calm down! What is going on?"

"Meat, man!" he bellowed.

Mom, Leslie and I stared at Cameron, who was wildly nodding and gasping, "Big, really big with horns!"

Sean stood up and added, "Inside!"

"Inside? Inside where?" Leslie's question held a note of alarm which made Sean grin.

"Inside the fence!" Sean said.

Reality hit me like a two by four. We had elk in the compound! How they had gotten in I didn't know, but perhaps we could get one before they got out. The same thought occurred to everyone, and we suddenly scattered to get dressed and find hunting paraphernalia, according to Floyd's shouted directions.

"Rope! Big knife! Axe? No, a saw! Need something to put the meat in! No shotgun – too hard to dig out pellets. Gun! – I'll get mine!" He bolted out the door.

We regrouped in record time. Mom had some rope and the biggest knife we owned. Cameron had gotten the saw. Leslie had a clean sheet and a slightly green face. She turned toward Teresa, who was standing by the door restraining Jason.

"Teresa, could you take this so I can stay with Hope and your kids? I don't think the little ones should be outside the cabin." Teresa nodded in agreement over the protesting cries of Jason and Stephanie. "I wanna see the elk, too!" Jason wailed.

Sean paced around, bugging us to hurry up. I picked up a box of ammo for my pistol. We exited the cabin just in time to have Floyd join us with his handgun, which looked like a toy in his big paw.

"Whatcha got there?" I asked.

"My .356 magnum. It'll kill a moose if it connects."

"Come on, everybody! We gotta get one!" Sean urged.

We followed Floyd into the woods, all the while peppering him with questions. Finally Floyd stopped and turned around. "Look, this is a hunt. We need to be quiet, 'cause right now every four-legged critter in the county can hear us. You gals need to stay back out of the way and low to the ground. We'll call for you once we shoot something. Boys, you need to stay behind me and your pa, so you don't get hit. Now, which way is the breeze blowing?" He licked a finger and held it high above his head as he slowly turned in all directions. "Northwest, okay. Let's spot 'em and circle toward 'em from the southeast. That'll keep our scent away."

I sniffed. Probably not, but I guess it couldn't hurt. I wondered how he knew.

"Floyd, how do you know how to hunt?"

"Grew up in Tennessee. My pa put me in the hunt when I weren't no older than little Steffie. I may be a worthless lump, but I do know how to hunt. Now you all gotta whisper or better yet, don't say anything." I nodded and we walked toward the herd.

Sean saw them first and swallowed a yelp. The gurgling, strangled sound made me turn to look at him. He was pointing urgently toward a small ridge to the north, his other hand clamped over his mouth. I didn't see anything at first. Then it moved. The rack of antlers stretched up and back in graceful arcs and curves. Numerous points tipped the various branches, and I wondered how old he was. He was a beautiful animal, shades of dark and light brown blending across his back and ending in a cream-colored butt. He had a huge neck and shoulders and powerful haunches. His head slowly turned, surveying territory beyond the rise. Then he thrust his neck forward, tipping his head and antlers back and blasted a note that echoed through the valley.

Floyd signaled to circle around to the right to stay downwind. This would take us over a gully and around the ridge the big bull stood on. I gestured to Floyd, mimicking the motions to shoot the bull, but Floyd shook his head. I shrugged my shoulders and lifted my hands palms up, asking why not, but he just shook his head again and waved me on through the narrow creek bed that took us out of sight of the elks. I wanted to protest. We had a clear shot and Floyd wouldn't take it. I couldn't figure out why.

We slipped stealthily through the gully and rounded a corner that opened into a large semi-cleared area. I came to an abrupt stop and stared. Four or five elk cows in the area were feeding or lying in the grass. This bull actually was repopulating his world and had the harem to do it with.

It was all I could do to refrain from taking pot shots at several of them. Again Floyd held me back. He seemed to be looking for a particular cow, or some indication of critical information that I couldn't detect. Finally, he nodded his head and pointed to a female standing near the edge of the trees near the base of the bull's lookout.

She was grazing farther away from the main group. She turned gracefully and presented us with a view of her white backside. The bull had been watching her and bugled again as he descended the hill. The cow made an odd sound and started to urinate as the bull approached. He quickly sniffed her stream, then nudged her. She turned and licked his face and antlers. He laid his head on her back and she stood still. The bull then quickly positioned himself behind her and mounted.

Sean and Cameron had moved up beside me and each had a different expression. Sean as a prepubescent boy looked vaguely horrified while Cameron had a curious thoughtful expression.

Floyd meanwhile gestured for us to move farther down the gully, alongside the meadow. While the bull was otherwise engaged, Floyd spotted a nearby cow, took aim and pulled the trigger. As the female dropped to the ground, pandemonium broke loose in the herd. The bull bellowed and the cows took off for the deeper woods with the bull herding them with calls and outright pushes. Within seconds silence filled the meadow and a lone animal lay in the grass.

We walked slowly over to it. She had died almost instantly, from the hole near her ear. Fortunately, she had fallen with the exit wound down, but I could tell a good portion of that side of her head was gone. Floyd squatted and placed a hand on her side.

"I'm sorry you had to die. We wouldn't a done it 'cept we need to eat too. I hope you're in elk heaven. Thank you." He didn't cry, but he swallowed a lump in his throat and his words were choked. I placed a hand on his shoulder as he knelt on the ground.

Teresa moved close to me as I stood next to Floyd. I could smell the sweet odor of flowers from her above the muskiness of the elk that lay before us. I looked at her. Her dark eyes were wide and I could see her pulse pounding at a hollow near the base of her neck. She seemed to be excited by the hunt. The boys were standing together five yards away, regarding the dead elk as if it had fallen from space. I heard a noise and turned towards it. Mom was walking up with a rope.

Floyd took the rope from Mom and scanned the surrounding area. He found a tree with a sturdy lower branch and walked over to it. He slung the rope over the branch and left it dangling. Coming back to the elk, he had us all take a leg and drag the body over to the rope. He tied the rope around one back leg and one front leg so the belly was exposed. We all hauled on the ropes to pull the body into a stable position. Mom handed Floyd the knife and he slit the belly skin from anus to throat. He used the knife to carefully separate the skin from the underlying muscle and pulled the left side of the skin down. We all stood in a semicircle watching him work. This was a side of Floyd we hadn't known existed.

Sean was in awe of the operation. "Why are you doing that?" he asked as Floyd made a cut completely around one ankle. "How do you know where to cut?"

Cameron jumped in, "Don't you have to gut it so the blood drips out? And where's the liver? I think Indians ate the liver, and heart –"

Sean interrupted with a gagging sound. "That's gross! I'm not eating any liver!"

I wondered what we'd do with all the meat. The weather was getting colder, but unlike Omaha it wouldn't be cold all winter. Maybe we could make jerky or smoke some of the larger hunks. Floyd interrupted my thoughts.

"First, we gotta cool the meat. Heat ruins it. Then we hang it to make it tender. Then we cut and smoke it over a fire pit."

"What's a fire pit? Do we have one?" Sean asked.

"Well, it's a hole in the ground for a fire. The fire needs ta burn jus' right. Mrs. Mac can flavor it – the smoke I mean, with different wood. Hickory is best. We got some growin' near the stream. Can you dig a pit?"

"Sure, Floyd," Sean said. "Where do you want it?"

"Near my hidey hole. We put some fresh meat in the freezer cooler and smoke the rest."

Mom, who had turned a definite shade of gray when Floyd stuck the knife into the shoulder joint and started to cut through to remove the leg, quickly spoke up. "Son, I'll take the boys back and we can get the shovel to start the hole."

"Grandma, I want to help Dad and Floyd," Cameron announced.

I looked at Mom and we silently agreed. "Okay, Cameron can stay to help us. Mom, can you and Sean dig?"

"Absolutely!" Sean said, answering for both of them.

Teresa remained behind with us, entranced by Floyd's hunting prowess. She was behaving as if he was Tarzan and she was Jane. They engaged in some small talk that I could not hear, and then the next thing I knew, Floyd and Teresa had disappeared.

Cameron and I were left behind with the hanging elk. Finally, about thirty minutes later Floyd reappeared and showed us how to dress the elk. There was no sign of Teresa.

The next few days were consumed with preparing and preserving the meat. My desire to actually eat this meat began to fade the moment we started to clean it in earnest. The smell was overpowering and the entrails were disgusting. It was a good anatomy lesson for the boys at first, since the liver, lungs, stomach and heart were all recognizable, but when they realized how nasty this process was, they disappeared. Leslie and Mom were nowhere in sight, but Teresa occasionally came by to check on us. This left all the processing work to Floyd and me, and I knew how skittish Floyd could be. I did everything possible to keep Floyd on task, but it just wasn't in his nature. Before I knew it, I was butchering this meat by myself. Floyd did reappear from time to time, offering suggestions on how to smoke it and lay it in long strips over an old screen to dry it into jerky. But he had reverted back to the old Floyd, lounging around and doing nothing more to help out. The skilled and focused man intent on his work had appeared briefly.

We later learned that the elk population had held steady at around a thousand for the entire state of Arkansas over the previous ten years. Our efforts weren't the only ones to whittle down their population, and we never saw another elk.

One evening, as I grilled some elk tenderloins, I asked Floyd about his shot. "So where did you learn to shoot so well? It seemed like you brought her down almost without aiming."

"Nah, I was aiming. I always had decent aim, but I got really good in the Army. They made me a sniper. One shot, one kill, every time." He was moving his arms as if he were holding a rifle steady. He suddenly appeared to remember something and looked startled. He quickly changed the subject. "Say, dis jerky gonna be okay, Mr. Mac."

CHAPTER TWENTY

Floyd Fixes a Failure

FALL 2016, ARKANSAS

"Zeus does not bring all men's plans to fulfillment."

— HOMER

Early in the fall, we noticed the nights in the cabin were uncomfortably cool. It was only September, I thought, worried. What would January feel like? We needed to think of all the details that had to be taken care of before winter. We had been almost single-mindedly focused on food and the weather had been so hot until recently, we really hadn't thought through the implications of cold weather. After all, we weren't in Omaha anymore. How bad could a winter be around here? Our cabin in the woods ought to have some type of provision for cooking and heating during cold weather – or did it?

The cabin wasn't well prepared for winter. We had no cooking stove inside and the fireplace wasn't functional. I went looking for Floyd.

I found him later by the creek playing with Jason and Sean. They all had their shoes off and were sitting on the bank with their feet in the water. Floyd noted my arrival and gave me a big grin.

"Floyd, something has been on my mind this morning. Can you tell me how you've stayed warm in the winter since you've lived here?"

"Oh, that's easy." Floyd said. "I simply went over to Michael's trailer, my old Army buddy. Whenever it got cold for a spell, I'd always bring some food, so he was glad to have me. He was in the artillery and is almost deaf – so he never complains about my snoring." Floyd laid this on me like it was a logical and simple explanation – which it was for him. But his solution would not work for us and confirmed my fears that the cabin was not suitable for cold weather.

There was no established heating system that would keep the cabin warm for all of us that now lived here. How were we going to solve that?

Maybe Floyd had some ideas. "How do you think we might be able to keep the cabin warm this winter?"

Floyd gave me a blank stare. "Think you probably ought to burn some wood."

Now I was getting really worried. We had no means to burn the wood inside. Even if I could find a way to fix the chimney and locate a replacement damper, I had my doubts whether this would be a viable solution. I remembered how inefficient our chimney had been in Nebraska. The fire would heat the living room, but as soon as the fire started to die down, the chimney would suck all the heat out of the room. When the temperature dropped, we would be in trouble. Now what?

Dad had died before he could modify this place from a summer vacation cabin to a year-round home. We would have to upgrade the insulation to keep the air out and provide some type of heating system for the cabin, but how?

We needed a wood stove and didn't have one. I made some inquiries into trying to get a wood stove, but had little success and suspected that these items were in such incredible demand that we'd never be able to afford one.

I pulled out my "How Things Work" set of reference books I had brought with me and thumbed through it looking for ideas. It had been a low-cost investment made a few years earlier to help me understand the mechanics of a bunch of applications. It now became a quasi repository of useful technology.

The first book discussed steam engines and industrial plants with lots of piping, and it made my mind start churning. What if we had a heating source outside and brought hot pipes full of water into the cabin? Wouldn't that keep us warm?

As I started sketching out details of this approach, I discovered a number of drawbacks. How would we control the temperature? What type of vessel would we use to heat the water? Would we need a pump? If so, what kind? After all the low tech solutions we had used to plow and farm, a more sophisticated solution seemed attractive – as long as it worked.

We acquired some leftover stainless steel pipe from Floyd that looked like it had once belonged to a still. Upon further questioning, more of the still was located and we had both a container and the piping. The piping was screw pipe and was easily assembled and run a short distance from the house – just to be safe. An old faucet handle might give us the steam control we needed. In just a few days we had constructed a rudimentary steam system that we could heat with wooden logs to provide hot water pipes to keep us warm. We experimented with the system all through October and worked out all the structural bugs. Application in cold weather would be the real test.

Halloween came and Margaret came over to invite everyone to a Harvest costume party and potluck at their barn. The idea of dressing up without the convenience of Wal-Mart pre-made costumes was initially a little daunting. We rummaged through our meager closets and supplies while offering and rejecting suggestions from each other. Mom found a white shirt and skirt that she combined with a shower cap to become a nurse. Mom thought Leslie and I should go as Fred and Wilma Flintstone with Hope as Pebbles.

"You would be so cute," Mom argued. "And we certainly have enough rags to make your costumes."

"Ha! That's the truth, we're definitely equipped for the Stone Age," I retorted.

"I think we should go as that farm couple in the painting," Leslie suggested morosely.

"American Gothic?" I asked her. "Why on earth for?"

"Well, I already look old and tired. I could just pull my hair back in a bun and we could borrow a pitchfork for you."

Mom and I exchanged glances. "You know what would be perfect?" Mom quickly said. "Why don't you go as a suit and a secretary – but Leslie's the suit and Alex – you be her guy Friday. Besides, Leslie already knows the executive role." Leslie smiled tightly and nodded.

Teresa came in followed by Floyd. He pulled out a folded package of red cloth and handed it to Teresa, then placed a couple of other packages on the table.

"I – I got some stuff from a friend." he stammered. "I can just be myself, but here's some extra stuff for you all."

We all started talking and looking at Floyd's packages of accessories and clothing. Teresa took her package but didn't open it, so none of us knew what she was coming as until the night of the party. As we assembled for the walk over to the Kingstons', Teresa finally appeared – as a Spanish dancer. Her voluptuous figure filled the frilly red dress, and her long dark hair cascaded down her back.

Cameron, Floyd and I stared with our mouths hanging open. Mom arched an eyebrow and glanced at Leslie. She had been upbeat about her suited executive outfit, but took one look at Teresa – which was really just one glance at me staring at Teresa – and her joy visibly dimmed. She withdrew into silence and gave me the cold shoulder for the rest of the evening.

We had managed to assemble some simple costumes for the kids. Cameron got talked into wearing an old dress of Mom's with a hat and gloves. I found a curved branch in the woods to be a crook for "her". Leslie made a nose and ears out of some of the elk hide to make Sean a wolf, and we turned Teresa's kids into fluffy sheep with the batting from an old quilt. As it turned out, Bo Peep

Floyd Fixes a Failure

and her sheep and the big bad wolf were the hit of the party. Teresa came in a close second.

The party was deemed a huge success by everyone, especially the guys, who all made a point of talking or dancing with Teresa. We had taken some of our garden goods to trade, and we came home with several jars of preserved fruit in exchange for our corn and other vegetables.

The Kingstons also gave us a pumpkin. In other years we might have been tempted to make a jack o'lantern, but under our present circumstances, we opted to convert it into pies and side dishes immediately so that we wouldn't risk spoiling it.

As it started getting colder, I learned some painful lessons in mechanical engineering. The first challenge was the huge heat lost from the pipes before they even made it into the cabin. The outside was so much colder that despite our rudimentary insulation of rags and mud, most of the heat was released into the great outdoors. Our efficiency was horrible, and we burned a great deal of wood for very minimal benefit.

The next problem had to do with the question of who was going to freeze their tail off to make sure the water was heated properly. We generally ensured the water was boiling in the tank right before we went to bed, however, we felt we couldn't leave the fire going. The heat in the kettle would continue to build and the steam could burst the whole system. We tried banking the fire but managed to burn the kettle dry instead when a small release valve blew off. So the heat needed to be almost completely removed before we went to bed. In an emergency, one of us could serve as night watchman for the heater, but this would have to be the exception rather than the rule – there was just too much work to be done during the day, even in winter.

At the first cold spell we fired the system up. Day one, we managed to burn the heck out of Hope's hand when she grabbed a pipe to keep herself from slipping as she toddled along. The next day, we almost set the cabin on fire when Jason dropped some old paper he was coloring onto the floor next to the pipe. Worst of all, the system provided almost no heat. We would have been warmer had we heated bricks on the fire outside and brought them into the cabin. Since Teresa and Stephanie were still sleeping in the main room of the cabin, she was very interested in whatever solution we were going to come up with.

"Can't we just let the steam heat the room?" she asked. "Wouldn't it be like a sauna?"

"I'm not sure the steam will be enough to heat the whole room." I told her. "We might just get everything damp."

"Do you have a better idea?" she asked. "Even a fire in the fireplace would help."

"We'd need a large piece of metal for the flue vent so we can keep heat in. We just don't have the right piece of metal," I told her with a frustrated sigh.

"It's just that I get so cold at night. I'd love to find a way to stay warm," She said softly with just a hint of invitation.

I was about to reply when Leslie walked into the room. She took one look at Teresa standing close to me, frowned and walked right back out. I wanted to go after her, but needed to get this job done so we wouldn't freeze.

I proceeded to drain the water out of the holding tank and out of the piping to the house. I then disconnected the piping and simply terminated the intake pipe with the water faucet. We then heated up the holding tank to a boil and opened up the faucet slightly. The steam hissed out slowly and a few minutes later the windows started to fog up. I closed the valve slightly so just a hint of steam escaped.

I wasn't sure what good this was going to do, but night was coming again and it was starting to get cold. Everyone sleeping in the cabin's main room moved their bedding away from the wall where the faucet was and went to sleep.

When I awoke, sometime in the middle of the night, I could see my breath in the cabin. Both Hope and Sean were squeezed between Leslie and me. I got up to check on the others. Shivering in the icy cold, I could see that everyone seemed to be snuggled up against someone else trying to stay warm. Jason and Cameron were huddled together and Teresa and Stephanie had curled up with Mom. Even Floyd had gotten into the act. I could hear the two goats bleating between his snores from the bunkhouse. Apparently he had not gone to his friend Mike's place for the night. Strike two.

I tiptoed over to the faucet and opened it fully. Nothing happened. No steam, no water, no hiss. Without a fire at the holding tank, we had frozen pipes instead of hot water and steam available. Rather than risk flooding the house with water once the pipes thawed, I turned the faucet completely off and went back to bed. I tried to curl up behind Leslie, but she turned toward me and shifted Hope between us. I wasn't sure if she was doing this to keep Hope warm or to keep me away. The end result was the same.

The whole episode was a perfect example of trying to do something without really knowing how. This type of learning curve haunted everything we did. In our previous mode of living we would have just said, "Nuts to this," and called in some experts. Now we had no option to quit, because if we did, we would freeze our tails off all winter.

The next morning, I felt like a scoutmaster making all the kids get out of bed so that they could go warm themselves by the fire I had built outside. We checked the youngest kids to make sure that they weren't getting frostbitten toes or noses.

Floyd came in mid morning. "Damn it's cold in here," he said, walking over to watch me tinker with the faucet. "I guess this idea didn't work?"

"No, it didn't work and I'm about out of ideas," I growled, mad as hell about my experience. "Plus, I'm tired and cold and hungry."

In sympathy, he pulled a small bottle out of his jacket pocket, took a swig and handed it to me. I took a swig and felt a burning sensation running down my throat. It was moonshine he had apparently made himself. It was potent and remarkably flavorful.

"Floyd, this is great hooch, but it isn't going to solve my heating problem for the cabin. Can you think of anything that might work better?"

Floyd looked at me as if he were now in charge. "Can you loan me the keys to your wheels?" he asked. "Also, I'll need to take all the parts of my old still. I'll go get the condenser and tubing. Just load everything else in the back."

I fretted over the potential cost of gas that Floyd would burn, but was desperate for a better solution.

When Floyd returned with an armload of parts and pieces, I helped load up the rest of the still parts we had used in our home-heating experiments. It left two holes in the wall of the cabin where we had run the piping, but we just stuffed them with mud and straw and covered them with a board. "Tell Teresa that *I'll* be back with a heating solution shortly."

"Oh, she's been working on you too," I joked.

I wasn't sure if Floyd knew how to drive and doubted that he had a current license in any case. He started the vehicle up and then tried to restart the engine again after it was running. A grinding noise could be heard throughout the camp.

"Sorry!" Floyd yelled out the window as he headed out down the road rather slowly.

Part of me wondered if we'd ever see Floyd again this winter.

Yet six hours later Floyd returned and in the back of our vehicle was a genuine wood burning stove. There was no sign of Floyd's still.

Floyd had a grin from ear to ear. "I think you're going to like this better."

I was dumbstruck. "Better? This is wonderful! Mom and Leslie can cook on the top, and we can use the residual heat for warming the cabin. Where did you get it?"

We had made repeated inquiries for several months, and no stove had surfaced. But in just a few hours, Floyd had mysteriously found one. Furthermore, he had a pallet of mason jars that we could use to store additional nuts and seeds in. My mind started calculating. The cold outside was going to suffice as a refrigerator during the winter as long as we could keep animals away from our storage shed. The mice were particularly good at knocking over bottles and chewing up anything that wasn't protected by glass. These jars had become almost as rare as wood stoves, and I was floored that Floyd had been able to return with both items.

I can't fully describe the happiness this brought to our farm. We could now stay warm in the cabin with an efficient heating system and, best of all, the stove allowed the women to cook inside. I had never seen Teresa more excited or more appreciative, and she jumped up into Floyd's arms and gave him a giant hug and kiss on the cheek.

"Darn," he said. "If I'd a known you'd be this happy, I'd a gotten one months ago."

"But, Floyd, how did you do it?" I asked. "You didn't do anything illegal, did you?"

"I simply traded my still and a little hooch for the stove," was all Floyd shared with us. He didn't go into any details regarding who he had conducted the exchange with, but when I checked the odometer on the vehicle, it showed that Floyd had traveled about a hundred miles since taking the car. At current prices it might cost us a half a grand to replace these five gallons, but the stove was worth it.

It was clearly stamped "Made in the USA." The workmanship was slightly shoddy and it was obvious this wasn't well manufactured. Someone had built this stove with what might have been a local blacksmith operation. It appeared that it had never been used before, which made me believe it hadn't been stolen from anyone else.

    I thanked Floyd profusely and called Cameron over to help me install the stove in the house and run a vent pipe out the top of the roof. The next night we slept warmly. During the rest of winter, all any one of us had to do was to mention how nice it was to have a wood stove and everyone within earshot would send up an "Amen" and "Thank God." It seemed that Floyd was helping us find religion.

CHAPTER TWENTY-ONE

Hitting the Wall

FALL 2016, ARKANSAS

"Courage is fear holding on a minute longer."

— GEORGE S. PATTON

As much as I wanted to pretend that everything was okay between Teresa and Leslie, there was increasing tension between the two women. Little unintended comments from Teresa sent Leslie up in smoke. Teresa would remark that there was a cockroach in the kitchen – a pretty normal occurrence in a cabin that was a long way from being airtight – and Leslie would spend the next two days scrubbing the floors in addition to everything else that she was already doing. Leslie would say she felt claustrophobic and Teresa would interpret this remark as a comment that she wasn't wanted and proceed to sulk for the next three days. I tried to stay on the right side of both of them, but living in such tight quarters was challenging.

Admittedly, I was part of the problem. During this same time, I did find myself rerunning the image of Teresa's nude body in my mind over and over again and didn't feel guilty about conjuring up lurid images on occasion – even if the object of those visions was a natural beauty that lived on the same compound. I wasn't proud of myself, but I fed off sexual energy to put up with all the hardships that we faced.

From time to time Leslie caught me feasting my eyes on Teresa. I didn't mean it, but Leslie was so closed off to me most of the time, I couldn't help it. I loved Leslie unconditionally – the committed way that people love their kids. So, what harm could a little innocent fantasy do?

The tensions reached a head with the coming of winter. We spent a couple of frantic weeks picking, cutting, cleaning, canning and trying to preserve all the food we had struggled to grow. Mom's canning knowledge and the teamwork of the women in completing this essential chore struck me as the crowning achievement of our meager existence after months of backbreaking labor. When we had finished putting up everything we could, Leslie thought our work would subside.

"Alex, we've finished harvesting the bulk of our crop. The kids need some school time. Even farm kids attend classes in the fall and winter," she pointed out. "Let's work out some regular schedule."

I didn't like the idea at all. "Leslie, I need Cameron and Sean to help me plow under the stalks. It's like fertilizer and we need to turn the soil before it gets cold. We also need to clear some more of the forest so that we can farm more acres next summer." Seeing her stricken face, I offered a bone, "You can set up something with Teresa for Jason and Stephanie. They need to learn to read and write, but our boys are fine for now."

"No!" Leslie cried. "Cameron would be in high school right now. He needs some higher math and literature. His writing skills need to be maintained. I only need a couple of hours a day."

In my mind, working to keep us warm, alive and fed counted far more than traditional education. The boys had to know how to plant and harvest and hunt. They didn't need algebra and history now. "Can't this wait until the weather gets colder? It's still warm enough during the day to work outside," I pointed out.

"It could, but then I'd be trying to get a year's worth of education into them in only a couple of months." That didn't bother me and she went on, "by the end of February you'll need them working again. If we can have a few hours of school first thing in the morning, then Teresa and I could help in the field some and Mom could take over the cooking. Look, I've made out a schedule for everything."

She handed me a three by five note card with what looked like a school schedule printed out in her compact handwriting.

This is a waste of my time and their time, I thought as I glanced at the card and handed it back. "Look, dear, school just isn't that important right now. A little delay in their education isn't going to matter. On the other hand, not having their help in this work will make a difference to our survival. Let's wait for another six weeks and then we'll see, okay?"

She was outraged by my obstinacy.

"I never thought you'd be stupid and shortsighted about your own sons' future!" she snapped.

"I'm not stupid or shortsighted!" I shouted back. "If we know the boys are most likely going to be farmers, shouldn't we focus more of their efforts in learning that trade? I'm not against teaching them to read or write or even to appreciate academic subjects like Shakespeare or history. I do, however, think that our farming efforts are their best preparation for whatever their future holds and, besides, we really do need to get a few more projects done this fall while we still can."

She glared at me, threw the note card on the floor and slammed out of the cabin. I looked around and noticed numerous heads ducking back behind openings and doorways. I hadn't realized everyone was listening, waiting for my decision.

Mom came out of her room and headed over to the kitchen sink. She said. "I think you need to find her and make some compromise," as she came out of her room and headed over to the kitchen sink. "She's only trying to establish some connection to the life we've all lost. You owe her some credit for that." She held my gaze. This is not the life she planned for herself or the kids. She's used to being in charge."

"But Mom, school can wait for a couple of months. The work can't!"

"It's not about the work, Alex," She said mildly. "It's about a routine and tradition and how we all grew up. It's late fall and the kids haven't had much schooling recently. Can't you just give it a chance? This is important to her."

I wasn't conceding my point. I knew very well that we were on the raw edge of survival. "Then she can just make a schedule of all the work that needs to be done before winter. If we get through that – fine. Then there can be time for school, but not before!"

I grabbed my work boots and yelled for the boys. "Come on, guys, we've got some dirt to turn!"

Sean and Cameron slowly came down the loft ladder, followed closely by Jason. None of the boys looked at me. They dutifully donned their work boots and followed me out to the corn field.

Over the next couple of days everyone was sullen. Leslie gave me the silent treatment, refusing to even acknowledge my presence. Any attempt to touch her was shrugged off. I decided my best option was to ignore the whole situation and act as if nothing was abnormal.

The boys continued to work hard. They enjoyed the short respites from our labor when they terrorized each other with dirt clods and gave Jason bugs to scare his sister with. Our efforts to turn the corn stalks and other leftover vegetation progressed slowly. I was starting to feel positive about our chances for a better crop next year. If the weather held, we would make a lot of progress clearing the trees and cutting firewood.

As I worked, though, my mind kept coming back to what I had really wanted to say to Leslie. I too wished that our kids could have a quality education and all the advantages that we had grown up with. At the same time, I feared that we'd be setting them up for expectations that they might never be able to meet. How many accountants and consultants now found themselves tilling fields like these? What good was their degree doing them?

A week later, Leslie still wasn't speaking to me. She really deserved a more thoughtful explanation from me, but I just hadn't fully processed what I was willing to compromise on yet. The work would taper off soon and she could start her teaching program.

Mom cornered me one evening to break the impasse. "Alex, you've got to consider this from Leslie's perspective. She had a life that was comfortable, productive, and relatively easy. Now she's poor, she's been so sick we thought she'd die, her daily work is endless drudgery and she still wants to devote what little energy she has to giving the boys and Teresa's kids some academic preparation. Can you fault her for this?"

"No, Mom. I can't." I admitted. "But is education the key to their future? We really do need to finish our fall farming requirements."

"Alex, you need to make peace with your wife," she told me sternly. "This is too small a place to feud and she's still not doing well. After her E. Coli bout, I think she faced her own mortality for the first time and it scared her. She's worried about our future. She's on edge a lot and resents our living circumstances."

"And I don't? What happens when we don't get our crops all in or the plow doesn't have spare parts?" I asked. Seeing her strong expressions I sighed. "I'll talk to her, but my feelings on this aren't going to change."

"Then I guarantee your marriage will," she warned.

"Leslie, you can't keep this up. You can't not talk to me." No response.

Leslie was washing clothes by the creek after another silent breakfast, and I decided to try to convince her that my position was the best course for the family. I picked up a shirt and made a token effort to rinse it in the creek water as I stood next to her.

"Look, the boys and I have cut down enough stalks and crop waste to warrant getting Will's wagon and hauling it all over to his place for some ethanol. Then maybe we can use his tractor and turn our field in a few hours. We're also starting to clear another eight acres of land in preparation for next year. If we can get this done, we can grow more food next year and maybe even generate some real income. The boys can study during the winter months and maybe a couple hours each day in the spring once the crops are planted. How does that sound?"

She grabbed another pair of worn jeans and started rubbing the stains with little chunks of soap. The washboard was propped up near her feet, and she quickly doused some water on the jeans and started scrubbing. She didn't even look at me.

"Leslie. Please, say something." She continued to scrub silently. I dropped down on my haunches and grabbed her hands. She froze. "Leslie, come on. Talk to me!"

"And say what, Alex?" Her voice was soft and sad, and she refused to look at me.

"I don't know – you understand? You can see my point?" I ventured.

She snorted and jerked her hands away and started scrubbing furiously. "I can see your point. I've always seen your point. It's too bad you can't see mine!"

"What does that mean?"

"Exactly what I said! You're so caught up in what you think is right – your timeline, your issues, your priorities. You've completely lost touch with anyone else's ideas, needs or feelings."

"That's not true! I've been busting my butt to keep us all alive. I think school is important, but I also think we need the boys focused on farming right now."

"Exactly my point!" She turned to me at last, "when you're certain, when you decide. Do you really think the rest of us aren't doing our best?" She stood up abruptly, "Fine – I quit! You do what I do every day and see how you like it. I ask for just one thing and it's not important to you. Screw this!"

She slapped the wet jeans across my chest, kicked the water bucket at me and stalked off into the woods. I stared after her. What was I supposed to do now?

I left the wet shirt I'd rinsed with the pile of dirty clothes by the creek and walked back to the cabin. "Mom!" I called. "Where are you?"

She appeared from the path to the outhouse. "What is it?"

"Leslie just stomped off into the woods in a rage."

"I tried to warn you."

"I know and I was trying to reason with her like you suggested."

She put her hands on her hips. "I'm not taking sides here. You may be the only man in the family, but we've all had a really tough time too."

"That's not fair," I complained. All of the frustration of the past months poured out. "Dad seemed to think this would be a great place for us, but it sucks, and I keep having problems to solve –"

"Alex! You've been so caught up in fending for our needs that you haven't been thinking about the emotional side of all this. Leslie's hurting and you seem to have missed it. When was the last time you told her you loved her? And I don't mean having sex with her – I mean just treating her like a woman you care about instead of a maid?" She shook her head wearily and walked back into the cabin without a backward glance.

Leslie didn't come home for lunch. I was still mulling over everything she had said to me. If Leslie was still mad, I reasoned, maybe a day off would help her. Mom had taken care of the laundry and Teresa made some soup and brought me a bowl.

"I hope you like the soup, Alex." she said softly. "I made it special for you."

"Yeah, thanks Teresa, it's good," I responded, distracted. My mind was on the things Mom had said to me. I didn't even notice

Teresa's frown. Could everything Mom had said really be true? Was I such a jerk? Had I let the daily grind blind me to Leslie's needs?

Lunch was a silent affair. I didn't have much appetite but ate anyway. I gruffly complimented Teresa on the soup again and returned to work.

Mom brought a pitcher of water out to the field mid afternoon. Cameron and Sean dashed up and gulped down huge swallows, then kissed their grandma and thanked her. I walked up slowly.

"Thanks for taking care of the clothes, Mom. How's Leslie?"

"She hasn't come back yet" she said, "and I'm getting a little concerned about her. If you can take a break you should probably go look for her."

"Leslie hasn't come home?" I frowned, wondering where she might have gone to.

"I haven't seen her since breakfast."

That was not a good sign, not with her being depressed all the time. "Okay, can you make sure the boys keep working?" I sighed. "I guess I'll need to go look for her."

"I've got more work of my own to do," she replied in annoyance. "Just tell the boys to stick with it for another hour or so and then head home. If you aren't back by then, we'll all need to look for her." She gazed around with a strange expression of fear and fatigue. She gave me a look that spoke volumes. "She doesn't need to spend the night in the woods when she's depressed."

I didn't reply but headed in the direction of Floyd's cave. My thoughts were spinning, trying to figure out where she'd go.

I arrived at Floyd's cave out of breath, but there was no sign of her. The river and swimming hole were undisturbed too. The woods echoed with my calls, but I heard no response. I worked my way to our fence line and followed it around the compound, looking for signs that she had passed. All the while I continued calling her name. Two hours flew past and I heard the boys' voices calling in the distance. She might ignore me but I couldn't see her deliberately worrying the children. I followed the sound of their yelling and soon saw them moving through the woods toward me.

"Hey, guys! I'm over here!"

Sean spotted me first and dashed toward me. "We started searching at our gate and walked all around the east boundary. We haven't heard anything. You don't think she fell down and is hurt – do you, Dad?" His worry was apparent. Cameron trotted up in time to hear me assure Sean that his mom was fine and that she just needed some time to think and take a little break from the work.

"Grandma rode my bike over to the Kingstons' to see if Mom walked over there. She said she'd be back before dark."

"Has she ever told you guys of a special place in the woods or off the Ark?"

"No, I don't think so," Cameron said. "All she's ever said is she likes the creek – easy to think and forget there."

That gave me an option, at least.

"Well, let's walk up the stream then. Maybe she likes a spot beyond our property."

We followed along the bank, calling and looking for footprints. Our shouts startled a number of birds and small animals, but we saw no sign that she had passed that way. After twenty minutes of scrambling along the bank and calling without a response, we realized she probably wasn't in the area. Sean didn't seem too worried but Cameron did. "Dad, she had some breakfast, but did she have food or water with her?" he asked.

I tried to remember if she had a canteen or a pouch when she stormed off. I didn't recall seeing either. "No, son, I don't think she did, but she could get water from the creek and there's always something in Floyd's freezer. Plus, she might be able to find some berries, if there are any left."

"Are there bears or wolves around here?" Cameron asked. Sean's ears perked up when he heard bears and wolves.

"Bears? There are bears here?" Sean said.

I groaned inwardly, wishing Cameron had never brought it up. "I've never seen one, but I suppose there might be. We also need to be on the lookout for snakes, poison ivy and rabid animals. Just be careful, okay?" I said.

"Floyd and Teresa said they'd check some places he knows once Grandma comes back." Sean blurted.

"Places on the Ark or in the area?" I asked, wondering if Floyd had some additional "hidey holes" and the like.

"Outside I think – he mentioned someone named Mike. He sleeps there in the winter?" he asked, his voice flecked with panic. "I can't remember. Mom wouldn't go to some other man's house, would she?"

"No, Sean. A friend's place maybe, but not a stranger's."

Our search had taken us near Floyd's cave again, so we took a detour inside. There was still no sign of Leslie having been here.

"Where, besides the boundary line, did you guys search before you met up with me?" I asked them.

Sean started counting on his fingers. "The outhouse, the garden, the road to the gate, Floyd's bunkhouse, the cornfield, and the woods along the fence line over that way." He pointed his thumb over his right shoulder.

"Okay she isn't in the southern portion of the property then and she did head off upstream. Let's follow the creek to see if we can see any sign of her."

"But it's mostly dry, Dad" Cameron pointed out. "She might not think it's so nice now." He was very distressed, and his next remark was more like an accusation. "Why did she leave anyway?"

My expression must have told him something because his concerned look flashed into anger and suspicion. "Did you make her cry again?"

Again? When had I ever made her cry? "No," I replied. "Actually, she was mad at me and slapped me with a pair of wet jeans."

"Humpf!" He snorted. "Yeah well… she must be pretty tweaked."

"I guess so. She wants you and Sean to get some schooling, but I need you to help me right now. We've been discussing it."

He laughed out loud. "Arguing is more like it!" Then his tone turned wistful. "It sure would be nice to get a break from all this farm work." He kept his eyes down and didn't glance at me.

"Really? I thought you enjoyed the freedom of no school."

He laughed again. "Jeez, Dad, get a clue! It's not freedom if you've got us working every day. At first it sort of felt like summer vacation, but this is real work." He paused and kicked the dirt and leaves on the trail. "We don't really have friends, or sports or anything like that anymore. A couple hours of some type of schoolwork would make me feel like we hadn't lost everything."

Sean, who had been ahead leading us up the dry creek bed, suddenly stopped and yelled. "Dad! I think I see some footprints. Come check!"

Cameron and I ran up and squatted beside Sean. Sure enough, the prints looked like Leslie's size foot, but there were also some large animal foot prints in the mud nearby. Leslie's prints were deep as if she had sprinted away from the creek in a hurry. When I looked at the prints more closely they appeared to be pig-like. Now I was really worried.

Razorbacks were a dangerous threat. While technically feral pigs, they were essentially wild boars. They could grow to several hundred pounds in size and could move at great speed. I had never actually seen one, but I had heard that they were in the area and Will had warned me about them, telling me. "Their tusks can slice you to pieces and they are not afraid to attack if they are disturbed." If one of these guys had been chasing Leslie, her only escape would have been up a tree. I just hope she understood that.

I made a sign to Cameron and Sean to keep quiet and cautiously looked around for any sign of these creatures. I didn't see any and we followed Leslie's prints away from the creek. I was relieved to notice that there were no more animal tracks visible. This suggested that Leslie had not been pursued when she left the creek.

The trail went on for a little ways, but then dead-ended in a large bramble. The ground was dry and I could no longer spot any trace of prints.

"What now, Dad?" Sean asked.

"We spread out and keep heading in this general direction. You go that way and Cameron, you go over that way. Go just out of sight but yell so we can keep in hearing range of each other. Look for any prints or broken branches maybe – bent weeds, whatever. Keep yelling but listen for a reply. If you get chased by a hog, then climb a tree. Let's move quickly. It's going to get dark soon."

"Okay! Got it, Dad," Sean replied and headed left. Cameron headed right in a parallel line to me. We searched for an hour without finding any sign of Leslie. By then the boys were tired and I was getting very worried. We had crossed through parts of the woods that I had not had any time to explore. Some areas had been easy going with large trees and relatively low ground cover. Other areas were dense with brush and tangled blackberry bushes or wild roses. I couldn't imagine her entering this mess. But we didn't have a better direction to search in.

"Hey, Dad!" Cameron called from my far right.

"Yeah?" I yelled back.

"I think I found something. Come see."

"Sean!" I yelled. "Stop and wait a minute. I've got to check something for Cam."

"Okay," his voice floated back. I raced over to Cameron. He was looking at a scrap of fabric snagged on a low branch. It was the same color as the top Leslie had been wearing. The small twigs near the scrap had been broken recently. She had passed this way.

"Leslie! Mom!" I yelled, hoping to hear a quick reply. There was only silence.

"Cam, go get your brother and come back this way some. I'll head forward. Make sure you can hear me and let's move a little faster."

"Okay, Dad" He ran off toward Sean's position, and I advanced deeper into the woods calling and listening. A few minutes later my yell was faintly echoed by a desperate tone. "Alex! Can you hear me?"

"Where are you?"

"I don't know. I'm lost," Leslie said plaintively.

"Just sit down, stay put and keep calling out. I'll come to you" I called back then yelled for the boys. "Sean, Cam! I found her!"

"Woo hoo!" Sean yelled. I could hear the boys pounding through the woods toward me. I took more steps forward and called. "Leslie?"

"Alex" Her voice was shaky but it was closer. In typical fashion she had ignored my advice and was moving toward me.

"I'm here. Can you see me?" The growing twilight made it hard to see into the darker shadows. The boys were making their way toward me, whooping and calling in relief. I didn't need to yell for Leslie. The noise from the boys would guide her. I turned from the guys' approach and saw Leslie stagger out from a dense growth of saplings. She was bedraggled, muddy and scratched up. I ran to her and held her tight. She was crying and choking down her sobs as the boys reached us and we all hugged each other.

"Mom, where have you been? We've been looking and looking!" Sean stepped back and looked up at his mom, noticing her scratches and torn shirt. "Are you hurt?"

"No, I'm okay." She snuffled and wiped her eyes. "I had been walking up the creek when I thought I saw a giant pig. It scared me to death, and I got away from the creek. I've been trying to get back home, but I don't know where I am or which direction to go. I don't recognize any landmarks."

I looked quickly at the sky to see which way the sun was setting. "Boys, I think if you head in that direction, we'll run across a trail we'll recognize. We can follow that home. Why don't you see what you can find? But don't get too far ahead so we lose touch with each other, okay?"

The two took off together and stayed about fifty yards ahead of us. They soon found the trail that I thought they would find, and after excitedly pointing it out to Leslie and me, they raced each other home.

"Are you okay?" I asked quietly when we were back on the path.

"I banged my knee when I slipped in the creek," she said sullenly. "I'll be okay."

"Want to talk about it?" I was leery of broaching her feelings now given that she was both tired and hungry. But privacy was difficult to arrange, and I knew she would shut down once she got back to the cabin.

She was silent for a few steps, then stopped and faced me. "I feel old, dirty, and like there's no escape from this hellhole. I don't want this life anymore. I just want to leave, but where could I go? Maybe it would be better for everyone if I were just dead."

"Leslie, don't say that! I love you and I don't want to lose you." I took hold of her shoulders. "The whole time that I was looking for you, I was worried sick that something might have happened to you. Don't you know what you mean to all of us?"

She didn't warm up to my appeal. "Look, this isn't about you. I haven't had a hot bath in almost a year. I live in a cabin with no running water, no kitchen and no electricity. My kids don't have a school. I don't have a job and I work from dawn to dark just to survive," she glanced downward. "My hands are callused, my nails broken and dirty. My hair is going gray and there's no way to care for it or my complexion. Meanwhile, I'm foolish enough to invite a woman that has the looks of a movie star to live with us in tight quarters."

"Is this about Teresa?" I asked.

"No, not really...." she said. "It's more that I don't have a real bed or a toilet or a washing machine. I miss calling up some girlfriends and going to the movies or playing bunko. I can't go anywhere. I can't do anything that I once would have considered normal. No shopping, no relaxing, no traditions. Just work, work, work! And to top it off I feel ugly which is only compounded every time I see you leer at Teresa."

"Look, I know I look at Teresa, sometimes, but I'm absolutely not in love with her. I love you."

"Are you listening to what I'm saying?" Leslie stopped and looked me dead in the eye. "Sleep with Teresa if that's what you want. Maybe it will get it out of your system. At least you're still feeling something that takes your mind off of all this." She shook her head in discouragement. "I've never felt so worthless. We don't have a future and I'm going to die out here in the backwoods of nowhere with nothing to show for my life. I hate it!" Tears were streaming down her face. "I hate everything and I want my life back!"

I didn't know what to say so I gave her another hug. She let me hold her but she didn't respond. She just stood in the circle of my hug and pressed her forehead against my chest. Her despair was cloaking simmering anger. I couldn't give her what she wanted. I didn't know how to cheer her up or make things better. Leslie was in her own personal darkness. She was emotionally worn down by our crude living circumstances.

Perhaps I could let the boys study a couple of hours. Cameron seemed to think it was a good idea. Maybe it would help Leslie.

We headed back to the cabin in silence, both lost in our own thoughts. A crisp wind blew strongly at our backs, and we shivered as we hurried toward home.

CHAPTER TWENTY-TWO

The Meeting

LATE FALL 2016, ARKANSAS

"The greatest danger for most of us is not that our aim is too high and we miss it, but that it is too low and we reach it."

— MICHELANGELO

We settled in for the winter, dreading what this unforgiving season had in store for us. The volunteer firefighters at the station about five miles down the road hosted a get-together for Thanksgiving. They had had a tough year since they had little fuel for their truck. They never left the firehouse until they were absolutely sure that it was a real fire, and by that time, the blaze was frequently out of control. In addition, half the time when they arrived on the scene, there was no water pressure or their equipment did not work properly.

We took a large piece of back strap from the elk meat and had them grill it and slice it. We didn't mention where we had gotten it or what type of meat it was and no one asked. Others brought chicken and stuffing. One family who lived up in a remote canyon actually brought a turkey. Each family took the opportunity to offer thanks for something in their lives. Cameron asked to speak for us.

"I am thankful for a man I never met," he said when it was our family's turn to speak. "He was a great man who told folks things they needed to hear, but mostly they didn't listen. But he could see into the future. He bought some land here, and started work repairing the cabin and putting up a big fence. I'm alive and my family is alive because he prepared a way for us to survive. So the

MacCasland family is thankful for Aiden MacCasland and his visions. He was my granddad."

I was proud of my son and my father, and realized I was a link between these two men who would never lay eyes on each other. How much Dad would have loved the kids. I looked over at Leslie and caught her rolling her eyes. Obviously she was getting pretty tired of hearing about the world from my family's viewpoint and wasn't particularly thankful for the life that we were living.

I noticed Teresa eyeing Leslie thoughtfully. I suspected that she had noticed her response to this discussion. I didn't realize that she was thinking in terms of opportunity.

The next day, I found myself alone in Floyd's shed when Teresa walked in. She headed straight towards me.

"Teresa, why are you here?" I asked.

"I was looking for you." She pulled her hand through her long dark hair as if to accentuate it for my benefit.

"Yes?" I felt my mood improve just from being close to her.

"I wanted to say how impressed I am with your father. He must have been a very smart man to have had the foresight to purchase this cabin when he did."

Her tone was silky and I started to get nervous. "He was out of my league. I can't imagine what would have happened to us otherwise."

"Oh, I don't know about being out of your league. You've done a terrific job here as our leader."

I felt my chest swell up and felt a rush of gratitude. "Teresa, I'm sorry, but I've got a confession."

"Yes?" she said, leaning in close.

"I accidentally saw you bathing a few months ago, and I'm afraid I can't seem to stop thinking about you. You're so beautiful..."

"I thought that was you," she said flattered by my compliment.

"Look, I love my wife, but she's been sick lately and..."

She stared at me with her soft brown eyes and my words stopped short. Our eyes met and I sensed that we were both feeling the same need.

Teresa finished my sentence for me. "You'd like to find a way to make her better."

Her sexuality infused the entire trailer and I'm not sure if I could have held myself back had she finished my sentence differently.

"Yes, exactly," I said weakly. My heart was still pounding from her proximity and I was frozen in place. She took my face in her hands as if she recognized my condition, but also, I sensed, as a way of saying goodbye to any possible further intimacy between us.

Without notice Floyd walked in. "Hey, what you two doin' in here?"

Teresa looked at him as if she'd been caught in the act of something and quickly responded, "Nothing! Don't you ever knock?" She whisked right by him as she left abruptly.

"Knock, hell, this is my shed," Floyd growled at her passing figure.

"Floyd, it's not what this looks like," I said quickly. "I was just getting some cans of food for dinner and Teresa came in to get something."

Floyd didn't believe me for a second. "Look, you're a married man. You're lucky it was me that came in here."

"Floyd, there's nothing between us. She's really pretty, but you're right, I am a married man. We're not going to allow anything between us." This last remark came out wrong, filled with too much regret. "Nothing happened, okay?"

I left the room in confusion and Floyd just stood there and watched me leave. But something struck me as funny. The dope smoking, hooch-making, lazy bastard didn't give a hoot for moral rectitude. He was not looking out for Leslie's interest. No, he was jealous.

215

CHAPTER TWENTY-THREE

A Christmas Surprise

December 2016, Arkansas

"It was always said of him, that he knew how to keep Christmas well, if any man alive possessed the knowledge. May that be truly said of us, and all of us! And so, as Tiny Tim observed, 'God Bless Us, Every One'."

— Charles Dickens

Christmas in close quarters required considerable compromise between Leslie and Mom in how they decorated the house, what we would eat, and how the day's events would be organized. They also had to decide which one did what for which kid. There was considerable opportunity for disagreement and I was pleasantly surprised that they seemed to be working together harmoniously on this. One evening before bed Mom cornered me.

"Alex, here's my plan for Christmas," She said, pulling a much folded piece of paper out of her pocket. "I've got a list of what everyone wants or would like for gifts. Wanna go over it?"

"Yeah, sure Mom, whatever you think, although I'm not sure we can do much to make it a real Christmas."

"Ha! Shows what you know," she announced smugly" "Sean will be easy. He has a basketball and the start of a concrete playing court, but he doesn't have a hoop or backboard. You could design and build that combination, and I can knit a net. Stephanie and Hope will each get a knit doll I've figured out how to make. Jason wants a wood truck with wheels. I think we can come up with wheels from a couple of my old wooden thread spools."

I was impressed. "Wow, Mom! You've put some thought into this."

"Yes I have, but Cameron is a problem. At fourteen, he isn't really into toys anymore, at least not ones that don't need electricity or batteries."

That was almost true. He had bartered for a telescope at the Fourth of July event and spent many nights this past summer sleeping under the stars after looking at them with his prized possession. He safeguarded the telescope closely, perhaps sensing how unlikely it was that such a precision-manufactured instrument might come his way in the future.

Of all the kids, he would most remember what old Christmases had been like – spending frenzies with too many presents for everyone. We had always had a perfect tree, decorations, and a beautiful dinner with all the trimmings on the good china.

The china had been sold, the decorations were in boxes in a house in Nebraska we probably no longer owned, and we had no money to buy a tree. Of course, that wasn't a big problem – we could go into the woods and cut our own. We could improvise everything else too, I hoped.

"So what do we do about Cameron?" I asked Mom. "And Leslie is an even bigger concern. You know how much she loves Christmas."

"Yeah, unfortunately, I haven't got any new ideas for her, but we can do things for the kids at least. Now take notes. There's stuff you need to do. And we only have a few weeks to get everything done."

It snowed for five straight days the first week of December. We bundled up the kids and let them make snowmen. Then we all took a bucket and skimmed the top layer of the snowfall into it. We hiked to the cave and started dumping the snow into Floyd's freezer. It wasn't ice, but for right now it would help keep a few things cooler.

Mom brought out small bowls, filled them with clean snow, and drizzled a little honey over each. Once everyone was cold and wet,

A Christmas Surprise

we came in for hot herbal tea. Leslie had heated the water on the wood stove and made the tea from herbs we had grown in the garden. When I looked up to thank her for pouring each of us some, I noticed her eyes were filled with tears. I put my hand out to her, but she shook her head and edged away.

The kids went to bed early that night, and Leslie soon followed. Mom and I stayed in her room working on the Christmas gifts for the kids.

"Mom, have you thought more about what we can do for Leslie to give her a proper Christmas?"

Mom sighed and stopped knitting for a moment. "I've been giving it thought, son. But I think it's going to be up to you."

"Me? I don't know what to do for her."

"Alex, we've gone over this before." Her tone held a note of exasperation. "For starters, you need to try and reach Leslie. She should talk about things, not hold them in. Depression can feed on itself. Her silence isn't good."

I thought about Leslie's recent excursion into the woods. I had been in denial about her pain and had come close to physically losing her. But I still hadn't done anything to help her emotionally.

Mom interrupted my dark thoughts. "Be sure you include her in the basic Christmas plans. Since it's Leslie's favorite holiday, ask her advice on little things. We need to put as much festive work into it as we can. That may cheer her up."

The next day I took the boys out for a short walk. I explained the situation and asked them to help me think of ways to decorate and make Christmas special for their mom. They agreed and we all started comparing memories of things she had done in previous Christmases.

At dinner, I announced that we needed to conduct a Christmas tree-hunting expedition. Numerous cedars and pines were scattered around the property. We needed to find the perfect tree, and we would start looking tomorrow after chores were done. Everyone perked up at the thought of some fun in the woods.

The next afternoon, we bundled up, put Hope in the back pack carrier, grabbed the saw and some rope and set out. I casually asked Leslie what she liked in a tree.

"I like fir trees, but I'm not sure there are any around here," she said, caught up in the spirit. "The traditional triangle shape of the Christmas tree farm trees always bugged me. A Christmas tree is a little bit of nature brought indoors, so it should look like nature. And it should be tall. Floor to ceiling but with room for the angel on –"

She abruptly stopped and I saw tears roll down her face. "What's wrong, babe?" I gently asked. She didn't answer, just silently sobbed, so I put my arm around her. Mom quickly suggested the boys take her ahead to a good stand of trees that might have possibilities. I nodded my appreciation to her and said. "Come on, Leslie. I can't help if I don't understand why you are crying."

She laid her head on my shoulder, and I could feel her collapse in my embrace. "The angel is gone. All our decorations are gone. No stockings, no dishes, no Christmas dinner, no cards, no friends, no phone calls, no parties –"

"Leslie, honey, it's not that bad."

Her head jerked up and she glared at me.

She sank back into my arms, beating her fists weakly against my chest. Hope, alarmed at her mother's outburst, started to cry and kick my back in her carrier, trying to reach Leslie.

I held Leslie and murmured all the things I loved about her and how we would build a new life. She continued to sob into my shoulder. Hope was now pulling my hair, trying to climb out of the pack and over my shoulder to reach her mom. "Momma, Momma! No cry, Momma!" she yelled in my ear.

Hope finally managed to squirm up over my shoulder far enough to grab Leslie's hair and pull. It seemed to shake Leslie out of her funk, and she reached up to pull Hope free.

"Don't fuss baby, Momma's okay." Leslie's mothering instincts kicked in and she drew a curtain around herself again. Hope gradually calmed down once she was sure her mother was okay. I knew better but didn't want to aggravate her further. We managed to get Hope repositioned in the carrier just as Mom and the boys reappeared.

"No good trees over that way," Sean announced. 'I think we should head over toward where we shot the elk." He seemed oblivious to his mother's tear streaked face. Cameron eyed us both silently, while looks of concern and curiosity flashed across his face.

Mom assessed the situation and announced, "I think Sean's right. I do remember some nice trees over near that ridge line. Can you remember the way, Sean?"

"Yup! Everybody, follow me," he replied.

We kept walking and looking.

Hope found the tree. Actually, she saw a cardinal in the tree, but it was her high pitched squeal of delight and babbling about the "wed birdie, purdie-birdie, want da-birdie" while she jumped up and down in her carrier that made us all stop and stare in the direction she was reaching. The tree was awesome. It was about seven feet tall with well-formed branches and great proportions. It had a vaguely blue-gray color, and Mom said she thought it was a white pine. Whatever it was, it would do just fine. I shrugged off the baby pack and handed Hope to Leslie.

Cameron, Sean and I were just about to cut when Leslie yelled "Stop! Let's not cut it. It's about perfect and we will probably live here a long time. Let's let it grow and be the permanent MacCasland family Christmas tree. We can cut one of those over there for the house."

Her face was blotchy and her nose was red, but her eyes were shining with emotion. I wondered if I was looking at some bipolar behavioral manifestation. I made a mental note to ask Doc Mitchell the next time I saw him. Meanwhile, we cut down a less perfect specimen and hauled it home.

Decorating the tree took imagination. We had no lights and no electricity. Leslie was still too nostalgic for our old Christmas ornaments to make any suggestions, so Teresa and Mom stepped in to help. Mom got out her yarn and cut lengths of red and golden yellow. Sean collected pine cones according to Teresa's instructions.

"What are you going to do with the pine cones, Teresa?" he asked.

"I'll show you. It's something my grandmother told me she did as a little girl."

She put a cup of bleach in an empty can and dipped in each pine cone. "We have to let the cone soak for a couple of minutes so it fades. Now comes the magic part." She took an old compact of eye shadows and dusted each cone with a different color. She added a piece of yarn as a tie and hung the different colored cones on the tree.

"Wow, they are really sparkly," Sean said, admiring them. "I like them. Maybe we can frost some leaves, too."

Cameron came back from the Kingstons' with a decorating idea from Judy. She had suggested we string popcorn and holly berries and leaves. It took some patience, but after two weeks we had several long strands of this kind of garland, too. He also had a handful of colored paper that had been cut into squares. He folded them up into thirds and started cutting. Then he unfolded the paper to display a snowflake. Using yarn, he tied it to the tree.

Sean and I worked on our own ornament addition out in the cave. Sean took the smallest empty cans he could find. He punched a hole centered in the bottom of the can and ran a narrow wedge-shaped piece of metal through the hole. The top and narrowest part of the metal strip he turned and crimped over the yarn to be a holder. The other wider end he turned over a pebble and crimped closed. He had made a clapper. If he swung the can and bell gently, the can rang out a tiny tinkle. Meanwhile I had taken a much larger can and cut up from the bottom in several sections. I flared these sections out slightly and inserted a slightly smaller can underneath with similar but smaller flares; I secured the two cans together and then attached them to the bottom of a very narrow can that looked like a tomato paste can. I attached two arms a set of wings, a pebble head with a tiny copper halo. She wasn't as beautiful as our former angel tree topper, but I hoped she would do.

We walked back to the cabin with a box of our metal work. Sean placed the box on the table in front of Leslie. "These are for you, Mommy."

Leslie opened the box and carefully lifted out a number of small bells. She held one up and rang it gently. The tinkling sound made her smile, but when Hope toddled over, lifted her arms to be picked up, Leslie broke down and sobbed. She lifted Hope up in her lap and hugged her.

Hope stared at her mother in momentary confusion then reached out and pushed the corners of Leslie's mouth up into a caricature of a smile. Leslie broke into tears again, scaring Hope, who started crying herself. Leslie hugged her, hoping to reassure her that everything was okay.

Sean, Jason and Stephanie started hanging the little bells on the tree. We all added our own efforts to the tree decorating. The end result was homey but quite pretty.

Leslie looked in the box again and realized she had missed a bulky object wrapped in a rag. She carefully lifted it out and unwrapped it. The angel was rustic but was truly a labor of love, and Leslie saw that. She looked at me and smiled. "I love you, you know," she said softly.

I was greatly encouraged that she had liked my gift. "I know. I love you too."

She handed me the angel and then asked Hope if she wanted to go way up high to help Daddy put the angel on the tree. Hope clapped her hands.

I lifted her up onto my shoulders and handed her the angel. We maneuvered as close into the tree branches as we could. Hope lifted the topper and I pulled the trimmed tip close. The angel slipped onto the top. Gently I tipped the tree back to vertical.

We all stepped back and looked at our handiwork. It was not the ornate color-coordinated Christmas light themes of our past. It was the most special tree we had ever had. It was beautiful. Mom slipped into her room and came back out with an armload of fabric. I didn't recognize any of it at first, but Leslie jumped up out of her seat and hugged Mom tightly.

"How did you do this? I thought we left everything in Nebraska!"

"Well, I just left a few more clothes and made room for these. It's just not Christmas without the stocking you've had all your life." She laid the pile on the table and sorted out hers, mine, Leslie's and each of the kids – including a beautiful sequined angel stocking with Hope emblazoned on the top. Then she flipped open a flat box and presented Teresa, Jason and Stephanie with personalized stockings as well.

Teresa looked down at the stocking and burst into tears. Hope looked worried and went over to pat her on the leg. Teresa smoothed Hope's curls and said. "Hope, I'm okay." Hope brightened up and started rocking back and forth like she was dancing. Teresa laughed.

"Okay, everybody," Mom directed. "How about we hang our stockings on the mantel?"

The days before Christmas were full of sly activity, hidden projects, and whispered conversations. Strange requests were made to borrow tools or materials, even feathers from the roosters' tails. We did our best to provide. Anticipation grew and Leslie began to sing again as she went about her chores. She and Teresa consulted with Mom and Judy Kingston for menu options. The trading of

223

A Christmas Surprise

canned and preserved food and cooking ingredients escalated among the neighbors. I had my own project in the works.

A special truckload of items came into town from Fayetteville with sugar, flour, fresh oranges, and an assortment of toys and household items. Everyone was invited to come into town for a pre-Christmas swap and shop. Once again we piled into the Kingstons' wagon, loaded with boxes of handmade items, outgrown clothes, and preserved foods to swap. Everyone was buzzing about the big truck shipment, because no one knew who had sent it, not even the mayor.

Much like on the Fourth of July, the town laid out categories of stuff in different locations. This time, though, everyone in our crew scattered to "shop" on their own. We had given the kids a pillowcase so they could make their transactions in secret if necessary. Leslie and I had discussed what to do about Cameron's gift off and on for over a week. Everything else on Mom's original list had been taken care of. We were now focused on finding something for Cameron, but would keep our eyes open for small things for the other kids. Mom circled one table, made a quick exchange, and came back to us with a star chart of the constellations. She grinned and walked on. It was a start. We found a couple of books the kids had mentioned, and I found a complete ball pump with inflation needles for Sean. Leslie found a toy farm set for Hope, and I found a whole basket of yarn for Mom.

I had a project underway to create a gift for Leslie, but I had no idea what she wanted. Then I walked into the town hall and saw an emerald green quilt with a lush design of spring grass and jeweled tulips. Something about the quilt was vaguely familiar and I knew I had found the perfect gift. The lady behind the table smiled as I walked up. I reached out to stroke the silky fabric and asked how much.

"Well, I don't exactly know unless you've got cash."

I hesitated in my response. I did have a little cash, but did not want to use it, since we no longer had credit cards for emergencies.

"Hum, didn't think so," she said dryly. "Do you have anything for sewing to swap for?"

I didn't think anything we had was in that category, but I thought I'd look in the basket of yarn I had just purchased. In the bottom of the basket was a small box. I hadn't seen it before and didn't know what was in it. When I opened it, I still didn't know what it contained, other than the tiny bottle of oil. The rest of the items were weird little contraptions with odd moving shuttle-like parts and curved metal. Each piece had an arm with a slot and a tightening nut and screw. I had no idea what this stuff was for. I held out the box to her.

Her reaction was anything but nonchalant; her hands practically trembled as she took the box, and she sucked in her breath. "Oh, mister, you can have anything here you want – take two, take three! Just please let me have these!"

I picked up the emerald green quilt and a much smaller one with horses and bunnies in lovely pastel colors. Hope could use a good quilt.

"You can have those if you tell me what they are. I've never seen anything like them before."

She laughed, "Deal! These are all special attachments for a sewing machine." She picked up the most convoluted piece and told me it was a "ruffler" – whatever the heck that was. Another was a blind hemmer. She was ecstatic over each piece and thanked me profusely. I stuffed the two quilts into my pillowcase and walked away confident that I had gotten the better deal.

I did some trading for my special project, then met up with Leslie again and asked if she had had any luck with a gift for Cameron. She opened her bag and dug out a science book that covered a variety of topics, most of which Cameron had expressed interest in. I guess it was progress. I told her I would meet her again in an hour and made my way to an area of antiques. I wandered around the tables looking for anything Cameron might want. Nothing popped out at me. I was ready to leave when I noticed a small table in a corner with unusual equipment on it. I walked over. Some of it looked like old medical and dental tools, but I also spied a small scale with weights and some chemistry set equipment like beakers, vials, test tubes and so on.

The wizened old man who was displaying the stuff noted my interest. "You got any tobacco?"

I shook my head.

"What about girly magazines?"

"I'm afraid not."

The old guy sighed, then asked, "Okay, what about moonshine?" Now that I did have. There was a bottle for me to trade and two from Floyd, who had another specific request.

"Yeah, I got a bottle of that."

"Okay, it's all yours. Give me the hooch."

"What do you mean, it's all mine?"

"Just what I said, sonny." He reached under the table and handed me a box and began putting everything in it. "My pap had all this. I've been hanging on to it forever for no damn reason. I got less than three months to live and I want to enjoy them. Take all this away so the bank don't get more than they need to." He held out his hand. I put the bottle in it. "Thanks," he said, tucking it into his coat pocket. "I'm out of here." I watched him walk away whistling.

Cameron – check. Leslie – check. Sean – done? Oh yeah, at home. Hope – check. Mom? – ah the yarn. Okay, now do I get Teresa something or not? Something simple maybe.

I wandered off to find something suitable that wouldn't give anyone the wrong idea. Teresa was a perpetual distraction, but I knew I couldn't do anything that would stress Leslie any more. I might fantasize about jumping her bones, but my reality was grounded in the woman I had married, for better or for worse.

At the end of the day, everyone met back at the wagon, hugging close their pillowcases, now showing strange bulges. No one said much, but everyone was grinning. Christmas was three days away. The next couple of days were a flurry of cooking, wrapping and tying. We used old paper and string to wrap packages. The kids were constantly under the tree looking for their name on a bag or box and shaking packages in an attempt to figure out what they were getting. One of the adults was always telling them to get out from under the tree. The setting had changed, but the Spirit of Christmas was still with us.

About mid-afternoon on Christmas Eve, a stranger walked up to the cabin and knocked on the door. Teresa answered it, grabbed the man's hands and kissed them, mumbling, "Thank God, thank God, praise God," over and over. I walked over to the door and saw a priest standing there trying to get his hands free. He escaped at last and we invited the priest to come in. Teresa hurried forward to pull out a chair for him.

"Thank you, my child."

He had jet black hair shot through with silver. His green eyes were weary, attesting his current fatigue and to the difficult things he had no doubt witnessed over the past year. "Father, what brings you out here? We don't see many Catholics in this part of the woods. Around here it's mostly Baptists, Methodists or Presbyterians."

"I was just passing through town when I met Teresa in town earlier this week. She thought I might be of spiritual service to your family."

"Well, we haven't been to a real service in a long time and never around here. But it is Christmas Eve. Let me get my boy. Hey, Cam! Come on down for a minute."

Cameron appeared at the drop down and leaning his head out said, "Yeah, Dad?"

"Come down for a sec. I might need you to run an errand."

"Okay."

"So, Father...?"

"Miller."

"Father Miller, did you walk here? Are you staying somewhere?"

"Actually, I'm on a horse. She's hitched to a tree down the drive a ways. And I am a traveling priest – sort of a modern-day circuit rider. When the troubles began, my parishioners couldn't get in to church – so now I go to them. I cover a lot of territory and only get by here about once a year."

"Father, your timing is perfect. Will you stay for supper? Do you need to spend the night with us? I know Teresa and my wife would appreciate a Christmas blessing."

"Thank you, I was hoping we could have a Christmas Eve mass."

Leslie and Mom came in from feeding the goats and collecting eggs. They were surprised to find me talking to a priest.

"Father Miller, this is my wife Leslie and my mother Janine. Father Miller would like to hold a Christmas Eve service. There aren't any other churches within walking distance and my bet is that everyone around here would welcome the chance to join us. Shall I send Cameron over to the Kingstons' and see about using their barn?"

"That would be nice. They can also use the emergency contact procedure to send out word to the other neighbors, if it's okay. What time, Father?" Leslie asked.

"Say nine pm? Normally, we might want to conclude at midnight, but everyone still has to be able to get home afterwards. What's your emergency contact procedure?"

"Basically, we have some neighbors that still have phone lines," I said. "They provide the backbone for the system. A few neighbors also have electricity, access to the Internet or cell phones. When something happens that everyone needs to know about, we send out phone calls, emails, and text messages. Each of the recipients blows their horn if it applies to their area, and this notifies everyone that can hear a horn that there's a message that they need to get. At that point, everyone then contacts their designated emergency contact to get the message. It's kind of designed as a local defensive system, but I think people wouldn't mind if we used it on this occasion. The Kingstons have a phone and they can start the process for us. Cam, run and ask them."

"Come back quickly," Leslie added. "Dinner will be soon."

Fifteen minutes later the sound of horns could be heard echoing all around us.

The barn was crowded. My guess is that only a handful of people in the room had ever been in a Catholic mass before, but it didn't matter. It was Christmas and this was very special. Father Miller was overwhelmed and had to ask if anyone had bread or wine. He was prepared for about ten and nearly a hundred people showed up. Judy supplied some extra bread and some wine and we started the service. Teresa, Mom and Leslie listened intently to the words of the service, but I'm afraid my mind wandered off.

I wondered when I had begun to question everything I had been taught and accepted as a kid. Some of it had to do with Dad, some with the people I had met and worked with over the years. Dad's messages had since been proven true. The jury was still out on all this church stuff. I was pretty sure it wasn't God's fault we were in the mess we were in – if there really was a God. I felt both a deep comfort in the familiarity of the service and a vague uneasiness about my presence here when I wasn't sure what, if anything, I believed anymore. The whisper of "Alex" grabbed my attention and I looked over to Leslie, but her eyes were closed and she seemed to be lost in prayers. I wasn't sure I should take communion, but decided to do so when I realized it might mean something to Leslie and the kids. After the final blessing we walked out of the barn to find soft flakes of snow drifting down here and there. We hustled home to beat the weather.

I got everyone settled in bed, moving Teresa and Stephanie into Mom's room for the night before I finished the last details on my

A Christmas Surprise

project. Father Miller, who was setting up a bed roll by the fire, watched.

"What are you putting together?" he asked.

"I'm completing the inside wiring to an old wind turbine that I'm hoping just might work. It was a one-of-a-kind unit and the bearings are shot – so it's on its last legs. But maybe, just maybe we can get a little juice out of it before it gives out for good. I couldn't test it out, so I just set up everything. Tomorrow will tell."

"Batteries?"

"Yeah, I have a bank of two so far. Don't know how long they'll hold, but all the circuits seem to be good. You know anything about wiring?"

He laughed softly, "Yeah, I wasn't always a priest. Used to help my dad. He was in construction. I'll look things over for you, if you'd like."

"I'm not entirely sure of what I've done. My toolbox is on the shelf there, if you need anything."

"Go on to bed, Alex. I'll check it out."

"Thanks, Father. Merry Christmas!"

"Same to you."

Christmas morning dawned dark and still. There was no wind, no sound. Everything felt muffled like the pure silence of a deep forest. I got up and went to the kitchen window. A world of white greeted me. It must have started snowing heavily after we went to bed. There looked to be a foot or more on the ground. There was not a sound or movement outside – perfect stillness.

"Good morning" greeted me from behind.

I jumped and spun around. Father Miller was squatting near the wood stove with a piece of wood in his hand. He poked the glowing coals and laid a stick over them. He blew softly and a flame began to grow.

"So, when will the children be up? Frankly, I'm surprised it's you and not one of them."

"I think it's the quiet from the snow. Didn't sound right to me and probably has allowed the kids to really sleep well. And, well, I did kinda want to see if my surprise worked. Why are you up?"

"Habit," he responded. "I spent a couple of years in a monastery. We had services every three hours round the clock. I've just finished Matins. And if you'll pull that chain over there…" He pointed at a thin chain that hung down the wall by the front door.

I walked over and gave it a gentle tug. The room lit up with a soft glow from the lights I had strung from the ceiling near the tree, around the kitchen, and over the fireplace mantel.

"Oh man, this is great! Leslie will love this! Thank you!"

He smiled. "I didn't do anything but check the connections. You did everything right."

"Do you need to sleep more? Or should I put hot water on for tea?"

Overhead, we heard noises and knew the silence was ending. I quickly turned off the lights.

Cameron, Sean and Jason scrambled down the attic ladder and pushed it closed again. Jason ran to the tree looking for a package to open, but stopped at the fireplace when he realized the stockings were full. Father Miller, whose sock had also been added and filled, was taking his down.

"Can you get mine down, too?" Jason asked.

"You better wake up your mom or she'll be pissed," Sean advised him, then realized what he had said and clapped his hand over his mouth. "Sorry, Father. Am I in trouble?"

The priest and I started laughing which confused Sean even more.

"No, I don't punish children for crude but truthful sentiments. Teresa would probably be upset if she missed sharing your joy on this blessed day. Jason, why don't you wake her up – gently! And

231

Sean you should check on your mother, too." Father Miller cocked an eyebrow at me with a nod to Mom's room. I grinned and went to wake her up.

When everyone had gathered, some excited, some sleepy still, Father Miller gave a blessing and handed out everyone's stocking. "Let the bedlam begin," he intoned with a grin and the kids cheered. Our stockings had simple things: a new toothbrush, plastic pocket combs, pens, pencils, small writing pads, some hard candy, a book, some tiny toys for the kids like marbles, playing cards, and little dolls. Everyone got an orange, a pair of mittens from Mom, and a flashlight. We were thrilled.

Sean asked to be the present passer and took up his post by the tree. He picked up a package, located and deciphered the gift label, and then passed it to that person. For presents without labels he would sheepishly look at Mom, and she would motion with her head who the recipient was supposed to be. Soon everyone had a package – even Father Miller, who seemed pleasantly surprised. Everyone opened their presents. Hope and Stephanie had their homemade dolls, Jason had his truck, Sean had a sweater from Mom with a basketball design, Father Miller had a muffler and knit hat, Mom had a basket of yarn, Leslie had a set of hand molds of Hope, Sean and Cameron's right hand, Floyd had a shadow box of all his medals, Teresa had a set of clips and bows for her hair, and I had a wooden box lined with fabric to keep my watch and ring in.

Sean got a card with a map that led him outside, around the house, and to his concrete pad. When he looked up and saw his backboard and hoop with a knit net from Grandma, he whooped it up.

Leslie loved her emerald quilt. "Raina made this from my old party dress! I love what she did." So that's why it looked so familiar. When she looked at me, her face was flushed, and her smile told me I had done well.

Teresa got a faux fur jacket and Mom got some warm work boots. Cameron loved his chemistry stuff and scale. Father Miller got a small satchel of elk hide big enough to hold his Bible and traveling communion set, and I got elk hide slippers. Hope snuggled up with her little quilt to play with her farm set while Jason and Stephanie played with the little toys they had gotten.

Leslie had more color and spirit than any time since her illness. She was everywhere at once, laughing and talking and hugging the kids. Maybe she had come out of the darkness. I sent a prayer out to anyone who might be listening. It couldn't hurt.

"Leslie?" She glanced over at me and raised her eyebrows. "Pull the chain by the door there."

With a quizzical look at me, she walked over and pulled. The silence was immediate; everyone except Father Miller and me was stunned. Then everyone was talking, cheering, and clapping. Mom and Teresa grinned. Hope stared and kept looking around the room as if she had never seen lights. Leslie dashed over and threw her arms around me, her eyes shining and her smile as bright as the lights I had made.

"Any chance of getting some quiet time with Santa a little later?" she asked as she stroked the back of my neck.

"Yep, I'll bet he'd sure like to fill your stocking."

"Even if I haven't been good?" she quipped.

"Babe, you've never been better." I said, hoping that this might actually be the case.

CHAPTER TWENTY-FOUR

Business of the Day

January 2017, Arkansas

"Only as a warrior can one withstand the path of knowledge. A warrior cannot complain or regret anything. His life is an endless challenge, and challenges cannot possibly be good or bad. Challenges are simply challenges."

— Carlos Castaneda

Winter was an adjustment. We worked inside a lot. The ground was frozen and snow-covered or wet and muddy. We couldn't do much in the fields. By the end of January, things had really gotten tough. We had no money, little to barter with, and we were running out of Floyd's food cans. I was pondering what to do when Dr. Mitchell knocked on the door.

"Hi Alex, is Floyd around?"

"He spent the night at Michael's place and hasn't come back yet. Can I help you with something?"

His expression became guarded. "Ah, I'm not sure. Has Floyd ever spoken to you about his medicinal sources?"

I was quick to put two and two together. One of the few things Floyd did that resembled work was maintaining a small plot of land in the woods. On it were some very healthy and potent pot plants. Originally Floyd had grown these weeds for his own "medicinal requirements," though for the life of me, I never knew anything that was wrong with Floyd in a health sense other than his apathy. Occasionally, he had sold some to other veterans and friends. No one ever reported him, however.

Armed with this knowledge I answered Doc's question more directly. "Do you mean do I know about Floyd's pot crop? Yeah. I know."

The relief on Doc's face was obvious. "Alex, I can't get any drugs from anywhere anymore. It's a real problem, because several of my patients need something for pain. All I can think of is medicinal marijuana. I know we aren't out west where it's legal, but I'm willing to write prescriptions for anyone who needs pain medication. The sheriff's mother – for Pete's sake – has cancer and there's nothing I can do. I told him pot might make her comfortable for her last few weeks. He's all for it. You think Floyd would be willing to sell small amounts on a regular basis?"

"I don't know, Doc. I'll bet he'll do it, though I suspect he'll probably let you make the delivery to the sheriff's mother. I'll ask."

"Thanks, Alex. Here's a list of my patients in priority order. Many won't make it to spring, but they don't need to die in agony if Floyd can help." He turned to leave then stopped, "How's your wife doing?"

"She's doing much better, thanks for asking." I said.

The doctor studied my face with a little more interest than seemed normal. "I'm glad to hear that. She seems like a special lady."

"Yes, she is." I replied a little taken back by something I couldn't quite put my finger on.

He smiled and walked down the drive.

Floyd appeared an hour later. I explained what Dr. Mitchell had said and he nodded gravely. "I heard a long time ago medicines were getting scarce. I planted extra last year."

While I hadn't smoked pot since college, I was pleased to discover a value for our new cash crop. Before I knew it, I was on a bicycle pedaling grass to the neighbors on Doc's list in exchange for food, cash or anything they thought useful to barter with. Some laughed about having a pre-death estate sale and offered anything

235

Business of the Day

they owned. It was sad, but most of them were glad for anything to ease their pain.

Will's interest, expressed casually to me one day after he had heard about our recent efforts, was certainly a surprise, though in hindsight, perhaps it shouldn't have been. He had a number of ailments and pot was available while other medicines were not. We gladly bartered our weed for food and seeds for the next year's crop, and eventually we even obtained some livestock in this fashion. From my perspective, Floyd was finally earning his keep, albeit not in the way I had expected ten months ago. How long ago that seemed!

For the first time we added a small pig. We could ill afford pets of any kind and Sean latched onto our newest addition immediately and spent hours playing with him. I sighed and figured he would probably have to learn about life on a farm the hard way. We would see.

A newly weaned gray kitten who wandered in the gate one day kept Hope entertained for hours as she followed him around the house. I questioned whether we really needed a cat, but I was sold on the idea by our determined children who swore it would pay for its keep by controlling vermin. Given the lack of mousetraps, I agreed the idea had merit. And Leslie smiled every time Dorian curled up with her and purred. She wasn't as thrilled when he started leaving the remains of his catches on the front porch for us, but he was just trying to make a contribution.

Like our neighbors, we were a long way from a medical facility and would be hard pressed to get help in an emergency. We had maintained a few gallons of gas in our tank, just in case we needed to get the twenty miles to Harrison. We prayed we would never have to use it.

The first warning that we had some unexpected medical issues coming our way became apparent in early January when Teresa started showing. Knowing our limited capacity to help Teresa with pre-natal care or childbirth, I feared for the well-being of this soon-to-be member of our little band.

I knew I hadn't helped father her child, so I headed to the cave. It was the most likely place to find the one who had.

"Hi, Floyd!" I said, walking over to the freezer for a peek. "How's the ice holding up?"

"Pretty good this year. Course, I haven't been eating so many Popsicles. Gotta think about the future more."

"What's wrong?"

"Ah….well, it's … ah…" He flushed bright red and blurted out "I'm the dad of Teresa's kid." Seeing my nod of agreement, he went on, "I never had much family, and I don't know what to do. I know she ain't in love with me or nothin'. I'd probably marry her if she wanted, but I don't think she'd do it. I been tryin' to think what I want my kid to know about me when he's grown. Damnation!"

"So, Floyd, what do you think Teresa wants?"

He murmured something to himself and cocked a bushy eyebrow at me. "Hey, I got eyes." He proceeded to roll them toward me. "What she apparently wants is standing right here. And I can't say as how I blame her." He sighed, finished his treat and stood up. He reached out a big paw to me and said, "I'd be much obliged if you'd be sweet to her. I'm not askin' you to leave Leslie and marry Teresa, but if it falls out that way, would you just let me be Uncle Floyd to the kid?"

"I have no intentions of having a relationship with Teresa or leaving Leslie." I blurted. "If you have an interest in her, I'd suggest you get after it. You never know when competition is going to show up."

Floyd just shook his head as if he couldn't believe that he could get that beautiful girl.

CHAPTER TWENTY-FIVE
The Stranger
Spring 2017, Arkansas

"Man is the only animal that laughs and weeps, for he is the only animal that is struck with the difference between what things are and what they ought to be."

— William Hazlitt

On a cold, drizzling day in February, a stranger arrived on foot, walking slowly and wearing a pair of sandals made from old tires. He wore a dirty ski jacket, and his shirt and pants were in tatters. He was unshaven, bony, and worn by wind and sun. He carried a tattered bag over his shoulder. Several of us watched with apprehension as he made his way to the cabin door. I assumed he was just another beggar on the road wanting food, and Mom met him at the door with a piece of bread and a glass of water. When he saw Mom, his eyes grew wide. He stood stock still for a moment, and then dropped his bag and rushed toward her, but she threw the bread and the plastic glass at him in surprise. She grabbed a broom and gave him a whack.

He let out a yelp wailing, "Mom, it's me!"

Mom froze, while recognition turned to joy, and her scowl became a look of gladness as she finally recognized her youngest son. "Ace!"

The rest of us, who had started forward to help defend Mom, instead caught hold of Ace in hugs and kisses, and shared Mom's joy.

Ace had found us from the directions Mom had given him before we left Nebraska. Everyone was talking at once. Mom was telling Ace about the place; Cameron was telling his long lost Uncle

Ace about our crops and the pot operation; Leslie was asking him what he wanted for dinner; Sean was asking him where his motorcycle was; Teresa was introducing herself; and I was trying to figure out where he had been and what he had been doing. The last time we had seen him, he had been muscular and in good health. This scarecrow who had come back to us shocked me.

After a hot lunch of soup and a couple of hours' rest, I finally managed to take Ace aside. The rest and the food were starting to recharge him, but I was still stunned by his appearance.

"Ace, what happened to you?" We were walking in the woods. The usual smell and haze of wood smoke hung in the air, but it was dry and not too cold for this time of year. I had wanted to get him away from the others to talk, especially if news came up that were not for children's ears, or perhaps the kind of things that he didn't even want Mom or Leslie to hear.

"Alex, the country isn't what it used to be." He glanced at me with a look of disappointment and pain. I waited for him to finish this explanation, but he just continued walking.

"How so?" I asked, not wanting to probe, but also not willing to accept his cryptic answer as the last word on this subject.

"I heard stories of gulags in Russia, but never realized that it could happen here. Not in America." He let these words sink in and then continued his explanation.

"Last summer I left Los Angeles on my motorcycle to head here. My plan was to take I-40 straight across and cut up Highway 7 once I got into Arkansas. Anyway, I was approaching Barstow, where I-40 splits from I-15 to Vegas. I was traveling slowly to save gas, with my helmet on, my bike in good shape – all the lights working – everything." He paused as if replaying a too often run scene in his mind.

"Ace?"

He shook his head and continued "This police car came up behind me, turned on his siren, and pulled me over. I stopped and waited for him to come up to the bike. He approached me and said something about being on the lookout for a criminal on a motorcycle. He looked me over and then asked for my driver's license, and said something about my being from out of state. He called in on his radio, and before I knew it, I was in the back of his police car and my bike was being hauled away by a tow truck."

"He thought you were the crook?" I was trying to piece together why a cop would do that.

"Naw... but they figured out pretty quickly that I wasn't anyone who'd be missed in that part of the country. I was exactly what they were looking for. They locked me in a cell with some real dirt bags, and the next morning they put me in front of a judge who sentenced me to six months of hard labor. I still don't know what the charges were.

"The next day, they put me on a prison bus that took me west to a heavy oil mining operation that used prisoners for dangerous jobs and manual labor. About thirty of us were housed in a compound with a fence around the site and concertina wire above the fence. There was a guard tower on the east side of the compound and we lived in military style Quonset huts with a bunch of beds lined up on either side."

He paused, and though I was sickened by his tale, I let him gather his thoughts.

"Each morning we were handed a shovel and told to dig this oil and sand mixture out of the ground and dump it in a bin to be treated and the oil extracted. We got lunch some days, other days not. We were told to knock off around dark for dinner, though sometimes we worked later, and sometimes there was no dinner. The oil deposits were only a few hundred feet deep," he explained. Mostly our job was digging out the deep deposits and then handing them off to other guys who would carry them to the surface. It was an open pit mine – no roof, and all along the walls you could see the oil oozing down the sand along the side of the hole. A gas flare at the bottom of the pit burned continuously and jumped up in size occasionally as gas seeped out of the walls at various rates." He spread his arms to demonstrate. "The mine was about two hundred feet deep and it was expanding, getting deeper and wider daily. They said we were the 'Tulare tools'– some joke about the oil zone, I think." He paused, then went on with his account.

"We barely had enough food to keep going, and they didn't go easy on anyone that couldn't pull his load. Punishment was nasty and vicious; most of the guards were real sadists. Some guys died from beatings. Other guys couldn't keep up after a while, and got taken away to God knows where. It was pretty clear to us there wasn't a good way out." He looked over at me after this last remark, and the look on his face told me he might not be sharing everything with me.

"You're saying the government held you prisoner and forced you to do hard labor even though you hadn't committed a crime?" He was my brother and I knew he must have been telling the truth, but his story seemed incredible.

"Yeah, Alex, that's the way it was. I was an out-of-state male in a place that needed slave labor, and I paid the price. I didn't even try to make my one phone call – maybe that's what tipped them off that I wouldn't be missed. With oil prices what they are, they must have made an incredible amount of money for the county or city or whoever it was. I never did figure out who was actually getting the money. They used us instead of steam to extract this sludge oil and I'd bet we got close to 100% of it out of there. Their only energy cost was our food and that was severely limited." He paused, sitting on a rock to catch his breath or rest his legs.

"I know you know more about oil extraction than I do, but from what I've learned about these types of oil fields, they're lucky to get half the oil out with steam or other methods. Having us dig – well, it was a pretty astute way to extract oil, if you didn't put any value on human life. A few of the guards weren't really into this whole operation, but most of them were real bastards."

"How did you get away?" I was starting to wonder if the police might still be after him, and what that might mean for us if they came looking for him here.

"At the end of the six months I had been sentenced to, they just told me I was done. All the other prisoners couldn't believe it, since only one or two had been allowed to leave in the previous six months and more than that had died or disappeared. Maybe letting a prisoner go occasionally just gave the other prisoners hope that they would get out one day if they were model prisoners – I don't know. Maybe it was because I was sinking physically, and they weren't going to get much more labor out of this mule. I just accepted my release as a gift from God and kept my mouth shut.

"I was returned to police headquarters in Barstow and was given a set of clothes and shown the door. I asked about my bike that had been impounded, and they wanted me to pay the back storage fees that I couldn't afford. I didn't think it was a good issue to push – not sure they would have given it back to me even if I could have paid, because I really doubt it was really still there. I'll bet some cop has a nice bike at home now. Anyway, I was mainly thinking about putting miles between the police station and me before they changed their minds. On my way out, I noticed a load of fresh faces sitting on the mining bus. I felt sorry for those poor guys, but didn't want to risk getting crossways with any of the cops by talking to the new prisoners; they'd learn soon enough about their new home."

He scowled harshly at the memory, at his feelings of helplessness.

"Barstow had changed so much I couldn't believe it. Almost no cars were on the roads – trash was everywhere. There were a lot of bicycles around, so I guess the town was small enough to get around without a car. The fast food places and restaurants had shut down and looked like they'd been looted. Most of the stores were boarded up, just a few still open. It was bizarre."

"How'd you get here?" I asked.

"Determination mostly. I snuck on an eastbound train passing through. It's about the only way to get across country now. Lots of folks doing it – whole families even. I guess it's like hobos a hundred years ago. Share the ride, share food if you can, don't eat in front of others if you can't. I just kept hopping trains until one made it to Little Rock, and I walked from there. Got a couple of rides from trucks and wagons along the way."

"God, Ace, I had no idea things were this bad. How do they get away with it?"

Ace looked at me soberly, "I don't know, bro, but they do. I know it seems unbelievable, but it's happening. People are desperate, and oil is like gold. It's a bad combination for bringing out some vile aspects of our natures." He grinned, which made me feel a little better about how he was handling this, but I was still furious.

"Damn it, Ace! I'm shocked, no, I'm pissed you were treated like that. I can't believe this happened in the United States. There must be something we can do to stop these bastards. Write our congressman? Inform the media? Sue them? How the hell did they get away with this?" I was seething and vicariously felt the moral outrage of the violation Ace had experienced. But all my ideas for retribution sounded hollow and impotent.

"Bro, give it up. I'm just happy to be here," Ace replied weakly. "It's going to take a while, though, for me to recover." He coughed up a piece of coarse black phlegm and spit toward a tree, then just sat there gasping; his breath rattling in and out like he had asthma. He closed his eyes and seemed to be just enjoying the sun on his face.

My thoughts were still in turmoil. I guess we had little choice but to accept what had happened and move on. I swear to God, however, had we been closer to them, I would have taken my shotgun, gone down there and… and done what? I thought finally. Take on the whole police department? Find the crooked judge?

As my anger eased, I wondered how to help Ace. Besides food and sleep, he mostly just needed us to be here for him. We needed to work hard at making him feel like his old confident self. That was the best belated Christmas gift we could give him.

Welcome home, little brother, welcome home.

By March, Ace was strong enough to hunt and went out several times, returning with little to show other than a few birds almost too small to eat. He didn't care – hunting beat farming any day, which was probably why Cameron frequently asked to go with him. They had developed a special bond and I let them both go when I could spare them. One evening Ace mentioned he wanted to follow an old elk trail toward the Buffalo River. According to Cameron, who later told me the events as he recalled them, their midnight departure from the cabin and compound was uneventful. They never dreamed things would end up as they did.

Ace carried a rifle he had borrowed from the Kingstons', and Cameron carried my shotgun. Ace had a water bottle and some jerky in a small pack. They both wore long pants, wood colored clothing, and well worn tennis shoes with holes starting to appear in the sides. I wondered when we'd get the chance to buy them another pair of shoes, but for now they were reasonably shod. They carried some cord in case they were fortunate enough to shoot something large enough to carry home. Cameron was tall but lean. Any day we expected him to hit a growth spurt and start filling out a bit.

The landscape was changing rapidly. What had been isolated woods when we had arrived a year ago had begun to show the presence of many more people. A series of new trails were scattered through the woods, and small tree stumps were left along many of the trails. The trails made it easier to get around the woods, though we saw fewer wild animals.

Ace picked out a location in a large tree just on the edge of a worn trail that allowed him to see down its length toward the water. They both climbed up about ten feet and each looked down the trail in a different direction waiting for a deer or a rabbit to cross their vision.

They were silent, waiting for game, and Ace dozed a little, intermittently, leaning against the tree. Just as he closed his eyes, he'd catch himself and sit upright in a losing effort to keep awake.

Suddenly, Cameron blasted at a small object down the trail. Ace turned just in time to see a small deer stumble, then stagger back to its feet and head into the woods.

Cameron had only wounded the deer, and they needed to track it to finish the job. Cameron bounded down the tree and Ace jumped after him. A small limb snagged Ace's shirt and his forward movement was redirected into a misstep that sent him crashing to the ground. When he put out his arm to stop his fall, a sickening crunch sounded. Cameron stopped dead and turned back toward his uncle.

"Are you okay?" Cameron asked. From the way Ace was groaning and writhing in pain, it was obvious that he was badly hurt.

"My arm!" was all he could get out between groans.

Cameron strained to roll Ace over, and as he did so the groans coalesced into a scream of pain. Cameron could see the damage clearly, a compound fracture with the bone protruding from the skin of the upper arm. Cameron felt sick.

"Uncle Ace," he said, "I'm going to have to work on your arm and stop the bleeding. You've broken your arm bad and we need to get you back home. I'm sorry, but this is going to hurt."

Cameron flew into motion, trying to stop the blood and splint the broken bone. It was a tough task to get the bone back in place as blood poured out of Ace's arm. Finally, the bone returned beneath the skin – nowhere near where it needed to be but at least in a position where Cameron could apply some pressure to stop the bleeding. Ace coached him through, between gasps, applying a loose tourniquet. Cameron splinted the arm and used his rope to lash several solid pieces of wood around the arm. Ace was trying to be stoic, but he was nearly delirious with the pain.

In the good old days, Cameron would have used a cell phone to call ahead for an ambulance, but not now. He had to get Ace out on his own or go for help. Once he had Ace's arm strapped down, he tried a couple of ways of lifting him to see if he could carry him. Ace weighed less than a hundred and fifty pounds after his recent ordeals, but even so, Cameron weighed even less. He just couldn't move Ace any distance by himself, not without hurting him, and he didn't think Ace could walk very far.

The issue was settled when Ace passed out, which Cameron knew was not a good sign. So Cameron covered him with his shirt, left the water and the jerky and the gun near by and lit out to get help.

His heart racing, Cameron reached the house twenty minutes later, covered in blood, and breathlessly explained what had happened. Cameron knew how to reach him by the woods, but neither he nor we could reach him by road. I sent Leslie to the Kingstons' house to see if they could call an ambulance and left immediately with Floyd and Cameron.

We set out at a run, stopping only for Cameron to get his bearings and direct us on toward Ace. Despite Cameron's good sense of direction and woods sense, though, we got lost twice and had to retrace our steps, finally finding Ace after what seemed an hour but was really much less.

Ace was on the edge of consciousness, groggy and weak from loss of blood. We looked for branches we could tie together to construct a stretcher. Floyd simply reached down and put him over his shoulder, letting his broken arm hang in front of his chest. "Let's go," he said.

We walked alongside helping keep his hurt arm from banging against anything, but even so Ace moaned constantly. As willing as Floyd was to carry him back by himself, he wasn't as young as he used to be. We had to switch about every ten minutes, carefully protecting Ace's arm as we handed him back and forth. The trip back to the house cost us more than an hour. Leslie was waiting outside alone when we arrived.

"Leslie, where's the ambulance?" I asked blankly.

"They won't come," she said. "We don't have insurance."

"What?" I asked incredulously.

Instead I loaded Ace into the back of the van. Cameron jumped in and tried to keep Ace awake and stable during the trip. He wiped his forehead with a wet cloth and held him down on the seat so that he wouldn't fall off if the vehicle came to an abrupt stop. Ace wasn't looking good, and he was barely conscious.

I sped to the hospital in Harrison. We knew where it was and had always planned for such a trip, yet had never actually been there before. We offloaded Ace at the emergency room entrance and I went to park the car.

I raced back into the emergency room reception area. It was a poorly-lit, grimy area with a number of broken floor tiles and soiled chairs. I was met at the door.

"I'm sorry," the attendant announced, "we can't help you. You don't have insurance. We tried to tell you before you made the trip."

"Wait a second," I stammered. "This is a hospital. Isn't there anything you can do?"

"Well, you could pay cash," she suggested. "In the old days we were set up to handle charity cases, but that funding dried up long ago. Most of our staff has left, and we are now down to a small cadre of workers. We don't have the latitude to offer free medical care."

"This is an emergency," I pointed out. "What can we do to get some help?"

"Like I said, sir, you could pay cash," she persisted.

We didn't have any cash, and there was no way we could convince them we'd pay them back in the future. I fingered the wedding band on my hand praying that it might be worth enough to get them started.

"Would you accept our car as payment?"

She shook her head. "Sir, cars are cheap these days. I could have my choice of cars for practically nothing, and I'm afraid that your van is a big vehicle even if it is a hybrid. There just isn't much of a market for it."

"What if we borrowed against our property?" I asked.

"You have property? Property you own?"

"Yes, about forty acres down near Jasper."

She brightened up. "Have a seat."

Over the next fifteen minutes we exchanged details about our property and signed a promissory note against the property to pay for the cost of Ace's medical treatment. Only after this long negotiation did they roll Ace into the treatment area of the emergency room and start working on his arm.

Ace was lucky not to lose the arm. If we hadn't gotten medical treatment when we did, the loose tourniquet would have meant the end of his arm.

The compound fracture needed a difficult and complicated operation to restore his arm to full function. The surgeon had long since moved to Australia, leaving surgery in the hands of a general practitioner. A shortage of titanium meant this doctor had to use less expensive metals to screw the bones together. When the operation ended, Ace was rolled into the recovery room where he came to several hours later. He was heavily medicated and seemed to be doing okay. We would just have to wait and see what the doctor said.

Cameron had met a girl his age in the waiting room. Sophia's grandfather was there for surgery on a blocked artery. Cameron and Sophia talked and discovered that she lived a couple of miles down the road from us. She was pretty and neatly dressed, and Cameron lost little time in introducing himself.

Though I heard various snippets of their conversation, I was too absorbed in my own thoughts to pay much attention to them. I had had to sign a note on our property to get treatment for Ace - which meant that everything we had worked for was not at risk. I had not thought twice about doing this, but maybe I should have. We did not have the funds to cover this procedure and earning enough money to pay this obligation was not an easy proposition in our current circumstances. What would happen to us if we lost the Ark? I shuddered in fear and worry as the reality of our situation sank in.

CHAPTER TWENTY-SIX

Spring

Spring 2017, Arkansas

"The best way to predict the future is to invent it."

— Theodore Hook

We were about to start another long growing season. Ace had returned from the hospital after a few days and seemed to be healing fine. Teresa had been a real help, tenderly caring for Ace as he recovered from his broken arm, and looking after his needs. The doctor had advised him to keep his arm immobilized for the next few weeks, so Ace was unable to do a lot for himself. Teresa was nearing term, so they made a good pair, each helping the other as they could. I stumbled upon Ace in the outhouse, and the two of us engaged in some brotherly conversation as we conducted the business at hand.

"Ace, what's the deal between you and Teresa?"

"I like her. I think she sees a lot more in me than I can see in myself."

"Yeah, that's a funny thing about women. They tend to see us in black and white, it seems."

He gave me a brotherly wink. "Well, I can't say that for all women, but this one seems to want me more than I think she needs me. I'm giving things lots of time."

"Sounds like a plan. By the way, keep an eye on the big guy."

He had already picked up on that connection. "This may sound funny, but Floyd has essentially told me that he's giving Teresa to me to look after, but wants to remain Uncle Floyd to his kid."

"Some things I'll never understand," I said.

There was plenty of work to do in preparation for spring planting, but Cameron asked if he could go visit Sophia. He would be working hard in the near future, and this seemed like a good chance for him to have some time with someone his age, something that had been almost completely missing since our move to the farm. We had heard from her that there was a push to get kids into small neighborhood schools for at least a few hours a week and that got Cameron's attention. He wanted to ride his bike to the proposed school location with Sophia.

Cameron had started to grow again, and none of his clothes fit very well anymore. Ace loaned him a shirt and some jeans, and while they were large, he had that pant-drooping teenage boy look that had been popular.

From what we could gather, he and Sophia had set a time to meet in advance, since we didn't have a phone. We weren't going to question him on this point, and he headed out down the side of the highway on his old bicycle with a sense of urgency I rarely saw in his farming efforts.

Sophia's house was nothing special by the standards of ten years before, but the fact that it had been unchanged over this period was quite remarkable. Her father was a roustabout on an oil platform and made good money. He shuttled back and forth on a three-month rotation, and they brought him out to the platform by boat, since helicopters had long ago been deemed too expensive for anything but emergency use.

I imagined someone taking a family picture of us at the farm. It would have featured a pathetic scene with a bunch of thin, worn characters in threadbare clothes standing in front of a rundown cabin. It would have looked like a portrait from the 1850s or any third world village – except that most of us had nice teeth.

Sophia's house, on the other hand, was clearly a middle-class affair. While they did grow some of their own food, they had

Spring

access to a small store that also featured a local butcher and frozen foods. They had electricity, phones, television, computers, a washer and dryer, a truck and a car, some dogs, and a swimming pool. Sophia had an older sister away at college. Cameron was careful not to let his awe regarding their lifestyle show and directed his attention toward Sophia and one of her friends that joined them for the day.

When Cameron returned, he was quiet and thoughtful. He remembered the way we had lived before the oil crisis, and saw that Sophia's family still lived this way. Suddenly after all this effort struggling to make ends meet on the farm, he didn't feel so proud of our accomplishments. He felt poor and backward and embarrassed by our living conditions.

As we returned to our fieldwork over the next several days, we had a number of opportunities to talk and pass time. At first it was just idle chatter about innocuous things like the methods we were going to try to use to enhance our crop production this year. Then one afternoon while we were having a drink of water after having spent the last several hours plowing, Cameron stopped short. "Dad, what happened to us?"

"What do you mean?"

"Well, how is it that we are out here living hand to mouth each day and Sophia's family hasn't seemed to change their way of life at all?" he queried.

"It has to do with economics," I said.

"Like?" he asked.

"Well, we would still be living like Sophia's family if your mother or I had been able to find a job like her father has. It's a very comfortable lifestyle and we miss it." I gestured at the field around us. "However, there are a lot fewer families like Sophia's out there these days. Sophia's father works for one of the few industries that survived and actually prospered from the oil disruptions. Crude oil derived products have been desperately short and the industries that extract or produce them have continued to make money."

"But didn't you work in the oil business?"

"Yes, I did, but I changed jobs. Here's the part you have to understand. Very few other sectors in our economy have been left standing. Many companies have collapsed and others were sold to corporations in other countries. There is still a lot of food production, but more and more of it is being grown at farms like ours. Large-scale food production operations can't function without fuel and fertilizer that are just too expensive these days."

"But why do we have to farm at all?" he asked.

"In many ways, Cameron, we now live in what is essentially a developing country. There are a small cadre of very prosperous people who own some of the most vital and lucrative resources in our country, a tiny Middle Class – Sophia's family is a perfect example of these people – and a large number of lower-class and very poor people trying to scratch out a living. I'm afraid we're at the upper end of the lower class at the moment. But our land gives us real wealth that we'll eventually figure out how to get more value out of."

"Are you saying that we're actually doing well?" Cameron asked in disbelief. He had only known two lifestyles and ours seemed a whole lot more frugal than the one still enjoyed by Sophia's family.

I started to get defensive and reflexively switched into my economics professor mode. "Cheap, abundant fuel made the United States a great power, but our economy was too oil focused and badly designed. All of our big houses in the distant suburbs and large cars basically turned out to be wasted investments in hindsight. We were living in La-La land."

"So we're in trouble?"

"I think we can do better, but we're going to have to retool, put up with a lot of short term inconvenience during the transition, and find some longer term energy solutions. Does this answer your question?"

Spring

Cameron looked puzzled. A number of these points clearly went over his head.

Cameron started to raise another question, but changed his mind. He shook his head and then headed back into the field.

Maybe I should have just told him in simple terms that we were screwed. I knew that all my intellectual arguments were smoke screens to mask our desperate circumstances. The path back to a better life was probably not even in our control. We would be hard pressed to earn enough income from our food operations to even pay off the note from Ace's operation that would allow us to keep our property and grow enough food to feed ourselves.

Teresa went into labor at three am. She woke Leslie and me with a soft knock on our bedroom door and a moan of deep pain. Leslie knew that sound and became awake instantly. I was awakened a split second later with a gentle elbow to the ribs. Leslie slipped out of bed and took Teresa's arm to lead her back to bed. Another moan rose from her before Leslie got her to a chair. "Oh, Christ! That's only a couple of minutes apart!" Our plan to get her to the hospital in Harrison was not possible.

Teresa had backed up against the corner of the kitchen counter and had a forearm along each countertop. As a contraction built, she would drop down into a semi squat and pant between moans.

Her moans awakened Stephanie, who stood by the table staring at her mom. Leslie knelt down and told her it was okay, and she would have a baby brother or sister pretty soon. She gently sent Stephanie back to her bed. Then she went in and woke Mom before dashing back to the kitchen. She grabbed the big kettle of water and put it on the stove, then picked up several pieces of wood, opened the stove belly and stoked up the wood stove. Mom hustled in, wrapping her robe around her and assessed Teresa's condition. We decided her bed would be most convenient. I went back into her room and stripped the bed, while Mom grabbed a tarp out of the cabinet under the kitchen counter. She brought it in and covered the mattress, then covered the tarp with an old blanket and sheet. We helped Teresa move to the bedroom. She didn't want to lie down yet, so Mom helped her walk around the room.

I checked on our supplies. Leslie needed sharp scissors.

"Floss, do we have any floss? Maybe yarn, towels, blankets?" Leslie said as she grabbed everything and went into the bedroom and I followed.

Teresa was on the bed with a towel under her and her knees propped up under a sheet. Mom was holding her hand and murmuring to her. Leslie laid everything out on the end table and went back out to the kitchen to check on the water.

Our boys were coming down the ladder into the main room of the cabin where Teresa and Stephanie normally slept. The cabin was so tiny it felt like we were continuously camping out there.

"What's all the noise?" Cameron asked

"Teresa's having her baby. You can go back to bed or you can help, but you can't be in the way!" Leslie barked.

"I'll help, Mom," Sean said.

"Okay, I want you to keep an eye on Jason and Stephanie. They might want to have some food or something."

Cameron looked a little pale when he saw Teresa splayed on the bed.

Cameron scrambled for the door and almost ran smack into Ace. Only then did I realize Ace hadn't been in the room already.

"Alex, ask Ace if he thinks we should let Floyd know," Leslie ordered from out in the kitchen.

Ace looked a little befuddled, but as a deep moan rolled out of the bedroom, the light came on for him.

"Ace, go get Floyd," I ordered. He looked up and stared like a deer caught in the headlights, then dashed out to the bunkhouse. I could hear male panic in one voice and escalating excitement in the other. They came back in, then tried to squeeze in the door to Mom's room together, Floyd wedged his way through the door

Spring

first and Ace quickly followed Floyd's red long john covered bulk into the room. Well, at least room heat won't be an issue, I thought wryly. I went out to see what Leslie was doing.

She seemed to be running a mental checklist of needed supplies and potential emergency equipment. The water was boiling in the kettle, so she poured some into our largest pan and threw in a sharp knife, the large tongs, and the emergency medical kit's suture needles. She left them in the pan and added more water to the kettle, setting it back on the fire. She rummaged through the box of medical supplies.

"Leslie, can I help?" I asked.

"I need some skin emollient or oil."

"There's a small bottle of massage oil in my toiletry kit."

She rolled her eyes at me, shaking her head.

"It won't work?" I asked, confused.

"Yes, yes that's fine; just go get it!" I returned quickly with the small bottle, and Leslie grabbed it and her sterilized equipment wrapped in a clean cloth. I followed her back into Mom's room.

Leslie directed Ace to sit behind Teresa and cradle her through the contractions. Floyd was positioned across the bed to hold one of Teresa's legs while I would hold the other when the time came for her to push. Mom moved to the foot of the bed to help Leslie.

The table lamp was positioned behind us for maximum light and Leslie and Mom lifted the sheet up a bit.

"Teresa, when did your water break?"

"Don't know... I bathed earlier... and felt some pressure... when I... ohhhhh... sneezed... but didn't seem like anything... aaauuughh!"

The contraction forced some fluid from her, and the aroma of amniotic fluid was clearly detectable. Mom nodded to Leslie as another contraction tightened her belly. I had seen Leslie wash her hands in the kitchen, but she now took out an alcohol swab and scrubbed her hands with it. As the contraction subsided, Leslie reached between Teresa's legs and felt for the baby's head. A new contraction gripped Teresa, and Leslie said to me. "I can feel her cervix move. I'm guessing she's eight, maybe nine centimeters? If she's not demanding to push, we still have some time." Leslie looked at her watch to count the contractions. "Okay, that was twenty seconds," she announced. A few moments later she said "Now this one is fifteen seconds. She's speeding up." Mom put a hand on Teresa's lower abdomen and felt around. She looked at Leslie and shrugged.

"I think everything is in the right position."

Cameron had assumed the job of door security, but he was fascinated by what was going on and not paying attention to the constant traffic in and out of the room as Mom, Leslie and I brought in things and left to get other items.

Another contraction and then another came almost immediately.

Ace wiped Teresa's forehead with a damp cloth. Floyd seemed perplexed, waiting for instructions and trying to figure out where he could safely look.

"I... need... to... push!"

Leslie showed Floyd how to lift her leg and cock it back toward her hips. Ace pushed her shoulders forward so she could bear down. Leslie checked her again and reported that this time she could feel the soft fuzzy scalp of the baby's head. She grabbed the massage oil, put some on her fingers and began to massage the peritoneum. Leslie indicated that Teresa appeared not to have had an episiotomy before and that she preferred to keep it that way. The oil was silky smooth and quickly lubricated the area.

Each push brought the head closer to crowning. Everyone was encouraging her as a contraction swept through her body and aimed its force at expelling the child.

Finally one push brought the top of the head into view. The entire compound's population was in the room at this point, and the children let out an audible gasp. I had seen a dog give birth when I was a kid, so I thought this experience would be a net positive for them. But the room was crowded and everyone was trying to get to a better position to witness the birth. We would be giving a lot of anatomy lessons with the children after this experience was over.

"It's only going to be another two or three pushes, Teresa. With the next one I want you to really push hard so we can get the head out. Then you need to pant for me until we can rotate the shoulder out."

Teresa grabbed her knees with the next contraction and pulled herself up and forward as the head started to emerge. Leslie slipped one finger in to make sure the cord wasn't wrapped around the baby's neck. "No cord, no problem," she announced. The head pushed out, and the body started to turn almost on its own.

"Don't push!" Leslie eased the turn to expose the top of one of the baby's shoulders. "Okay, now push with all you've got!"

The little boy slid out with a gush of fluid. The kids gasped. Floyd dropped Teresa's leg and stared. I glanced up just in time to see his eyes roll up into his head as he crumpled to the floor in a dead faint. The children scrambled to get out of his way so they wouldn't be crushed from his fall.

Teresa was fine. The baby was fine. Floyd was terribly embarrassed but good-natured about the ribbing we all gave him when he came to. Ace was in awe, as were all the younger kids as they came forward to examine the little guy's fingers and toes. Jason demanded to see "all of him" because he didn't want another sister and wanted to be sure this one had the right equipment. We all laughed.

We would need to go into town to find the doctor later so that we could get an official birth certificate for the baby. Thank God there had not been any medical complications. We were lucky.

"What will you call him?" Leslie asked Teresa.

Teresa looked at Floyd and Ace. "Any suggestions?"

"Aiden," said Ace.

"Jonathan," said Floyd "It was my dad's name."
"Hello, Jonathan Aiden," Teresa said. The baby yawned.

CHAPTER TWENTY-SEVEN

A Change for the Better

Summer 2017, Arkansas

"It's only when you grow up, and step back from him, or leave him for your own career and your own home—it's only then that you can measure your father's greatness and fully appreciate it. Pride reinforces love."

— Margaret Truman

The man from the bank sat at the table with Mom and me, reviewing the note on the farm to cover Ace's medical costs. He had come out shortly after Ace came home and reviewed our situation. We were able to show him how we would put more acres into a cash crop devoted directly to paying the note. Fortunately for us, food supplies were still short, which meant that our food crops would be worth more and allow us to generate more income. He calculated futures for various crops and recommended we plant three different ones: alfalfa for animal feed, corn for ethanol production and soybeans for human nutrition. We planned to implement all those suggestions along with our continuing production of our medicinal "herbs," but we didn't mention that.

This time he brought a packet of papers and questions. "When was this property purchased?"

"The summer, no, let me think. Alex, you'd left for school. It was October of 1993 when we signed the paperwork," Mom answered.

"And the two of you signed?"

He nodded to me and Mom. I shook my head and Mom answered. "No, it was my husband and me."

"And he was…"

"Aiden, but why do you need that? He's been dead for almost two decades."

"Oh really? Hmm, that may explain things."

I interrupted, "What do you mean?"

"We've had an account at the bank since the mid 1990s. It was an unusual account, set up under a special agreement with the previous bank manager. The account had a number, of course, but the contact information for the account was never completed. There were steady monthly deposits until just recently. In an audit of activity, the account came up as having had only one transaction this past year, and that was for the property taxes on this farm."

"But weren't those taxes escrowed from the mortgage payments I made? I guess I never paid attention to them." Mom said.

The bank officer seemed surer of his direction. "May I ask if your husband had a safe deposit box?"

"He did – we had several…"

"And was one here?"

"Here? You mean at the bank here in town?"

"At ours – Bank of the Ozarks. I don't know about First National."

Mom and I looked at each other. Mom had only checked banks in Houston and DC. It had never crossed her mind to even think he'd set up something here. Mom got up and walked into her room.

"I think she's got something to show you," I told the banker, who looked confused.

Mom came back, sat down and held out her hand, opening her palm to show a small key.

"Does this look like one of yours?" she asked.

He picked it up and turned it over. "I don't know," he replied cautiously. "I don't help open the boxes, but I've seen keys like this before. We can try it."

The safe deposit box vault wasn't much bigger than a closet. There were three sizes: large boxes on the bottom row, only a few of those, many mediums in the middle; and fewer small boxes on the top. The teller had the key from the numbered account box. She said it was to one of the small boxes. Since we couldn't give any identification or code for access to the box, she had to have the manager assist.

We were anxious and hopeful. We knew the box would not have the Ark's property deeds because those were with an attorney in Houston. Whatever Dad had put into the box here, if he had a box, might be relevant to the plans that he had made for this property.

The manager emerged with a letter. He looked at us and asked, "Mrs. MacCasland, can you tell me the name of your first family pet?"

Mom started to laugh and said, "T.O.R. We called him Tor for short."

He looked at the letter and asked, "And T.O.R. stood for?"

"Terminal Oil Resources. It was sort of a theme in his life," Mom replied.

The manager was satisfied that it was our box. "Yes. Well, the contents of the box now belong to you. When you finish, just stop by my desk and we can do the paperwork." He left us with the teller. She took Mom in and showed her the box in the viewing cubicle, then left the room.

"Alex, come in too." I entered the cubicle and looked in the box at a large packet of papers. Mom took them out and unfolded them. It was a series of mineral interests for land in Colorado, Utah and Wyoming.

"What are these for?" I asked Mom, having never seen them before.

She was reading an attached report and muttering to herself.

"Mom? What are they?"

"Mineral rights."

"I can see that. What good are they?"

She read a little longer, then turned to me and asked, "Do you think they'll let me use their phone?"

"Why?" Her question was a total non sequitur.

"I need to call one of your Dad's old geologist friends. If these are what I think they are, we'll be able to improve the property here."

She was still being too cryptic for me. "Mom, tell me what you think these represent."

She looked up and blinked a couple of times. "Let me see if they'll let me make some phone calls." She headed out the vault into the main office of the bank. I remained behind trying to make sense out of the few documents that she hadn't taken with her.

An hour later, she returned with a big smile on her face.

"Mom, what's up?" I asked.

"Alex, we've just hit the lottery!"

"What?"

"I was able to scan some of these documents and send them to Houston. Based upon our preliminary analysis, it appears that these assets are now very valuable. Essentially, these deeds are for the subsurface rights to minerals, gas, oil, whatever. The reports show good concentrations of oil, gas and other mineral deposits in some marginal fields. They would have been worth very little when oil prices were low, but are probably worth a whole lot more now. If we still own these – as these documents suggest – and extraction is viable, or has already been ongoing, then they are very valuable."

We returned to the cabin around seven o'clock that evening. Leslie had made dinner and everyone was sitting down around the table about to start eating. Mom and I walked in carrying several grocery bags. Everyone turned and stared at the bags.

"Would anyone like some ice cream?" I asked innocently.

"Yes!" cheered the kids in unison.

"Alex, have you lost your mind?" Leslie asked, but before I could answer, she added rapidly, "What flavor?"

"Chocolate and vanilla." Mom replied. "It's all they had."

"But we haven't eaten dinner yet," Teresa pointed out.

"That can wait," I said. "The ice cream will melt if we don't eat it." There was a rush to the head of the table as Leslie stood up and began scooping large dollops to each of the kids and even larger portions to the adults; no one was on a diet tonight. I also pulled out a battered box of Captain Crunch. Stephanie screamed in approval.

And there we sat at a table full of healthy uneaten vegetables gorging ourselves on frozen concoctions. We ate until the dessert was gone and the boys licked the containers clean. At that point most of the uneaten food was simply put away. We retired to the living room as Mom brewed a pot of tea for the adults and served hot chocolate for the kids.

"What are we celebrating?" Leslie asked at last as she sipped some green tea. We had just tried to put the kids to bed, but all the sugar had them tearing around the cabin. Teresa and Mom were still trying to get them settled.

"Ah, I think we're rich."

"You must! How much money did you spend on food?"

"You don't want to know."

"So, what was in the lock box?" she asked. "Gold?"

I folded my hands comfortably behind my head. "Even better. Dad apparently left us some mineral interests for some oil and gas properties that should mean that we should now have a steady income that will last us the rest of our lives."

"You're kidding, right?" she asked in disbelief.

"Can you imagine me buying ice cream under any other circumstances?" I asked.

"Frankly, no," she said, and we both laughed.

"Dad kind of knew what was going to happen. I guess he understood which assets had the greatest opportunity to increase in value. He's really set us up quite well compared to the way that we've been living. Had he lived longer, the cabin would have been completely remodeled and we probably would've known about the lockbox when we first got here."

"Really?" came back her answer. "Are you saying that all the hardships that we've just gone through, all the nights of going hungry, the bug infestations, and all this baking in the elements didn't have to happen?"

I turned serious again. "Perhaps, but can you imagine if they hadn't?"

She thought about this observation long and hard, and I could track her features moving through various emotional states –anger, ebullience, and then intense contemplation. Her focus finally came to rest like a ball falling into a slot on a roulette wheel. "No, I don't think I want to even think about that. But tell me, are we safe?"

"Well, we haven't really told anyone else yet, except for the guy at the bank. Most of the documents are still in our box there, but we made a note of which properties we own. If someone tries to assign our rights to someone else, we should be able to stop them before they could steal our assets."

"Okay, it sounds like the assets are safe – but will we be safe living a more affluent life style in this neck of the woods?"

"Well, that's a very good question that I've just begun to think about. When you have nothing to lose, there's very little that people can take away from you," I observed. "We've now apparently got a lot to lose and we need to be more careful."

"You mean from thieves?" she asked.

"Well, for starters. There are also kidnappers, pirates, gangs and a whole bunch of other potential threats to include lawyers and all kinds of public tax authorities that we are now on the radar screen for," I said.

"Should we move?"

"To where? You mean, leave the United States."

"Possibly. Your sister is in Europe somewhere, right? Moving may be safer for our family." There was a pause in the conversation as this thought sank in.

Near the woodstove, Floyd reached over and took Teresa's hand. She leaned back against him while Ace got up and went into the kitchen. Whatever happened to us, it looked like Floyd and Teresa wanted to stay here.

"Maybe," I said. "But you know, if we did that, I think that Dad would roll over in his grave. He didn't set aside all these assets just to allow us to go find some remote island to buy and live out the rest of our lives. He's given us the means to make a difference for many others less fortunate. How we do that is how we repay him."

"You mean that we should help others around here?"

"No, I think we need to think bigger and become part of the larger solution. I've suddenly got a strong desire to go finance some commercial-scale wind turbines or maybe put in some solar farms."

She hadn't expected that answer. "Wow, that's a lot to think about. Can this wait until tomorrow?" She leaned forward and whispered in my ear. "I think I'd like to go for a midnight swim. We could have a little private celebration... if you're in the mood?"

"Am I ever! Just think... we can now put in a hot tub and a working wind turbine." I whispered back.

At this her eyes rolled dreamily. "A Jacuzzi? Hot water? Electricity? Just the thought of them turn me on. Swimming hole, now," Leslie directed.

"Yes, ma'am," I said as I escorted her out into the open air.

Authors' Notes

"This world that we have made as a result of the level of thinking we have done thus far creates problems which cannot be solved by the same level of thinking in which they were created."
— ALBERT EINSTEIN

"All we have to decide is what to do with the time that is given to us."
— J. R. R. TOLKIEN

"We are what we think. All that we are arises with our thoughts. With our thoughts we make the world."
— BUDDHA

"I ask not for a lighter burden, but for broader shoulders."
— JEWISH PROVERB

When we first started writing this story three years ago the idea that our nation could experience an oil crisis driven by a weak dollar seemed unlikely or at least a long way away. As we finished the final draft, recent economic events had evolved in the direction that we've suggested. Obviously oil prices are not going to remain continuously high and have returned to more comfortable levels, at least for a while. Even so, there is little doubt that the overall price trend for crude oil over the next twenty years will be upwards. As this novel suggests the path of that price trend matters.

Neither of us knows what the future holds and it is our sincere hope that this story remains just a fantasy. But we also believe that as a nation we can and hopefully will transition quickly to new energy solutions – preferably renewable, sustainable, and clean – while we have enough fossil fuels to make the transition gradual, manageable and fiscally possible. This is our version of a warning order; a call to action, even if it's just a decision you make for yourself and your family.

The authors have served in the military and as officers have sworn to defend our constitution, the soul of our nation, against enemies both foreign and domestic; peak oil qualifies for both. We realize that energy solutions are indeed a national security issue and a global concern.

In many ways, the United States is still in a privileged position when it comes to energy. We have the world's largest known coal reserves, attractive unconventional natural gas resource plays (though the US's natural gas consumption is only about half of the size of the US's crude oil consumption as measured on a BTU basis), extraordinary wind and solar power potential, plenty of uranium, various bio-fuel initiatives, and the technicians, politicians, and investors that could energize a transition to another energy regime. We have the potential to avoid an energy train wreck.

But any crude oil crisis will be one where we have to "come as we are". While there may be possibilities to harness other energy sources over the long term, none of this matters when the world is suddenly turned upside down and we are still in a predominantly crude oil driven society. We will most likely get to confront some future crude oil disruption with something that closely resembles the energy infrastructure that existed at the time this book was published, our fleet of mostly gasoline dependent vehicles, lots of widely dispersed homes and a retail system that is profoundly transportation dependent from goods and foodstuffs from all around the world.

Now would be a good time to buy a highly fuel efficient vehicle and do all the things that can reduce our individual energy footprints, but in the end, this will not be enough. We need to be investing in alternative energy resources at a scale and rate that is almost unimaginable in order to avoid some type of future disruption like the one described in this story. As odd as it may sound, we're hoping that oil prices remain at uncomfortable levels in the near future to induce our society to head in this direction sooner rather than later. The last twenty years do not suggest that we will actually do anything of this sort as long as oil prices remain cheap or even modest.

We gave our characters considerably more benefits and opportunity than most of us could reasonably expect or hope for under their circumstances. Perhaps the potential reality was simply too harsh to imagine. Or, maybe serendipity or faith could indeed power a sequence of fortunate developments that would materialize for a family without such a farsighted parent. In the end, it is all about sustainability. Mankind inherited an incredible trust fund of fossil fuel energy and the party has raged for a couple hundred years. What impressive trash we will leave for future anthropologists.

Acknowledgments

We'd especially like to thank our editor, John Paine, who transformed our very technical narrative into a much more readable novel. As to our individual acknowledgements, we'd like to offer these separately. Laura first.

My deepest respect and appreciation to: John, and his family, for supporting an off the cuff suggestion and helping make it a reality. All collaborations are difficult, especially long distance; John, your fire was always my beacon and I thank you sincerely for that. To Babette Donaldson who first believed – may your Ark float! To Andrew Martin and Trish Pietrzak, who were there at the beginning and cheered me on. Thank you, George Buchanan for understanding our vision for a cover and bringing it to life visually and beautifully. Go, Google! Thank you for having a lead to everything I needed to learn and research. To Cookie Terry and your sons – now long grown, thanks for the Halloween memory of Bo Peep and her sheep. To my extended family – Be Prepared! Our children will thank us. And finally – my love and eternal thanks to Tom, Devin, Garrett and Morgan. It's just another adventure.

And, here are John's acknowledgments.

I'd like to dedicate this book to my father, Robert H. Cape, that recently lost his battle with cancer; Dad, we love and miss you and know that you would have appreciated this story.

Next, I'd like to offer a general credit to my immediate family members that have been such a meaningful and central part of my life for the last quarter century – especially my spouse for many years, Carol, and my daughters – Katie, Dani, and Michelle.

Now for the book credits: Laura, thanks for your energy, your support and your creativity; you are truly a gifted writer, forward thinker and good friend and this novel would not have happened

Acknowledgments

without you. A special appreciation goes to William Haas and Andrew John Kinney Jr. who spent an incredible amount of time and effort working through the early drafts with us. Also, we really appreciated the insights and feedback from Ed Hart; John W. McWhirter, Jr.; John Suddarth; Greg Hiebert; William Schoen, Mary Cozine Woodward, Myra Tenenbown Ephross, Lisa Tharaud, Kimberly Thomen, Barbara Chandler, Rick Zimmerman, Laurie Prah; Carol Cape (Mom); Natalia Garmashova, Kim Buchanan (sister); Robert H. Baldwin, Jr.; William Fullerton; and James W. Bowen.

We used numerous books as source material for the factual aspects of our story and have noted these in the bibliography in the back. We have also included web sites that we have found particularly interesting and illuminating regarding the implications of peak oil.

References

For back ground information on peak energy, interesting links, deleted chapters, the **Oil Dusk** theme song, and the latest pictures and news on the authors, this book and related products, see http://www.oildusk.com

Useful peak oil related links:

http://dieoff.org

Goodstein, David. 2004. *Out of Gas: The End of the Age of Oil.* NewYork, NY, The Courier Companies, Inc.

Kunstler, James Howard. *The Long Emergency: Surviving the Converging Catastrophes of the Twenty-First Century.* New York, NY. Atlantic Monthly Press.

www.lifeaftertheoilcrash.net

Simmons, Mathew R., *Twilight in the Desert; The Coming Saudi Oil Shock and the World Economy.* Hoboken, New Jersey. John Wiley & Sons, Inc.

www.survivingpeakoil.com/article.php?id=until_the_last_drop

Tertzakian, Peter. 2006. *A Thousand Barrels a Second: The Coming Oil Break Point and the Challenges Facing an Energy Dependent World.* The United States of America. McGraw Hill.

www.theoildrum.com

The End of Suburbia. 2004. www.endofsurbia.com. The Electric Wallpaper.

www.wolfatthedoor.org.uk/

About the Authors

John M. Cape is a graduate of the Stanford Graduate School of Business, the US Army Ranger School, and the United States Military Academy at West Point. A registered professional engineer, he currently works for a Houston company that drills oil and gas wells. John previously co-authored *Reconstructing Eden* and the *CountryWatch Forecast Yearbook (2003)*.

Laura Buckner has a bachelors degree in Sociology from Iowa State University and a graduate degree in Political Science/International Relations. Since retiring from the Air Force she has worked for the Census Bureau, run an environmental engineering company and developed a career coaching program for young adults.

Singing Bowl Press
http://www.oildusk.com